Scooby-Doo!

The Haunted Road Trip

By Gail Herman
Illustrated by Duendes del Sur

SCHOLASTIC INC.
New York Toronto London Auckland Sydney
Mexico City New Delhi Hong Kong Buenos Aires

ISBN-13: 978-0-545-00518-0
ISBN-10: 0-545-00518-3

Designed by Michael Massen

12   11   10   9   8   7   6   5   4   3   2   1   7   8   9   10/0

Printed in U.S.A.
First printing, January 2008

Bump, bump.

The Mystery Machine rattled down the highway.

The Gang was taking a road trip.

All at once, the sky grew dark.
Lightning flashed.
Thunder boomed.
Rain poured down in sheets.

"Ruh-oh!" said Scooby-Doo.
"Uh-oh is right," said Shaggy.
Minutes later, the highway was closed.
"We have to pull off here," Fred said.

Fred drove up to a roadside motel.
Its neon sign flashed: CREEPY MOTEL.
"Zoinks!" said Shaggy. "Can't we stop
somewhere less . . . *creepy*?"

"This motel might have a strange name," said Velma, "But it's the only place around."

"I'm sure it's fine," added Fred. "Let's get some rest."

Thunder shook the windows. Quickly, Shaggy closed the drapes.

"Now what?" he asked Scooby.

"Room rervice?" asked Scooby.

"Like, great idea, good buddy," said Shaggy. He picked up the phone to order room service.

There was no dial tone.

"Ree Vee?" Scooby suggested next.
Shaggy turned on the TV.

A spooky graveyard filled the screen. Ghosts floated in the air.

"Nightmare-athon," Shaggy read. "All scary movies. All the time."

"Quick!" cried Shaggy. "Change the channel!" But they couldn't.

No food!
Monsters on TV!
What could be scarier?

TAP, TAP.
Suddenly, something knocked at the window.
Shaggy and Scooby saw a ghostly arm.
Woooooh!
An eerie howl sounded.

"Like, let's get out of — "
CRASH!
Suddenly, the lights went out.

"Like, on the other hand," Shaggy said, "Let's stay right here."

Shaggy and Scooby started to shiver.

"Raggy?"

"Yeah, Scoob?"

"Rit's rold in here."

They stumbled around, looking for a blanket.
Shaggy opened a drawer. Inside, he found a
flashlight.

Shaggy opened a closet door.
"Bingo!" he said. "Blanket!"
But when he lifted it, he saw something
terrifying . . .

A ghost!
Shaggy and Scooby leaped onto the bed.

WOOOOH, WOOOOH!
KNOCK, KNOCK!
Shaggy and Scooby hid under the blanket as spooky sounds echoed around them.

They were too scared to get the rest of the gang.

They were too scared to do anything but fall asleep.

The next morning, the storm had ended. Velma, Fred, and Daphne woke Shaggy and Scooby up.

"Like, this place is haunted," Shaggy said. "Let's get out of here!"

"The TV only plays scary movies," Shaggy exclaimed.

Fred jiggled the remote control. "It's broken!" he said.

"But we heard moans and howls, too," said Shaggy.

"It was just the wind," Velma explained.

Velma opened the door. A tree had fallen on the power lines.

"So no phones or lights," said Fred.

"What about the monster at the window?" Shaggy asked.

"That was just a broken branch," said Daphne. "See?"

"But there's a real ghost! In the corner!"
Shaggy cried.

"It's an old dressmaker's dummy,"
Velma explained. "A traveling salesman
must have left it behind."

"We still need to get out of here," Shaggy said. "Like, this place is *creepy*. Remember?"

"Reah!" Scooby agreed.

"No it's not," said Daphne.

"The sign was broken. It's really the *Sleepy* Motel."

"And Restaurant!" Shaggy added happily.

"Restaurant?" Scooby wagged his tail.

A little later, Fred honked the horn.
"What's your rush?" asked Shaggy. "We've
got to have snacks for our road trip!"
"Scooby-Dooby Doo!"

NO MORE
LETTING GO

The Spirituality of Taking Action Against
Alcoholism and Drug Addiction

DEBRA JAY

BANTAM BOOKS

NO MORE LETTING GO
A Bantam Book / May 2006

Published by
Bantam Dell
A Division of Random House, Inc.
New York, New York

Author's note
All the stories in this book are based on actual experiences. The names
and details have been changed to protect the privacy of the people involved.
In some cases, composites have been created.

LIBRARY OF CONGRESS CATALOGING-IN-PUBLICATION DATA
Jay, Debra, 1954–
No more letting go : the spirituality of taking action against alcoholism and
drug addiction / by Debra Jay.
p. cm.
ISBN-13: 978-0-553-38360-7
ISBN-10: 0-553-38360-4
1. Substance abuse—Treatment—Religious aspects.   2. Alcoholism—
Treatment—Religious aspects.   3. Drug addiction—Treatment—Religious
aspects.   I. Title.
HV4998.J39 2006
204'.42—dc22   2005057155

Printed in the United States of America
Published simultaneously in Canada

www.bantamdell.com

BVG   10   9   8   7   6   5   4   3   2   1

FOR JEFF

CONTENTS

ACKNOWLEDGMENTS

WOULD LIKE to express my gratitude to the following people: Sandy Peddicord for suggesting I write another book. My agent, Jane Dystel, for making it happen. My editor, Toni Burbank, for her wisdom and kindness.

I'd also like to thank several good friends and colleagues for their support and help: Nancy Solak, Dr. Jerry Boriskin, Lori Forseth Koneczny, Michael J. Smith, and PJ McSweeney. My deepest appreciation goes to my dear husband, Jeff Jay, who gave patient and unending support as well as some good suggestions.

Go where your best prayers take you. Unclench
the fists of your spirit and take it easy. Breathe
deeply of the glad air and live one day at a time.
Know that you are precious . . . and learn to trust.

—FREDERICK BUECHNER

NO MORE
LETTING GO

INTRODUCTION:
IT TAKES A FAMILY

THERE WAS A TIME when drunk driving was fairly acceptable behavior. Bars provided drinks in plastic "to go" cups to take in the car. Repeat offenders still held valid driver's licenses, no one ever heard of a "designated driver," and friends regularly let friends drive drunk. Getting caught resulted in little more than a slap on the wrist. Then two mothers, whose children were victims of drunk drivers, began an organization called MADD (Mothers Against Drunk Drivers) and convinced the nation that driving while intoxicated was unacceptable. Today, we are much safer on the road because of the passion of these mothers. Now we must go a step further and contend with addiction in our families, so we can live happier, healthier, and more secure lives in our homes.

Having worked for years with alcoholics, addicts, and their families—and growing up with alcoholism among my own relatives—I have come to a profound realization: *Addiction must be denied a place in our families*. I think we have all been told that we must wait until alcoholics and addicts want help, but we also know that "wanting help" can take years or never happen at all. In the meantime, we pay a dear price for addiction's "right" to exist in our families unchallenged. This book is about the spiritual act of saying no to addiction. *Letting go* is often misunderstood to mean we are to do nothing. When I say *no more letting go,* I am saying that we must never let go of our right to take positive action against this destructive disease. Instead, we must let go of those things that *block our ability to take action.* When families make a commitment to work together in love, a power they didn't know they possessed emerges. They gain tremendous influence, becoming highly effective at motivating alcoholics and addicts to accept help. When taking the right kind of action, the well-being of families begins to take precedence over the will of addiction.

A few years ago, I wrote a book titled *Love First: A New Approach to Intervention for Alcoholism & Drug Addiction.* I wanted to give families who were ready to take action access to a detailed road map showing them how to intervene. Since then, I've talked to people who tell me their families are having difficulty making the decision to do something. They can't move forward. When a family is hesitant or wavering, it usually means they don't have enough information. *No More Letting Go* presents families with what they need to move from uncertainty to a place of clear and definite decision-making. *No More Letting Go* then provides a number of specific ways to help addicted loved ones, giving families the latitude to select a method that best suits their individual situation.

Once we decide that untreated addiction is as unacceptable as drunk driving, we will begin addressing the problem differently. Imagine a time when it will be unthinkable not to intervene when someone we love becomes addicted to alcohol or other drugs. Ignoring a friend or relative's addiction will feel as wrong as handing car keys to someone who is stumbling drunk. No longer will we enable the disease; instead we will put a stop to it by initiating recovery. We will be able to depend on most everyone to help us, because almost no one will find it tolerable to support ongoing addiction. Those who become addicted will get help years or even decades sooner, and families will escape endless days of anguish and distress. Small children will know they can depend upon nonaddicted family members to protect them from the pain of growing up in alcoholic homes.

Family is our springboard into life. If our family life is robust and healthy, we have a head start on the world. But when addiction distorts and twists our households, we begin at a disadvantage. The longer we are subjected to another person's addiction, the more we change and the farther we diverge from the world of the well-adjusted. We cannot sacrifice the sanctity of our lives to the rapacious nature of addiction. We are given only one life to live, and it is precious. Each of us, including the addicted person, has a responsibility to stop addiction from stealing away with the best of our lives.

PART ONE

Questioning Our Assumptions

HITTING BOTTOM:
A FAMILY AFFAIR

WHEN ADDICTION BEGINS causing serious problems, a family's greatest fears turn into reality. They watch with disbelief as the alcoholic continues drinking while their lives are falling apart. Unable to convince the alcoholic to stop drinking, families begin searching for answers. In my years of working with the relatives of alcoholics and addicts, I have found that families rarely reach out for help until the drinking and drugging hit a crisis point, and then they are often told: "There's nothing you can do until the alcoholic wants help. You'll just have to let him hit bottom."

Hitting bottom is an old idea, still imposed upon families as if it were an absolute. Many families sadly believe that they must wait for alcoholics to hit bottom before there is any hope for recovery. They rarely stop to consider that this belief sentences them to years of unhappiness and devastation. No one ever mentions the fact that alcoholics and addicts don't take the trip to the bottom alone—the family goes with them. Families are never warned that the journey to the bottom takes even the smallest children.

Hitting bottom should never be our first strategy; it is a strategy of last resort. Only when every reasonable intervention technique is exhausted should we let someone free-fall. Even then, there are ways to raise the bottom, to stretch out the safety net of treatment and recovery. Addiction always presents new opportunities. The trick is recognizing them and knowing how to take action.

The premise of hitting bottom is that addicts hit one bottom and, when they get there, either are struck sober or go running for the nearest treatment center. But addicts are resilient. They find people to rescue them. They often bounce along the bottom for years without a flicker of recognition that they need help. When they find themselves in a tough spot, drugs and alcohol whisper reassurances: *There's nothing to worry about as long as you have me.*

I was having dinner with some recovering alcoholics, and a particularly nice fellow in his late fifties was celebrating fifteen years of sobriety. He talked about living in a roach-infested one-room apartment above a bar for twelve years, drinking and doing drugs every single day. He said his life was miserable, but he just couldn't stop. He came close to dying several times before getting help. One of the people in our group said, "Well, you just weren't ready." Someone else piped up with, "It takes what it takes." Everyone's head nodded in agreement. Stunned that my dinner companions thought that this man had had to lose some of the best years of his life before he was ready to get sober, I asked, "Where was your family?" He said his wife divorced him and his kids never came around. "All for the better, really," he added. "I wasn't any kind of father worth having." I asked what might have happened if everyone in his family, along with his closest friends, had come to him with a solid plan for recovery and an outpouring of love. Might he have accepted their help? Could it have turned out differently for him and his kids?

Would his marriage have survived? He looked at me for a moment and then said, "I never considered that before. Who knows, I might've taken them up on their help. Maybe we could've saved our family."

Do alcoholics ever hit bottom and then climb their way up into sobriety? Of course they do. But we never know who'll be the lucky ones or what price they'll pay along the way. Three hundred and fifty people a day find a bottom with no bounce— death. Countless others go to prison, go insane, or just go nowhere. Families are torn apart, children lose one or both parents, and relationships are damaged beyond repair. But many begin a journey of recovery before hitting bottom—the path is tough and rocky at first but becomes easier to travel as time goes on. Many things motivate alcoholics to make a turnaround before tragedy strikes, but it is usually family, friends, or employers. When the Hazelden Foundation asked sober alcoholics what set them on their new course to recovery, 77 percent said a friend or relative intervened. Someone cared enough to *raise their bottom.*

The best cases against hitting bottom are the real-life stories: A college-educated, forty-seven-year-old divorced father of three loses everything, lives in his parents' basement drinking and smoking pot daily, and is unable to hold a job. A twenty-four-year-old trades his girlfriend's new car for crack cocaine. The police find a seventy-two-year-old grandmother half naked and passed out on her front lawn. Babies are strapped in the backseat as a mother drives drunk to buy more wine; the police stop her, taking the children to protective services and Mom to jail. A young father goes to bed drunk and suffocates on his own vomit. A successful thirty-two-year-old woman driving home intoxicated kills a father and his daughter when she slams into them on the freeway. All of these stories come from families I've worked with, and no words can express their pain or deep, abiding sense of loss. Waiting for alcoholics to hit unknown bottoms results in much tragedy and heartbreak.

"Bottoms" can be temporary. Alcoholics resist getting sober even when things are going badly in their lives. They are good at weathering storms. Perhaps they'll swear off alcohol for a while, but as soon as things cool down, they begin drinking again. The addicted brain can't make lasting connections between alcohol and the problems it causes. Once the problems go away, alcohol is their best friend again. Addiction is both invisible and sacred to alcoholics: they deny its existence yet sacrifice everything to it.

Addicts don't want to cause trouble or hurt the people they love. Quite the contrary: they struggle to be the person they *think* they still are, the person they were before the addiction took hold. They can't make sense of their own actions. As their addiction progresses and troubles mount, they work harder to manage their lives, but addiction never lets anyone lead a life free of trouble. There are always problems, big and small. Bad behavior, poor decisions, and emotional upheaval are all symptoms of this disease, which affects both the brain and the soul. Families are confused, too. Not understanding what is happening to their loved one, they mutter, "When will she learn?" But addicts can't learn because addiction keeps tightening its grip, demanding complete allegiance.

The apostle Paul could have been describing an addict when he wrote: "I do not understand my own behavior; I do not act as I mean to, but I do things that I hate. Though the will to do what is good is in me, the power to do it is not; the good thing that I want to do, I never do; the evil thing which I do not want— that is what I do." As alcoholics try to resolve the conflict between how they want to behave and how they are behaving, in the end, the only solution they can see is another drink.

FOOLING THE MIND

THE BEST-KEPT SECRET about alcoholics and addicts is that they can't survive in their addiction without the cooperation of others. They act as though they are self-sufficient, but that's a masquerade. They suffer from a growing desperation, which they try to hide by using a combination of tricks to persuade others that everything is fine. But everything isn't fine. There are problems, and the cause is alcohol and other drugs. To keep people from noticing, alcoholics create illusions.

Every addict is a master manipulator. They have a sixth sense for knowing how to convince people they're not seeing what they are seeing. Addicts are like magicians. They camouflage what is in full view. All the signs and symptoms of addiction are apparent, but the family's attention is diverted elsewhere. With a sleight of hand, alcoholics alter reality and the family believes. Magician Doug Henning could have been talking about an addict's ability to fool others when he said, "The mind is led on ingeniously, step-by-step, to defeat its own logic."

Loretta was a sixty-four-year-old mother with six grown children. She had a lifelong addiction to tranquilizers, sleeping pills, and painkillers. She took whatever drugs she could talk her doctors into giving her. She always used hefty amounts of gin. She drank close to a liter of alcohol a day and frequently passed out by midafternoon. She was bruised from frequent falls and hid liquor bottles around the house. Two of her children were psychologists and one was a doctor, yet none considered alcoholism a possibility. Loretta successfully directed their concerns toward depression and away from alcohol and pills. As far back as the children could remember, they were told their mother was depressed. When they came home from school and she was passed out, it was depression. When she couldn't attend school functions, it was depression. When she didn't take care of the house or her own appearance, it was depression. The children were so thoroughly trained to believe it was depression, they couldn't see anything else. When a relative finally stepped forward and suggested she needed treatment for addiction, Loretta's children were incredulous. They became downright hostile to the idea their mother was an alcoholic.

Magicians rely on the art of misdirection to create illusions, and so do alcoholics. Misdirection is a technique that directs people's attention toward what you want them to see and away from what you don't. The famous magician Harry Keller said, "If I have an audience's attention, I could march an elephant across the stage without the audience seeing it." Families of alcoholics, it is often said, have an elephant in the living room that nobody is talking about. In magic, misdirection is used to create wonder. In addiction, it's used for deception and breach of trust. Neither magicians nor alcoholics could operate without it.

Attitude is one way to direct someone's attention where you want it. If you act as if something is important, others will pay attention to it. On the other hand, act as if something has little or no relevance, and others tend to overlook it. When an alcoholic loses his job because of his drinking, he pretends not to be bothered. He tells his parents and his siblings it was a dead-end street and he couldn't stand working there anyway. They did him a favor, he says, because now he's free to find something better. His attitude is nonchalant, almost blasé. The family doesn't quite know how to react. If he's not worrying, why should they? When his wife begins interrogating him about the connection between his drinking and losing his job, however, he shifts the focus onto her. She is the problem, he says. Her nagging, lack of support, relentless arguing, and unending dissatisfaction are more than he can stand. He brings up old problems from the past and complains about her family. He pushes her into defending herself, and the real issue is dropped. Anything is fair game when moving attention away from his drinking.

Another way of misdirecting others is by creating what magicians call "the offbeat"—doing something unexpected. A cocaine-addicted son misses his aging mother's birthday party because he's too high, so he shows up early the next morning to mow her lawn and repair the torn screen door. He surprises her with flowers and explains that he wanted to celebrate her birthday with just the two of them. If he'd come to the party, he says, the rest of the family would have snubbed him. They sit and drink coffee and talk. He makes her laugh. Later, when his brothers and sisters criticize him, she comes to his defense. "If you weren't so hard on him," she says, "he might come around more often."

Creating an impression of honesty and openness is another misdirection technique. This plays on the family's desire to give the benefit of the doubt. When a father approaches his daughter about her drinking, she tells him she's been wanting to talk to him about her problems but couldn't find the courage. She goes on to explain how depressed she's been since her divorce and how alcohol is something to medicate her feelings. She says she's sorry for worrying him. She reassures him that everything will be all right. He leaves feeling confident they've had a breakthrough, never suspecting she successfully diverted his attention from her real problem—alcoholism—by focusing on problems

surrounding her divorce. The daughter did what magicians do
to gain trust from audiences: create an agreeable mind-set others are willing to follow.

Misdirection of time is another powerful tool in magic.
Allow enough time between the deception and the revelation,
and people are easily fooled. When alcoholics find themselves in
trouble with their spouse, for instance, they avoid discussing the
problem for as long as possible, hoping the spouse's anger will
dissipate. This method of misdirection buys time to put some
good behavior between them and the incident that got them
into trouble in the first place. For example, when a husband
comes home drunk for the third time in a week, his wife is furious. To avoid her wrath, he passes out in bed. The next day,
when he gets home from work, he announces to the kids that
he's taking them to the movie he's been promising. The kids are
elated and have such a good time that his wife doesn't have the
heart to bring up yesterday's drinking binge.

For magicians to be successful, they must have complete
control over their performance. If observers can identify their
tricks, the illusion goes flat and the show is over. The same applies to alcoholics and addicts. They must control their performance so others will see only what they want them to see.
Magician Tom Crone says close attention must be paid to two
questions that work as a "mental magic wand": *What might be
presumed? What must not be seen?* Alcoholics and addicts, to
survive in their addiction, ask similar questions: *How much do
they know? What must I hide?*

Some family members eventually become skeptical of every
move alcoholics and addicts make. They mistrust everything
and try to catch every trick. Magician Ben Robinson says, "You
cannot misdirect someone who *will not* be directed. That is, unless they do not realize a deception is afoot." When people
aren't easily directed and respond negatively to an alcoholic's

attempts to trick them, they think they are ahead of the game. But Robinson says: "Either way, I win. I've got them. I'm in control. They are either following my directive with action or with rebellion. Regardless, the web of my deceit is upon them. They do not know what is going to happen next and, obviously, I do." Everyone revolves around addiction; it resides at the center of family life. Some family members believe and others rebel. But everyone answers to the addiction. When I work with families, the rebels always tell me that they don't let the addiction bother them. They can't see that their behavior is a direct response to the drinking and drugging of their loved one.

Misdirection is an effective way of controlling those who recognize addiction's presence in the family as well as those who don't. If addiction is the last thing a family suspects, misdirection keeps them from discovering the truth. Once it is no longer a secret, the purpose of misdirection is to keep families from challenging the addiction. The addict's goal is to convince everyone to do things that will support his or her drinking. When families tell me how they've been reacting to the addiction over the years, it is clear to me that addicts are very successful at getting what they want.

Alcoholics and addicts are controlled and fooled by the addiction, too. They know there are problems in their lives and may even have some fleeting awareness that their troubles are related to alcohol or other drugs. However, they cannot hold on to the idea that drinking or drugging is a problem. For them, it is ultimately the solution. So they make sense of this contradiction between "problem" and "solution" by pointing to something else as the source of their difficulties. It might be the spouse, the kids, or the job. The drug remains blameless because their solution cannot also be their problem. This is what we call denial. It is the misdirection of the self.

ADDICTION ISN'T A LIFESTYLE CHOICE

A FRIEND OF MINE explained why he decided not to intervene on his alcoholic father: "It's the lifestyle he chose and I'm not going to interfere." Two years later his father died, but it wasn't a lifestyle choice that killed him. It was a chronic, progressive, predictable disease called alcoholism.

We make many choices that affect our lifestyle: where we live, what we eat, who our friends are, how we spend our free time. Lifestyle choices can have consequences, both good and bad. Some affect our health. We choose our lifestyles, but we don't choose disease. Addiction is a disease, not a choice.

Making the decision to drink is common in our society. Some people drink too much and too often. Consuming fourteen drinks a week, for instance, is categorized as heavy drinking. That's two drinks a day. Not all heavy drinkers develop the disease of alcoholism. Two friends can drink the same amount of alcohol over the same duration of time, and one becomes alcoholic while the other doesn't. We see this on college campuses. Reports of binge drinking and the use of other drugs are common, but only about 10 percent of students will develop an addiction. Genetics, not choice, determines their fate.

Labeling addiction as a lifestyle choice is a moral judgment and usually falls under one of two belief systems. The first and most common is the *wet moral model*. This model supports social drinking as an acceptable part of life as long as everyone follows the rules and drinks within the bounds of propriety. Alcoholics are defined as people who don't exert a proper level of willpower and, as a result, break the rules. The slogan "Know when to say when" is derived from this model, and the keyword is *control*. People who exert proper control, it is believed, won't become alcoholic.

The other belief system is the *dry moral model*. Drinking any amount of alcohol, under this model, is considered sinful. Addiction, it is believed, results from a person's unwillingness to do the right thing. It is a curse people bring upon themselves. Once alcoholics decide to live virtuous lives, they are cured. The slogan for this model is "Denounce demon rum," and the keyword is *righteousness*. According to this model, the righteous don't drink, and therefore they are never tempted to become alcoholic.

Both the wet and dry moral models fail to differentiate between a way of life and a genetically based disease. They underestimate the problem and expect addicts to get well by simply exerting a little control. Of course, all alcoholics attempt to control their drinking for varying lengths of time, and sometimes they succeed remarkably well for a while. But they don't make dependable and lasting changes. The moral models don't take into account the fact that addiction erodes willpower and undermines attempts to do the right thing. As the disease progresses, the ability to exercise control diminishes. Drinkers who are not alcoholics can change their ways, even when they are heavy drinkers; alcoholics cannot without outside help. This is explained in the book *Alcoholics Anonymous,* otherwise known as the *Big Book:*

Moderate drinkers have little trouble giving liquor up entirely if
they have good reason for it. They can take it or leave it alone.
Then we have a certain type of hard drinker. . . . If a sufficiently
strong reason—ill health, falling in love, change of environment,
or the warning of a doctor—becomes operative, this man can also
stop or moderate, although he may find it difficult and
troublesome. But what about the real alcoholic? He may start off
as a moderate drinker; he may or may not become a continuous
hard drinker; but at some stage of his drinking career he begins to
lose all control of his liquor consumption, once he starts to drink.

A friend of mine understood that alcoholism ran in his family, and we discussed the genetics on several occasions. Both of his parents and a grandmother were alcoholics, but he drank daily anyway. He once explained to me why he wasn't worried. "I keep an eye on my drinking," he said with a certain amount of bravado. "If I see a problem developing, I'll just stop." I asked him what he thought he was going to see and why it is that people who do become addicted don't see it coming. Of course, people who become addicted aren't forewarned. They don't see it coming.

No one who chooses to drink or take other drugs can predict whether she will or will not become alcoholic. There are some guiding principles, of course. Children with an alcoholic parent have a fifty-fifty chance of inheriting genes that make them vulnerable to addiction. A healthy lifestyle choice, in this case, is to avoid alcohol entirely. Yet large numbers of people take up drinking regardless of family history, and many become addicted. They're convinced they can control it. That's what the other alcoholics in their families thought, too.

The signs and symptoms of addiction, for the most part, aren't noticeable until the disease reaches its middle stage. In its early stage, the best addiction specialists have difficulty diagnosing the problem. Many alcoholics are highly successful people who are exceedingly attentive to every detail in their lives but still can't detect addiction. If people could see it coming, it's reasonable to assume that most, if not all, would move out of its way.

You may be thinking, *What about drugs?* Let's clear up what we mean when we use the word *drugs*. Usually we're referring to street drugs. However, alcohol is a drug, too. Many prescription medications, such as Xanax and OxyContin, are addictive drugs. We assign stigmas to different drugs, but views change from family to family, community to community. Alcohol is the most accepted and least stigmatized drug in our society. Drunk driving is looked down upon, but drinking too many martinis at a party goes unnoticed unless you end up in the punch bowl. Even then, everyone might laugh it off. But if you're addicted to prescription drugs and you pass out facedown in your dinner plate, you probably won't be invited back. Of course, if all your friends use pills, then your behavior might be accepted as fairly normal and laughed off in the same manner the drinkers laughed off the punch bowl incident.

How we feel about a particular drug may or may not be relevant to how dangerous the drug is compared to other drugs. A drug prescribed by a doctor may be as addictive as a street drug, but we feel no concern about taking it. Some believe that if a drug is "natural"—such as marijuana or peyote—that it can't be harmful. Many people are surprised to learn that alcohol causes a bigger problem in this country than all other drugs combined. It's also the drug that is most damaging to the human body.

Alcohol is often used as a stress reducer. Mothers overwhelmed by children or executives under constant pressure turn to alcohol to unwind. No matter how bad things get during the day, they know a drink will wash it away. A nightcap or two becomes part of the lifestyle. Of course, when alcohol is used to forget problems, problems don't get solved. Rather than investigating new parenting skills or joining a stress management class, drinking a half bottle of wine quickly shuts down the brain. Alcohol is the easy solution. It requires no effort, and rewards come quickly. Attending parenting classes or counseling sessions requires time and work.

Alcohol is a fleeting solution. Neglected problems grow. Sensitivity to stress spikes as alcohol wears off. New problems arise when intoxication leads to arguments or other regrettable behavior. Alcohol is linked to depression. A study showed that when people who have one alcoholic beverage a day quit drinking, their scores improve on standard depression tests after only three months. Other studies show that high quantities of alcohol reduce our body's ability to respond to stress, and heavy drinkers have greater difficulty facing challenging situations. Alcohol also causes insomnia, which in turn increases stress. The "cure" quickly becomes the problem.

Kathy found that she gradually needed more wine to get the same feeling. She saw the increase in her drinking as a normal response to her problems: "The kids are driving me crazy. I need a little something so I can relax." When one glass of wine became two or three or four, her brain began building a tolerance to alcohol. Every once in a while she drank less to reassure herself that she was in control. She made it a point to keep plenty of wine in the house, and when going out she avoided places that didn't serve alcohol. She had no idea she was beginning to exhibit symptoms of alcoholism: increased tolerance, attempt to control, and preoccupation with use. At this point, her drinking quietly crossed the line from lifestyle choice to disease.

Not all alcoholics drink on a daily basis. Some drink only on weekends. Others are binge drinkers. For instance, Peter stays sober for weeks at a time, but then he begins feeling restless and irritable. He needs a drink. So he calls a few buddies and meets them at a local pub. Alcohol leads to cocaine. Then, after a two- or three-day binge, he goes back on the wagon. He may not drink or use cocaine often, but when he does it's always trouble. He doesn't come home, he skips work, he spends money he doesn't have, and sometimes he's unfaithful to his wife. Later he suffers deep remorse. Binge and weekend drinkers have an easier time convincing their families that alcohol and other drugs are a lifestyle choice, not an addiction. However, addiction isn't determined by how much you use or when you use, but what happens as a result.

Good people become addicted. Smart people become addicted. People we respect become addicted. There are doctors smoking crack, schoolteachers drinking Listerine to keep steady during class, grandmothers swallowing Xanax with bourbon, ministers getting through long days on uppers and downers, middle-class coeds snorting heroin. In the end, whatever lifestyle choice triggered the disease isn't as important as what it is going to take to get well.

DETACHMENT AND INACTION:
ARE THEY SYNONYMOUS?

E VEN THE DAY seemed more hopeful as the morning sun streamed down on the flowers in her backyard. *Finally,* Jennifer thought, *I'm going to ask someone to help me.* Just finding the strength to break the silence was enough to give her a feeling of lightness. For several years she had been isolated at home, raising two small children and trying to keep up appearances. Today she was ready to admit her husband's long-kept secret.

John had a good job, but money disappeared and bills didn't get paid. They lived in a house they could no longer afford. Their two- and four-year-old sons often received the brunt of John's rage. Some nights he didn't come home. Friends and family had been carefully deceived, or so she thought. Lately people had begun asking if everything was all right. She dodged questions but couldn't forget the concern on their faces. She knew the truth had to come out. John was an alcoholic and a cocaine addict. Their young family was falling apart.

Staying home to raise children was what Jennifer had dreamed of doing, but now she felt trapped and powerless. She worried constantly. Things would be good for a few days, then he'd pick a fight and take off. He was going in to work late and sometimes not at all. She thought about getting a job but couldn't afford day care. Borrowing from her mother-in-law to buy groceries and pay electric bills, she always made excuses to cover for John. She never told anyone the truth. But that was about to change.

Her former neighbor was a knowledgeable and experienced nurse at a local emergency room. She was the person to ask. She'd know what to do. They arranged to meet at a fast-food restaurant with a playground for the boys. As they sat down, the story came pouring out of Jennifer in a torrent of tears, anger, and shame.

"My dear," said the friend, "I'm so sorry you're facing this terrible situation. Unfortunately, he has to want help before anything will change. The best way you can help him is through detachment. You've got to let go. Stop rescuing him. Let the cards fall where they may. You have to let him experience the pain of his own making. If you clean up his messes for him, he has no reason to get sober. When you detach from his problem, you force him to face the consequences of his addiction."

As her friend continued talking about alcoholism, Jennifer began to feel as if the world was crashing down around her. She couldn't listen anymore. While struggling to strap her sons into the minivan, panic welled up. *How can I continue living this way and for how long? He could lose his job and then we'd lose the house. Where would the money come from? How would we survive? Am I really supposed to stand by and idly watch it all happen?* Other than her friend's heartfelt sympathy, she was leaving empty-handed. Walking around the vehicle to get into the driver's seat, she began crying uncontrollably. As she drove out of the parking lot, the children started to cry, too. The sunlight nearly blinded her as she accelerated into traffic.

Jennifer's friend's advice was half right. Alcoholics do need to feel the consequences of their addiction. But she left out the rest of the story, wrongly interpreting detachment as a hands-off approach. Jennifer needed to hear that there were things she could do to encourage her husband to get into recovery. Instead, she was left with the belief that she had to stand back as their lives fell apart, waiting for John to reach out for help on his own.

When we believe that doing nothing is our only option, we give addiction an open invitation to infiltrate the lives of everyone in the family. Untreated alcoholics disrupt the lives of those around them, causing emotional and physical repercussions that persist throughout lifetimes. Every alcoholic, given a pass to continue in his addiction, exacts a costly toll on those asked to wait until he feels ready to accept help. Detachment, applied in this flawed manner, is a dangerous misuse of an otherwise powerful principle.

Addiction literature has paid a good deal of attention to detachment over the last couple of decades. When I read literature about detachment, the advice is primarily about taking care of ourselves, ceasing our attempts to force others to do what they don't want to do, letting go of our need to control, setting people free to do as they choose, minding our own business, and finding a place of peace for ourselves. This is very good advice under most circumstances, but when we are faced with the uncompromising and relentless addiction of someone we love, we need a plan that is proactive and gets decisive results.

Addiction is intrusive and unrelenting. It demands our attention and drops fear, pain, and sorrow in our laps. The burden is immense and keeps growing. It is difficult to feel good about ourselves when we live with constant fear and worry about the very real problems that come with addiction. Simple platitudes of detachment are insufficient when someone we love is losing everything to addiction and our lives are crumbling as a result. When we think of how we want to live our lives, most of us don't think of coexisting with somebody else's addiction. We know we deserve better.

When I scrutinize how the word *detachment* is commonly used today, several questions come to me: Is motivating an alcoholic to get sober the same as forcing someone to do what he doesn't want to do? Is an alcoholic really doing what he wants to do when he drinks and takes drugs, or is he doing what the addiction makes him do? When we give an addict the freedom to live the life he chooses, aren't we simply giving addiction the freedom to imprison him? When alcoholism affects the family, isn't it everybody's business? How realistic is it that we'll find a place of peace when we are immersed in the daily distress of living with alcoholism? Why do we have to suffer because an addict doesn't want to get well? Why is addiction given more leeway than the family's needs? All these questions expose the inconsistencies and flaws in the idea that detachment means we should let addiction run its course. It makes no sense that the "solution" should cause turmoil and pain in the lives of those closest to the alcoholic. Isn't it better to interrupt the cycle of addiction as early as possible?

Detachment is not a synonym for *inaction*. Rather, it is a spiritual quality that makes action possible. As Kathleen Norris describes in her book *Amazing Grace,* detachment is "a healthy engagement with the world and other people." She explains further: "This sort of detachment is neither passive nor remote but paradoxically is fully engaged with the world. It is not resignation, but a vigilance that allows a person to recognize that whatever comes is a gift from God." Detachment, in this sense, is a willingness to take action while knowing you cannot guarantee the results.

DETACHMENT AND
THE BRAIN

E ARLY ATTEMPTS AT CPR created quite a stir. Was it our place to snatch man back from the arms of God? If someone drowned, did we have the right to interfere with divine will by jump-starting the heart? It was easy to contemplate such questions until it was your loved one pulled from a lake. The same can be said of detachment. It's much easier to talk about until it's your daughter who's smoking crack or your husband who's descended into alcoholism. When we're told that detaching is the right thing to do, why can't most of us do it consistently? Perhaps, since detachment has been distorted beyond recognition to mean doing nothing, this directive goes against our deepest nature: our will to survive.

Detach from the alcoholic with love is the advice commonly offered to families. It's usually taken to mean we should remove ourselves from the situation without being harsh or punitive, and let the addict figure out for herself what she must do. It's also the advice most families resist taking. The idea of not doing anything seems to run against the grain of families and, as it turns out, against our very nature. With the use of brain-imaging techniques (the ability to take photographs and movies of brain activity), science is beginning to discover why we react the way we do.

When something threatening enters our world, our brains are programmed to tell us we should feel fear and prepare to take action. Hearts beat faster, breathing becomes shallow, stomachs jump, blood pressure rises, and adrenaline starts coursing through veins. This emergency system kicks in before our conscious mind even detects trouble. It quite literally happens before we know it. A little almond-shaped part of the brain called the amygdala reacts with lightning speed to pick up signals from the environment and then send emergency messages throughout the body. You might say our survival instinct resides in the amygdala. Carl Zimmer, in his book *Soul Made Flesh,* describes how it works:

> *Fear strikes us suddenly because the amygdala doesn't have to wait for higher regions of the brain to work over sensory information or run it through some abstract set of rules. Neuroscientists have been able to activate the amygdala by flashing pictures of angry faces at people for only forty milliseconds—too fast for them to become consciously aware of them. In that brief time, the amygdala may be able to take a rough measure of a situation and detect anything that looks or sounds particularly dangerous. It then sends out a signal that makes hormones race through the body to prepare it to react. In other words, the amygdala acts almost like a little brain unto itself.*

The amygdala works unconsciously; it is hardwired to *do something* without asking permission first. It has domain over our most powerful unconscious drive—the will to survive. To successfully protect us, the amygdala doesn't wait around for our higher brain to fiddle with the details. There's no avenue for detachment here; the amygdala will react whenever it senses threat. When our alcoholic comes home intoxicated and we know from experience that he's belligerent when he's been drinking, the amygdala sets off the alarm before we've had time to think.

Of course, we are more than our amygdala. We have a prefrontal cortex, which is the seat of our consciousness. This is the part of the brain that thinks about what we do before we do it. Often referred to as the chief executive officer of the mind, the prefrontal cortex uses higher judgment to reevaluate the messages sent out by the amygdala. For instance, the amygdala sees a snake in our path and alerts us to freeze immediately. The prefrontal cortex realizes the "snake" is a stick and announces that we can move forward safely. The amygdala reacts almost instantly; the prefrontal cortex needs time to do its job. If we had to rely on the prefrontal cortex to keep us safe, we'd step on a lot of snakes before we ever saw them.

While the amygdala puts us on notice as soon as it senses the alcoholic pulling into the driveway, the prefrontal cortex tries to determine if he has been drinking once he walks through the door. *Does he smell of alcohol? What kind of mood is he in? What course of action will best protect me?* It is not unusual for kids to scatter as soon as an alcoholic parent returns home, hiding in bedrooms or leaving for a friend's house. They often don't bother waiting around to hear what their prefrontal cortex has to say, since they might be dragged into a tirade before their higher brain completes its evaluation.

Our internal emergency system also sounds an alarm whenever our loved one's addiction begins generating negative consequences: When an addict loses his job, the family is thrown into uncertainty. When she is endangering her life and the lives of others by driving drunk, family anxiety skyrockets. By stealing from his grandmother to buy crack, he creates a fear as to how far he'll go to satisfy his addiction. When she leaves her small children alone at night to go out drinking, she puts them in harm's way. The prefrontal cortex reviews the problem and determines: *Yes, this is serious, and we'd better do something fast because this affects our lives, too.* We aren't just rescuing the addict; we are trying to save ourselves.

People closely related to alcoholics and addicts are susceptible to higher anxiety levels, or what is referred to as free-floating anxiety. Brain research shows that when we are exposed to repeated trauma and stress, the amygdala is affected. More connections grow between neurons, increasing cellular communication. Synapses become more excitable. Our vigilance is heightened. This may explain why the wife of an addict jumps every time the phone rings or someone walks through the door. Her amygdala is hypersensitive; she sees peril where others do not. In response, she increases her efforts to control the addict's problems in a desperate attempt to quiet the alarms going off in her brain.

The spiritual tradition of Buddhism defines detachment as freeing oneself from the preconceived ideas that influence action. It teaches that detachment is the coming together of compassion and objectivity, and from this comes clarity of insight, which allows us to relieve the suffering of others while we simultaneously preserve dignity and justice. That perfectly describes how we want to approach the problem of a loved one's addiction.

Detachment frees us from false assumptions and paralyzing fears that block fruitful and dynamic action. Working constructively with our instinctual drive to find a way to end the cycle of addiction opens us up to new hope. As explained in the book *Al-Anon Faces Alcoholism:* "Detachment is not a wall; it is a bridge."

Franz Metcalf, in his book *What Would Buddha Do,* reflects on what actions the Buddha would take if a friend were addicted to drugs:

When someone goes wrong, it is right for his real friends to move him, even by force, to do the right thing. . . . (Jatakamala 20.23) *Buddha never heard the term "intervention," but that is exactly what he demands with these words. Even if it sometimes takes force, we should try to help our friends when their strength to help themselves is exhausted. This may be the hardest task in the world (other than helping ourselves). It is usually the least-rewarded as well. It is also deeply holy.*

WHEN DO WE LET GO AND LET GOD?

L ETTING GO, much like *detachment,* has been overused and underanalyzed. It has become an excuse to step away from problems that require our attention. We let go when we feel immobilized, or when we no longer feel like bothering with a problem that won't go away. When we hear the often-repeated slogan "Let go and let God," the question rarely asked is: "Let go of what?" Nowhere in the substantive meaning of *letting go* are we absolved of our responsibility. The essential principle of the slogan is to let go of things we are powerless over, not the things we have the power to change. However, sometimes we no longer can differentiate between what we can and cannot do.

In 1965, two scientists discovered a phenomenon called *learned helplessness.* Martin Seligman and Steven Maier exposed animals to prolonged and unpredictable stressors over which the animals had no control. They discovered that when these animals were then given a chance to avoid the stressors by retreating into a safety zone, the animals did not. For example, if rats were given a series of unpredictable shocks that they couldn't avoid, they very quickly developed learned helplessness. When they were moved into a box that had a safety zone and a light that warned of upcoming shocks, these rats continued to allow themselves to be shocked rather than retreat to the shock-free side of the box. In contrast, rats that were not previously stressed by shocks or were given shocks that they could control (terminate by hitting a bar, for instance) had no trouble learning to move to the safety zone as soon as they saw the warning light.

Once rats developed learned helplessness, they had difficulty handling ordinary living skills. Motivational problems prevented them from trying. They rarely engaged in simple life-improving tasks. They also began thinking differently than other rats. When they did attempt to cope, they weren't able to determine if their attempts worked or not. Robert M. Sapolsky, author of *Why Zebras Don't Get Ulcers,* explains:

> *If you tighten the association between a coping response and a reward, a normal rat's response rate increases (in other words, if the coping response works for the rat, it persists in that response). In contrast, linking rewards more closely to the rare coping response of a helpless rat has little effect on its response rate. Seligman believes that this is not a consequence of helpless animals somehow missing the rules of the task; instead, he thinks, they have actually learned not to bother paying attention. . . . [The rat] has learned, "There is nothing I can do. Ever." Even when control and mastery are potentially made available to it, the rat cannot perceive them.*

People with learned helplessness are common in alcoholic families. Having a close relationship with someone addicted to alcohol or other drugs results in three things: prolonged stress, unpredictable stressors (never knowing what the alcoholic will do next), and a sense of having no control. These three conditions create learned helplessness in monkeys, dogs, cats, rodents, birds, and insects; scientists show that they render people helpless, too.

Donald Hiroto used loud noises to show how little it takes to create helplessness in humans. In one group, the noise was inescapable; in the other, an escape mechanism was available. Later, when both groups were presented with a task that would stop the noise when done correctly, those who previously had no control over the noise did considerably worse on the task. Hiroto also found that their helplessness spilled over into other areas. They were less able to solve simple word puzzles or perform well in social coping situations. The effects of learned helplessness include lowered self-confidence, poor problem-solving skills, social constraints, limited attention span, and feelings of hopelessness. All of these symptoms could be used to describe individuals living in a family system plagued by alcoholism.

Psychologists studying illiterate inner-city students were stunned to discover the far-reaching effects of learned helplessness. They set out to determine if the reading problems were due to limited intellectual capabilities. Rather than using the English alphabet, they presented the students with Chinese characters. In a few hours, the students were capable of reading sentences in Chinese they could not read in English. The psychologists found the students' inability to read English resulted from being taught to *believe* their mental aptitude was inadequate. How similar is this to the family that's been convinced they have no power to change the course of addiction?

When one family member suffers from learned helplessness, he or she can slow down the progress of the entire family. For instance, a sister decides to motivate her brother to get treatment for his cocaine addiction and convinces the entire family except her brother's wife to work toward this common goal.

The wife remains resistant even though addiction has cost her husband two jobs and might result in eventual bankruptcy. She complains about the addiction constantly but insists nothing can be done. She adamantly refuses to commit to working with the family to get her husband into treatment. When asked what she wants to do, she can't offer a solution. Working with her causes everyone to pull their hair out. What the family doesn't understand is that she is not being selfish, uncaring, or insensitive; she is suffering from learned helplessness. She believes nothing in the world can solve the problem. When solutions are presented to her, she cannot evaluate them properly. If she is presented with an escape route, she refuses to take it. Lacking the clarity of mind to know when things are going badly or when they're going well, she doesn't protect her children from the hardship of living with an addicted father. When the family insists she take action, she retreats further into helplessness and unmanageability. Like the shocked rat, she has learned "There is nothing I can do. Ever."

It is far better, if you suspect someone is suffering from learned helplessness, to present yourself as a source of gentle strength. When presenting solutions for the first time, gather together a small group of respected family members. The prevailing message from the group should be "We are your refuge." Reassurances can create a sanctuary: *Everyone is here to support you and the children. You don't need to worry about anything because we have taken care of everything. We have found the very best help. We will succeed by working together as a loving family.* Use the power of the group not to intellectualize or theorize but to calm the wounded spirit.

Letting go, when applied improperly, is used to explain away learned helplessness or make it appear noble. The definitive test is to ask ourselves: *What is our work? What will it take to accomplish what is necessary? Are we willing to work together as a family?* If we can answer these questions with positive determination and put what we learn into action, we are not helpless. When we do our part in a meaningful and constructive way, based on solid information and good planning, and have the courage to leave the results in God's hands, we are using *letting go* as it should be used.

In the book *A Place Like Any Other: Sabbath Blessings,* Molly Wolf gives us a wonderful sense of what it means to let go and let God:

The healthy people I know—the ones I respect—seem to allow themselves to be less than fully certain without being paralyzed. They're honest about having their fears, but they also face into them without running away. They debate within themselves and with others the right course of conduct, neither jumping for the simple answer nor being frozen into inaction. They haven't got the easy answers, but they're willing to go ahead as best they can. . . . They are prepared to put a lot of effort and pain into making decisions, while paradoxically trusting that, in God's hands and in God's time, it will all come round right.

IT IS EVERYONE'S BUSINESS

CHRISTINE EXUDES a casual elegance. She is slim and articulate. She and her husband, Andrew, built their dream house in one of the most affluent suburbs in town. When the children come home from school, she quickly sends them outside to play. By this time of day, Christine is finishing off her second bottle of wine and washing down another Xanax.

Andrew hired a woman named Lodi to keep house and monitor the children. He's worried Christine might not be fit to handle an emergency. Lodi came to the rescue more than once when Christine dozed off in the midst of preparing dinner. For Christine, cooking always requires copious amounts of wine.

Christine views herself as supermom: keeping a spotless house, chauffeuring the kids to ballet and soccer, making cakes and cookies from scratch, volunteering at the hospital, and entertaining her husband's clients. At one time she had done all these things and more, but as her addiction to alcohol and prescription medication progressed, it was other people who began taking care of her.

She begins the day with a cup of coffee and a sedative before driving the kids to school. Long telephone conversations with her friends and sisters—in which pills and alcohol fuel complaints about her husband and her life—take up her afternoons. Christine requires constant attention and reassuring.

Her sister Aimee carpools in the afternoon because she knows Christine will be too impaired to pick up the kids. Her other sister, Maria, escorts her to birthday parties or school functions, deathly afraid that, left alone, she would get into an automobile accident or make a fool of herself in front of other parents. Sometimes Christine isn't fit to leave the house and Maria takes over.

After a long day at work, Andrew comes home to face his wife's mood swings. The children try to cheer her up so she won't start a fight with Andrew, but they rarely hold her attention for long. She is a chronic malcontent and quickly becomes argumentative. If Andrew doesn't respond to her rants, she resorts to foul language or throwing things.

Andrew tries in vain to manage the situation. He helps the children with homework, tucks them into bed, and packs their lunches in the morning. He goes to the obligatory meetings with teachers and drops the kids off and picks them up at friends' houses.

But there is nothing anyone can do, or so it seems, to stop the ongoing unmanageability of Christine's life. When her sisters tried to talk to her about drinking during the day, Christine adamantly denied that she drinks before five o'clock. When her sisters pressed on, saying they'd seen her intoxicated by noon, she kicked them out of the house and refused their calls for six weeks.

A close friend tried reasoning with Christine about mixing pills with alcohol. Christine reassured her that the doctor who prescribes the pills says alcohol isn't a problem if she drinks judiciously. When the friend suggested that maybe her body was more susceptible to the effects than the doctor anticipated, Christine's demeanor turned icy and she changed the subject.

Andrew doesn't use the words *alcoholism* or *drug addiction* when talking with Christine's friends or sisters. He prefers *overwhelmed, depressed,* or *exhausted.* The children learned long ago not to mention their mother's drinking. They avoid her and know not to bring friends home after school. Her sisters and friends don't discuss their concerns with Andrew because they believe it isn't their business to approach him. If he wanted help, they reason, he'd come to them.

Declaring that a loved one's addiction isn't our business is a form of self-deception. Everyone makes it their business. The things we do reveal how involved we are: cover up, clean up, ante up, make excuses, rescue, overlook, discount, write off, run away, and keep quiet. Furthermore, our feelings divulge the power the addiction has over us: fear, frustration, sadness, depression, anger, and numbness. Saying it isn't our business is only a way of saying we're not getting involved in finding *solutions.* While Christine's husband, sisters, and friends were busy managing the drinking and pill-popping, finding a resolution to the primary problem of addiction was left undone.

If Christine were having epileptic seizures, the family would discuss it openly and look to the finest neurologists for answers. Why couldn't they do the same for addiction? Is it that everyone is afraid of Christine's anger? She's always mad at somebody and causing everyone else ongoing headaches and heartache. Or is the reason shame? Does the family engage in keeping it secret to preserve their reputation? Are they willing to live in ever-increasing misery in hopes that no one else notices? How about guilt? Do they think they are somehow to blame and fear retribution? (Incidentally, no one can cause someone to become addicted, any more than we can cause someone to become diabetic.) These various worries may all play some part in keeping families stuck, but the primary reason most families don't take action is that they don't know what their responsibilities are or how to carry them out. In other words, *they don't know what to do.*

Discussions about responsibility and who has it usually end up with all fingers pointing at the alcoholic. Someone in the family will say, "It's his responsibility to get it together, not mine." That's true, to a point. Addicts are responsible for their recovery. But here's the catch: addiction invades and conquers willpower and self-control. When addiction becomes the decision maker, addicts will not seek treatment. So if we choose to leave decisions up to alcoholics, we must be willing to say, "I leave it up to them no matter how much suffering we all have to go through as a result."

Are we robbing addicts of their responsibility when we motivate them to get treatment? J. R. Lucas, a fellow at the University of Oxford and author of *Responsibility,* says: "Responsibility is not a material object. If I take a material object, I deprive someone else of it. But I can take responsibility for an action without depriving you . . . of responsibility for it too." Because we take responsibility does not mean we take away the alcoholic's responsibility. Alcoholics don't wake up one day and proclaim it's a good day for recovery. There's always a motivating force—divorce papers, a court date, a boss's ultimatum, or a family's intervention—chasing them into treatment. When families take on the responsibility of learning how to correctly motivate an alcoholic to accept treatment, they are asking the alcoholic to accept responsibility, too.

It isn't our business whom people marry, whether they rent or buy a house, how many children they have, where they go on vacation, how they dress, or what career paths they pursue. But when something in an alcoholic's life adversely affects our lives, it becomes our business. Lucas continues: "It is not just your business: it is my and everyone else's business too, and I cannot acquiesce in your doing it on the grounds that it is for you alone to decide without reference to anyone else." We must reference the cost of untreated alcoholism to the price the *family* pays. In doing so, it quickly becomes clear that alcoholics don't have the right to say drinking is nobody's business but their own, and neither do families. This is a family disease. We're all in it together. It's going to take every one of us to conquer this cunning opponent.

A distinction needs to be made between two ways of helping alcoholics: one helps them stay sick and the other helps them get well. These different helping methods are often referred to as *enabling* and *intervening*. Enabling nurtures the disease; intervening interrupts it. Enabling helps us feel better in the short run; intervention sets goals for long-lasting change.

When alcoholism steals its way into our families, we cannot ignore it without paying long-term consequences. We are called to action in spite of our reluctance. Whenever I hear the story of the Good Samaritan, I think of how it relates to helping alcoholics and addicts. As Jesus tells it, a priest and a Levite are traveling down the same road, both making their way past an injured man without helping. Then a Samaritan comes along, sees the man, and stops. He tends to the man's wounds, puts him on his donkey, takes him to an inn, gives the innkeeper money to care for him, and promises to return to pay any additional expenses. Even though the injured man is an enemy of the Samaritans, the Good Samaritan never questions whether or not he is worthy of help. This story demonstrates more than good neighborliness; it reminds us that we must all make a decision: *Do I stop or do I not?*

When we make a decision, we are taking a stand. Decisions reveal our character, and they change us. Choosing a certain course of action can alter the direction of our life. How we choose to act determines if we will be a better person or a lesser person. Jesus was showing us that our stance toward others is our stance toward our self. When we decide, we define ourselves: *Who am I? Who do I wish to be? Am I the priest? The Levite? Or am I the Samaritan?* When we encounter addiction along the road of life, what will we choose? Families often tell me that they make decisions based upon what the alcoholic will do. They'll say, for instance, "Well, I can't do that. If I do, he'll become angry and stop talking to me." But it's not the alcoholic who determines what we can or cannot do. We set up our own limitations. When families tell me they can't do something because of how the alcoholic might react, I suggest they ask themselves: "Am I acting out of fear or courage, anger or love?" Whichever road we choose to follow, it always tells us something about ourselves.

Addiction lives in shadows, secrets, and silence. It whispers to the family, *Don't say anything, don't do anything, don't ask for help.* But when we decide to talk about addiction, we open windows and let in the light. Doors swing open to new ideas. Good decisions are made.

SEEMING TO DO
IS NOT DOING

THOMAS EDISON, the great inventor, was fond of saying, "Results! Why, man, I have gotten a lot of results. I know several thousand things that won't work." Families have similar revelations trying to straighten out addicts and can tick off plenty of things that didn't work. Most families give up after a while, but Thomas Edison says a few words about that: "Many of life's failures are people who did not realize how close they were to success when they gave up."

Addiction creates unmanageability, and families respond by trying to bring things back to "normal." Everyone, including the addict, works toward achieving equilibrium. The trouble is that the disease of addiction always knocks everyone off center again. As a result, two things begin to happen: families try harder to create balance, and they grow more accustomed to being off balance. Always seeking stability, families are forever inventing new ways to work out problems caused by alcohol and drugs. But rarely do they look outside the family for answers, believing instead that their lone resourcefulness will be sufficient.

The trouble with ideas hatched around a kitchen table is that they are almost always misdirected. They are designed to deal with peripheral problems, not the core issue. In other words, families take care of the negative consequences caused by alcoholism, but not the alcoholism itself. This makes alcoholics happy, because drinking is easier when someone is always cleaning up the mess yet never threatening the addiction. The family feels better, too. For a short time they feel they have everything under control.

The common thread among families coping with a loved one's addiction is the belief that improving the addict's circumstances in life will render the addiction unnecessary. Problems in the addict's life, it's believed, are what cause the addiction, not the other way around. If the problem is solved, it is reasoned, the addiction should go away on its own. Thinking of addiction in these terms results in enabling the disease to progress with greater ease. I have seen families try to solve all of the alcoholic's problems, in hopes the addiction would go away. Here are some examples: A twenty-four-year-old with a marijuana problem is given full financial backing to return to school. Retired parents bankroll the latest business adventure of their unemployed fifty-two-year-old alcoholic son. A condo is purchased for a cocaine-addicted daughter. An addict's brother-in-law gives him a job. Checks are written to cover mortgages, car payments, utilities, groceries, and more.

Everyone is confident that by giving an addict a fresh start, he can build a new life. As it turns out, most addicts do quite well for a while, thereby convincing the family they did the right thing. But addiction isn't to be ignored. It reasserts itself, and things begin to go badly. Addicts, of course, always offer sensible reasons why things didn't work out, but addiction is never one of them.

Families are often trapped in the "threaten, punish, relent" cycle. They think they can shake sense into an alcoholic. Straighten up, they say, or there will be severe consequences. A husband says he'll move out and take the kids. Parents threaten to take away the car. A daughter says she'll stop all after-school visits with the grandkids. A girlfriend promises she'll break it off for good this time. At first, threats produce some good results. Alcoholics shape up, and the family feels good about setting things straight. But changes don't last and families relent. It was easy to threaten, but not so easy to follow through: *If I move out, who will take care of the kids when I'm at work? If we take away his car, how will he get to school? How can I tell my mother she can't see her own grandchildren? If I break up with him, he'll probably have a new girlfriend in a week and I'll be left alone.* Once they've gone through the "threaten, punish, relent" cycle a few times, they've trained the alcoholic not to believe what they say. The addiction is empowered because it understands no one will get in its way.

Families sometimes put together ramshackle interventions. They send a few family members to speak to the alcoholic. There's no planning, no preparation, no format, and no arrangements for treatment. The family doesn't stop to learn anything about intervention; they wing it. They rush over to the alcoholic's house and initiate a discussion that quickly dissolves into a free-for-all. They are outgunned by the addiction and don't know it. They lose control quickly and are either bamboozled or trounced by the skillful manipulation of addiction. Later, when someone suggests they try doing an intervention, they say, "We've tried that and it didn't work."

Underestimating what they are up against is the undoing of many families. Because they think addiction is little more than a bad decision or an unfortunate turn down a wrong road, they take for granted that a little prodding, some tweaking, or a dose of admonishment should get the addict back in the right direction. They take their approach from an intellectual stance or a punitive one. The message is *shape up*.

We expect addicts to get their heads on straight. But therein lies the problem. The brain is one of the places addiction takes up residence; the other is the soul. We expect addicts to rely on the strength of their mind and spirit to pull themselves out of the quagmire, but these are the two areas crippled by the disease. Addiction has co-opted the power of the brain and the soul to work for its own survival. When we try to convince our loved ones to do the right thing, it is the addiction that responds. The disease is in the driver's seat, and it will not easily relinquish control. We must appreciate the power and cunning of this disease or we will not prevail.

It is a far better strategy for families to get *their* heads on straight. We tend to confront addiction with whatever idea feels right and without taking the time to find out if it is. For example, a father sat his seventeen-year-old, pot-smoking daughter down at the computer and told her to research the perils of marijuana. Dad was convinced that a little education would solve his daughter's problem. Instead, she found several pro-marijuana Web sites that reinforced her decision to use drugs. Seeing his idea backfire, he blamed it on his daughter's insolence. He continued to defend the workability of his plan and was unwilling to admit that it hindered more than it helped. Not being wrong was more important to him than learning the right way to help his daughter.

If our families are to succeed at defeating addiction, we must be willing to put our beliefs to the test and ask ourselves, "Is this working or does it just feel as if it should work?" Only when we allow ourselves to admit to being wrong can we find the right answers. Thomas Edison, after all, rejoiced in being wrong because he knew he was one step closer to getting it right. He also understood that while we might look as if we're diligently trying to solve a problem, it doesn't mean we are getting results: "Being busy does not always mean real work. The object of all work is production or accomplishment and to either of these ends there must be forethought, system, planning, intelligence, and honest purpose, as well as perspiration. Seeming to do is not doing."

CREATE A
SPACIOUS PLACE

THE HEBREW WORD *YASHA*, translated as "salvation" in the Bible, literally means "to bring into a spacious place." To find hope in the face of alcoholism, families must make their world larger. This requires the spiritual action of opening up to others and forming a cooperative spirit. *Yasha* breaks down barriers, heals wounds, makes room for new ideas, and teaches us to accept the support of others. Addiction, on the other hand, isolates families, keeping inner and outer worlds small. Working together is the key to reclaiming our family, and by doing so we find ourselves in a spacious place.

The first step toward recovery is identifying who in our family is most open to change. Look for the person who is discontent with the way things are and most willing to work toward something better. Discontentment, in the best sense of the word, sparks the desire for change. We evaluate old beliefs, and if they have been blocking our progress, we discard them. Discontentment opens our minds to explore new possibilities. It pushes us into a spacious place. J. Krishnamurti, the Indian teacher and philosopher of spirituality, wrote: "Discontentment will have an extraordinary significance because it will build, it will create, it will bring

new things into being. For this you must have education . . . that
helps you to think and gives you space—space not in the form of a
larger bedroom or a higher roof, but space for your mind to grow
so that it is not bound by any belief, any fear."

Asking for help is a daunting task in an alcoholic family. Our
training has been the opposite: don't talk, don't trust, don't feel,
and, above all, don't let yourself be vulnerable. Asking for help
makes us vulnerable. To keep the task from becoming daunting,
first approach those who will be the most supportive. Keep your
spark alive by uniting with family members willing to light a torch.
Don't allow it to be extinguished by the unwillingness of others.

In most families, there is a mixed bag of reactions toward initiating change. Some family members constantly complain, but
when solutions are offered, they are quick to shoot them down.
These people usually begin sentences with, "Yes, but . . ."
Others have washed their hands of the situation. When they're
approached, they quickly distance themselves from solutions:
"I'm done trying to help her. I've done everything I can."
Others are downright hostile to change. They reject out of hand
the idea of interfering with the addiction. They leap to the conclusion that all help is meddlesome, and mistakenly believe the
family is planning to treat the alcoholic unjustly. They object before they know what they are objecting to: "I could never do
that to him. He doesn't deserve it." Begin instead with the person who will say, "Yes, I'll help. You can count on me."

In some families, addiction has taken such a toll that no
one is willing to collaborate. Everyone is so accustomed to self-
protection that no one risks breaking out. Living in the chronic
dysfunction of the family becomes more comfortable than ven-
turing into the unknown. When this is the case, turn to the extended family. A respected uncle or aunt, grandparent, cousin,
or close friend can be a trustworthy ally. Approach this person in
a way that will make him or her feel comfortable rather than

overwhelmed. Don't begin by saying: "We need to intervene on our alcoholic right away, but no one will help." It's far better to proceed in measured steps: "I've found new information that I think could make a difference. I value your judgment and hope you will work with me to determine the best way to solve this difficult problem." Then together you can gain the necessary knowledge and make the best decisions. A good advisor is committed to your success and will go to great lengths working toward it. He or she can also help build your team. I have found that it is often a person removed from the emotional turmoil of the family who has the greatest success bringing everyone together.

If there are no relatives available, turn to a professional. Choose an addiction specialist experienced in family intervention techniques. A skilled practitioner can evaluate a situation and devise a plan for bringing the family together. After gathering some initial information, a consultation with everyone in the family—other than the alcoholic—is the next step. The meeting can take place in an office or in a telephone conference call. Reluctant families are often less resistant if they don't have to sit in a counselor's office with their entire family present. A conference call is less formal, everyone calls from his or her own home, and nobody has to make major schedule adjustments. This is also very convenient when family members are scattered across the country. Properly facilitated, a contentious family can find common ground and agree on a plan of action in a relatively short amount of time. If financial resources are scarce and hiring a professional is out of the question, turn to clergy. If your pastor or rabbi is unfamiliar with intervention, ask if he or she is willing to learn along with the family. If not, ask for a referral to someone else.

Family members who refuse to cooperate with the rest of the family usually do so because they are wounded. They may outwardly display anger or impatience, but the true emotion is hurt. Alcoholics cause so much pain and disappointment that finding the compassion to help them is sometimes extraordinarily difficult. However, when we come together, we do so not just for the alcoholic but also for every other member of the family. When it's clearly understood that confronting the disease begins a journey of healing for everyone, it is a goal most people can agree upon. Families who have defeated addiction often say, "Recovery is not a spectator sport." Everyone needs to get involved.

When family members refuse to participate in an intervention, they are usually telling us, "I need more information." Respect their need to know. Don't rush anyone into anything. Find out what they can comfortably agree to do now. Will they look at a Web site? Read a book? Talk to someone who can answer questions? Achieving some degree of forward movement is accomplished not by pushing or prodding but by understanding. If we take the bull out of the china shop and give it a wide-open space, it calms down. This is true of people, too. Free from the need to fight against something or somebody, most of us can agree to take a step in the right direction.

This is a small beginning, but one that leads to unexpected and powerful change. The disease of addiction protects itself by setting one family member against another and then finding safety by retreating into the chaos and confusion. It spins uncertainty, fear, and hopelessness. It tells us: *There is nothing you can do.* But when people come together, they discover there is most definitely something they can do. As explained by Molly Wolf in her book *A Place Like Any Other:* "Hope's slow sometimes. . . . But once hope gets a foothold, a little warmth, some promise, it *will,* in its very nature, simply grow. Once the Spirit gets one tendril in a person's heart, the spirit will persist, insist, demand, to keep on growing and becoming."

PART TWO

The Collapsed Spirit:
Inaction and Old Action

OLD ACTIONS PERPETUATE THE PAST

A N OLD RABBI used a favorite story, the parable of heaven or hell, to teach his students that our spiritual condition is determined by our willingness to cooperate with one another, and that past behaviors are the best indicators of how we'll behave in the future. Even when our actions don't serve us well, we resist changing them.

An old man knew he was approaching death and wanted to visit both heaven and hell before the day arrived. A wise man agreed to take him on a tour. First he took him to visit hell, and the old man was surprised to see long, beautiful tables laden with gourmet foods, each dish more gloriously prepared than the last. He turned to the wise man and said, "If this is hell, I can hardly wait to see heaven." But then he became aware of a most disturbing sight. The people seated around the tables were pale and malnourished. They were living skeletons moaning in hunger. As he approached them, he understood their plight. Everyone was supplied with twelve-foot chopsticks. As they attempted to feed themselves, they failed. With a broken heart, the old man left. He was haunted by the tortured expressions of people starving while surrounded with such abundance.

Next the wise man took him to visit heaven. He was surprised to see that heaven looked exactly like hell. Rows of beautiful tables were laden with the finest foods. Then he looked at the people and saw how happy they were. They were laughing and talking. Cheeks were plump and rosy, and a healthy glow emanated all around. The air was filled with a feeling of peace and contentment. The old man was amazed to see that the people in heaven had the same twelve-foot chopsticks as the people in hell. "How do they eat?" he asked the wise man, who then gestured for the old man to take a closer look.

As the old man watched, he saw a woman pick up her chopsticks and gently select a delicacy before her. She then fed the person across the table. The recipient of this kindness smiled and returned the favor. The old man suddenly saw that heaven and hell offer the same circumstances and conditions, but the critical differences lie in the actions of the people.

The old man turned to the wise man and said, "I must return to hell and relieve the suffering of those poor souls." The wise man, with a knowing smile, said nothing, but led him back to hell. The old man rushed up to one of the starving people and whispered, "I've been to heaven and you do not have to go hungry. I know the solution. Use your chopsticks to feed your neighbor, and he will surely feed you." The man looked up in indignation and self-righteousness and said, "You expect me to feed any of these despicable human beings? I'd rather starve than give such an undeserving lot a single morsel of this food." The old man walked away, shaking his head, finally understanding the vast division between heaven and hell.

How often do families act in the same way? We remain loyal to actions that have long failed to produce positive results. Even in the midst of a feast of new information, we refuse to change. Perhaps we think the alcoholic is not deserving of our efforts or that it's his job to get his life together, not ours. Whatever our reason for not changing, it usually comes down to a common rationale: *I'm not willing to expend the energy to learn something new. I'd rather keep doing what I've been doing all along and live with things as they are.* We continue to evaluate the alcoholic's state of affairs, of course, but fail to recognize that the entire family is paying the price.

By recycling old actions that don't work, we perpetuate more of the past. We go in circles with the addiction and get nowhere. Before we can break away from our past behaviors, we need to begin questioning *ourselves.* Ask yourself these questions, not with harsh judgment but with an honest desire to see how addiction has taken hold of your family:

How does my family reuse the same old actions, each time expecting different results?

Is someone always ready to manage the alcoholic's troubles?

Is someone else shaming the alcoholic and expecting him to magically overcome his problem without outside help?

Is someone trying to get as far away from the problem as possible?

Who plays which roles? Do some people take on more than one role? What rewards come from each?

When the alcoholic gets into a jam, how does the family react? Who throws her hands up in disgust? Who rushes in to fix everything?

Who feels as if something's been accomplished each time the alcoholic apologizes and agrees to do better?

Can anyone say he has a workable plan for conquering the addiction in the long term?

If a family member points out that the family's actions aren't helping the alcoholic, does this observation raise the ire of the others?

Does the family think the alcoholic is a bad person or a sick person?

Tally up all the old actions that haven't worked in your family. We must begin to recognize what doesn't work. Once we can see that our old actions require tremendous emotional, physical, and financial expenditures without giving us any good returns, we're more willing to open the door to fresh ideas.

When we continue to struggle with the alcoholic's behaviors but don't address the addiction itself in any meaningful way, we never get anywhere. We're relegated to the sidelines to wait and see how the game of chance plays out. It's always a roll of the dice, and the odds favor the addiction. We have no way of knowing how great our losses will be or how long the losing streak will last. Will our addicted loved one eventually find her way into recovery, or will the addiction take all? It's anyone's guess, but as a friend said to me after visiting Las Vegas for the first time, "It's easy to see who's winning. You just have to take a look at the hotels." With addiction it's easy to see who's winning, too. Congressman Jim Ramstead, speaking at a luncheon on Capitol Hill, made clear what the odds are: "Only 5 percent of addicts and alcoholics are in recovery," he said. "Eighty-two percent of people in jails are there because of addiction."

Families may not have signed on to play this game of chance, but they share the losses nonetheless. Even children have to pay. Of the nearly twenty-eight million children of alcoholics in the United States, eleven million are under eighteen years old. This means that one out of every six American children is paying the price for a parent's addiction. These are children living in our neighborhoods and our families. Claudia Black, author of numerous books on children of alcoholics, describes some of their losses: "The children wake up in a world that does not take care of them. They learn not to show their feelings, not to talk honestly, not to pay attention to what's happening around them." When we don't set up a zero-tolerance policy for untreated addiction in our families, the most vulnerable among us—our children— are abandoned. They cannot trust the addicted parent, nor can they look to nonaddicted family members to do what needs to be done. As children, they cannot get their addicted parent into treatment. Their only means of survival is to *change who they are* so that they can better fit into the alcoholic home.

We feel comfortable with the way we've always done things. When our actions don't bring about lasting results, we try the same things again anyway. We believe that if we keep doing what we're doing, the addict will eventually see the wisdom of our ways. Emmet Fox, scientist and spiritual philosopher, shares an anecdote that illustrates the insanity of clutching on to things that do not work:

> *A party of hunters . . . left their campfire unattended, with a kettle of water boiling on it. Presently an old bear crept out of the woods, attracted by the fire, and seeing the kettle with its lid dancing about on top, promptly seized it. Naturally it burnt and scalded him badly; but instead of dropping it instantly, he proceeded to hug it tightly—this being Mr. Bear's only idea of defense. Of course, the tighter he hugged it the more it burnt him, and of course, the more it burnt him the tighter he hugged it, and so on in a vicious circle, to the undoing of the bear.*

Before we can change, we must be rigorously honest about our resistance to change. It is easier to suffer than to change. It is easier to cry than to change. It is easier to curse than to change. We must ask: *Am I willing to leave behind the comfort of my old ways?* The pain of change always gets better, but the pain of staying the same always gets worse. We have to decide if our future will be determined by our past or by the changes we make today. As Francis Bacon, the father of deductive reasoning, said: "He that will not apply new remedies must expect new evils; for time is the greatest innovator."

THE ART OF CONTORTION

Trapped in the alcoholic system, everyone scrambles to find safety. As Tennessee Williams said, "It's almost as if you were frantically constructing another world while the world that you live in dissolves beneath your feet." Each calamity is met with a corresponding survival skill. When an alcoholic, out for dinner, drinks too much and becomes belligerent and loud, one embarrassed family member makes jokes to defuse the tension while another tries to calm the alcoholic down. With an apologetic smile, they slip the waitress an extra $10 bill as they leave. "He's a good guy until he's had a little too much," they say. Everyone in the family is humiliated, but they do their best to put a good face on a bad situation. They've become adept at the *art of contortion*.

Contortionists twist and bend their bodies into unnatural and seemingly impossible shapes. Some bend backward until the back of their head touches their calves. Others rest their chests on the floor and bend themselves over their head until they are sitting on their head. Still others squeeze their bodies into boxes that appear infeasibly small. In families of professional contortionists, each individual is skilled at a unique form of bending the body. Together they create a seamless balancing act. Similarly, alcoholic families, to keep the family system balanced, bend and twist their behaviors, emotions, thoughts, and spirits. By twisting themselves into different shapes, each member of the family compensates for addiction in his or her particular way. As addiction gets worse and shifts the family further out of balance, more extreme contortions are required to reestablish equilibrium.

I was listening to an interview with Gilles Ste-Croix, vice president of creativity for the famed Cirque de Soleil, as he described child contortionists they discovered while scouting for new talent. He said, "We discovered, in India, little contortionists and . . . they carry a little bowl with a little candle on their forehead while they're doing their contortions." As he continued describing these tiny little girls doing very difficult things while keeping these flames burning, I suddenly realized how similar these girls are to small children in alcoholic families, who twist and bend themselves to counterbalance a parent's addiction. They burn little lights, too, but these are lights of hope. They hope for love and acceptance in a family system that is increasingly impaired. These children contort themselves as a way of gaining approval from a parent who, beholden to addiction, is not able to fully attend to the family's needs. They delicately balance themselves between attracting positive attention from their parent and avoiding the wrath of the addiction. These contortions are *survival skills* and the beginning of *character defects*.

Survival skills target specific problems. Upon solving the problem, we no longer have need for that particular skill, unless a similar problem crops up. However, when a problem persists over time and we repeatedly rely on a survival skill, that survival skill begins to solidify into a character defect. Character defects become part of our personalities. For example, responding with anger to an alcoholic's behavior is a survival skill; becoming

chronically quick-tempered with everybody is a character defect. Survival skills fade away after alcoholics quit drinking;
character defects do not.

Even though self-protection is the popular explanation for
why we develop defects of character, could there be other reasons? Could it be that we develop them not just as an attempt to
endure our family but also as a way to interact with them? After
all, our most basic instinct isn't just survival; rather, as social beings, we are driven to connect with one another. If we don't
make social connections, we won't survive. Character defects,
therefore, can also be defined as necessary distortions of behaviors that help facilitate our attempts to connect to a family being
pulled apart by addiction.

Communication is difficult in alcoholic homes. Addiction dis-
courages healthy discourse, so families resort to extreme measures
to get their messages across. Exaggerated attempts to connect
become the norm. Anger becomes rage; concern becomes
panic; frustration becomes retaliation; authority becomes domi-
nance; persuasion becomes manipulation; disagreement becomes hostility. The volume is turned up. It's often the only way
to get anyone's attention.

Sometimes families keep the addict happy as a way of maintaining relationships. Everybody works to maintain peace by
quickly solving problems, taking over responsibilities, and acting as if everything is fine. As long as the home runs smoothly on
the surface, they're willing to overlook the underlying disrup-
tions. An uneasy truce with the disease holds the household together. It can go on that way for years until the addiction does
something impossible to ignore.

Martha and Art were married for forty years. Art was a heavy
drinker when they met, but problems didn't surface until the
kids were school-age. The drinking never interfered with Art's
work, but he became increasingly unavailable to the family.

Martha learned how to navigate his drinking. She knew the first couple of beers were okay. He'd become gregarious and relaxed. If she kept things light, they could have a good conversation. But after dinner, as he drank more, he'd withdraw. Martha knew that talking stopped at this point. He became brusque if she tried to discuss family matters or ask him to do anything around the house. Instead, she'd make him comfortable in front of the TV and herd the kids into their bedrooms. Art worked hard and deserved some downtime, she reasoned, and it was in the best interest of their marriage if she provided him with what he needed. As the years went by, Art drank more. Alcohol turned him into a chronic malcontent. The more difficult he was to live with, the more Martha strived to be the ideal wife. She was a perfectionist around the house and a consummate people pleaser. When the children, now grown, had a falling out with their dad, she smoothed things over. When Art was too intoxicated to fulfill promises, she made his excuses. She wasn't blind to the relationship problems, but despite it all, everything she did was geared toward their marriage. When Art did something thoughtful or paid attention to what she was saying, she counted it as a success. The tender moments they had together, she told herself, outweighed all the bad times. Connecting with her husband was Martha's primary motivation for changing her behavior. She did what she could to work around his addiction. The fact that connections with Art came infrequently made her work that much harder.

As human beings, we invent ways of connecting with one another. We come together by talking, playing, dancing, joking, working, sharing, touching, and helping. In alcoholic homes, addiction interrupts these normal coming-together activities. So families invent new ways to connect. One child becomes the *hero*, bringing accolades to the family by getting top grades or being the star football player. Another is the *scapegoat*, attracting negative attention by always getting into trouble. The *lost child* stays out of the way and is rewarded for being the one who entertains himself and is never a nuisance. The *mascot* makes everyone laugh. As the clown, he always has an audience. In small families, people take on more than one role. Over time, playing these roles reinforces our defects of character. In the book *Another Chance,* Sharon Wegscheider-Cruse explains: "Each role grows out of its own kind of pain, has its own symptoms, offers its own payoffs for both the individual and the family, and ultimately exacts its own price. . . . The longer a person plays a role, the more rigidly fixed in it he becomes."

Unspoken rules inhibit communication in alcoholic homes as a means to safeguard the addiction. Addiction is threatened by honesty, so the entire system shuts down—no information in, no information out. A rich and rewarding family life is impossible under such circumstances. A truthful expression of feelings— especially negative emotions such as fear, anger, frustration, sadness, and disappointment—is unacceptable. Healthy discussion of what's happening in the family is unthinkable. Outside information is unwelcome. Everyone adapts to these rules and by doing so constructs an unhealthy family system. This occurs without anyone being aware of what is happening, but this doesn't make the outcome any less disturbing. Family therapist Virginia Satir describes the result in her book *The New Peoplemaking:*

> *The atmosphere in a troubled family is easy to feel. Whenever I am with such a family, I quickly sense discomfort. Sometimes it feels cold, as if everyone were frozen; the atmosphere is extremely polite, and everyone is obviously bored. Sometimes it feels as if everything were constantly spinning, like a top; I get dizzy and can't find my balance. Or it may be an atmosphere of foreboding, like the lull before a storm, when thunder may crash and lightning*

strike at any moment. Sometimes the air is full of secrecy.
Sometimes I feel very sad and cannot find an obvious reason. I
realize that's because the sources are covered up.

When we live under stressful conditions we exert tremendous energy to cope, and most of the time we don't do this by avoiding one another. We desperately search for ways to connect, not only with nonalcoholic family members but also with the alcoholic. It's as if we are fighting to come together while the centrifugal force of alcoholism is pulling us away from one another. While avoidance is a common coping tool, it rarely triumphs over our urge to come together. Avoidance is more of a time out; then we get back in the game again. Avoiding family one day doesn't mean we won't try to connect with them the next, no matter how imperfectly. We may be an alcoholic family, but that doesn't mean we aren't *family*. As humorist Erma Bombeck put it, speaking for all families everywhere:

We were a strange little band of characters trudging through life
sharing diseases and toothpaste, coveting one another's desserts,
hiding shampoo, borrowing money, locking each other out of our
rooms, inflicting pain and kissing to heal it in the same instant,
loving, laughing, defending, and trying to figure out the common
thread that bound us all together.

FEAR

FEAR LURKS BEHIND every character defect: fear of being rejected, fear of being alone, fear of being hurt. Whichever character defect surfaces in our lives—perfectionism, people pleasing, anger, resentment, control, procrastination—when we peel it back, we find fear. Character defects are mechanisms for controlling fear. Perfectionism, for instance, is an attempt to do away with fear by applying unrealistically high standards to everything in our lives. If we can make our world perfect, there shouldn't be a reason to fear anything. Of course, perfectionism isn't an escape from fear but an expression of fear.

We're taught to perceive fear as a negative emotion, but fear is a great motivator and protector. It is nature's way of warning us we're in trouble and need to take action. It guides us through new experiences, telling us to keep our eyes and ears open because we don't know what we'll find around the corner. Sometimes a little fear is better than no fear. Before playing sports or speaking publicly, a moderate amount of adrenaline pumping through our bodies heightens our senses and improves our performance. It also helps us complete tasks we know will reward us if done well and penalize us if not—an exam or a project for work, for instance. Fear is our friend. Living in constant fear, however, changes everything.

When we're living in the closed system of addiction, fear has nowhere to go. Without a healthy way to eliminate or dissipate fear, it reverberates and begins to traumatize us repeatedly. Our sense of threat is ever present: it may be a looming danger or a vague sense of dread. Either way, living with addiction is like living with a tiger. One eye is always on the tiger, even when it's asleep in the corner. We can never stop thinking about it for long—hypervigilance being our best defense. We make sure it's content, and when it isn't, we quickly placate it or move out of its way. We know the tiger's potential: it can turn on us at any moment. When we live with it long enough, we live life on its terms.

When fearful conditions persist and we believe we have no power to change them, we adjust ourselves by normalizing what is abnormal. We absorb fear into our lives and make it ordinary. After a while it's routine, and sometimes we barely notice it. Once fear is the status quo, we sustain it as a normal part of life. Emotional shutdown allows us to put up with behaviors we once said we'd never tolerate. Overloaded brains reduce the output of emotion—fear is reduced to background noise rather than a constant drumming in our ears. In other words, if there's too much fear, we stop responding to it. Although the problem persists, we're desensitized, and thus we're inadequately motivated to take action. We're no longer *feeling* as afraid as we should, and we begin *underreacting* to the seriousness of the disease. For example, I've consulted with many wives who said they'd never stand by and allow their alcoholic husbands to drive while intoxicated, but then found themselves letting it happen all the time. Many rode in the car with their husbands, and some didn't step in when he drove the children. They still worried, but they didn't take the kind of action they had promised themselves. Once our brains shut down, they don't fully wake up again until something sufficiently serious happens—an accident or a DUI arrest, for instance. It takes a louder alarm to get a reaction out of the family, in the same way it takes more of the drug to get the addict high. Everyone's brain is building up tolerance.

Thrown out of equilibrium by persistent fear, our brains always seek to regain balance. But the price we pay by adjusting to the problem, rather than fixing it, is extraordinarily high. The human body responds to stress as if it's life-threatening. Whether we are chased by a grizzly or exposed to psychological stress due to a loved one's addiction, the body reacts by releasing the same hormones—adrenaline and cortisol. When a grizzly is after us, more adrenaline is released into the body. When the stress is long-term, more cortisol is released. When high levels of cortisol are sustained in our bodies over extended periods of time, serious consequences follow: weakened immune system, loss of hair, thinning skin (which makes it more susceptible to wrinkling), decreased muscle mass, and lack of energy. Our ability to concentrate is reduced and serotonin levels drop, limiting our capacity to control impulsive behaviors. We're at high risk for depression and insomnia. Elevated levels of cortisol are also associated with diseases such as stroke, diabetes, heart attack, high blood pressure, and osteoporosis. Our stress hormones are no longer saving us; they are aging us. Prolonged stress is destructive, biologically speaking, because we are not built to live in a constant state of fear. David M. Sapolsky, professor of biology and neurology at Stanford University, explains:

That the stress-response itself can become harmful makes certain sense when you examine the things that occur in reaction to stress. They are generally shortsighted, inefficient, and penny-wise and dollar-foolish, but they are the sorts of costly things your body has

*to do to respond effectively in an emergency. And if you experience
every day as an emergency, you will pay the price.*

The area of our brain most responsible for memory, called
the hippocampus, begins to decline during long periods of stress.
The communication lines between brain cells begin to shrivel.
We aren't forgetting things just because we're distracted by a
loved one's addiction; we're losing our ability to remember because stress is causing our hippocampus to atrophy. Brain cells
are shutting down. Once stress subsides, brain cells begin growing new connections and our ability to remember returns.
Allowing stress to persist over long periods, however, can cause irreversible damage, and then our memory is never fully restored.

Emotional stress that comes on suddenly—a jolt to the system
caused by fear, anger, or grief—may cause heart failure in people
with no history of heart disease. This is informally called "broken
heart syndrome," but research is showing that the old ideas
of frightening someone to death or dying of grief may be true.
Dr. Ilan S. Wittstein, a cardiologist at Johns Hopkins University,
says: "It's important for people to know that this is something
that emotional stress truly can do." Broken heart syndrome is
not a heart attack but stress cardiomyopathy, or weakening of the
heart, caused by high levels of stress hormones, which are toxic
to the heart. The heart is literally stunned by high doses of adrenaline and cortisol. Consequences range from mild to fatal. Older
people are most susceptible to this syndrome, but it's been reported in people as young as twenty-seven. This can happen not
only when the stressful event occurs but also when the memory
of the event is triggered. For instance, if a mother loses her son
to a drunk driving accident, the anniversary of her son's death
could cause enough grief to trigger this type of heart failure.

These are serious issues. Families who believe there is nothing they can do about the alcoholism are not just living with a

few inconveniences or an occasional embarrassment; their physical and mental health is eroding. The addiction's "right" not to be interrupted until the addicted person is "ready" costs family members their health. Temporary fear doesn't damage our bodies, but generalized, I-don't-know-what-is-going-to-happen-next fear slowly kills us. The older we are, the more vulnerable we are to physical and mental problems associated with this kind of fear. A loved one's addiction can cause repercussions in older adults that speed up the aging process and threaten health and cognitive abilities; eventually the decline can lead to loss of independence. I've worked with many older parents who, in their retirement, declined quickly due to the toll their adult child's addiction was taking.

Carolyn and Ernie expected to pass their retirement years traveling, playing golf, and spending time with grandchildren. They sold the family home and bought two condos, one up north near their children and one in Florida. They never foresaw their youngest son Kevin's addiction to crack cocaine. It threw the entire family into turmoil. They lived in constant fear, always imagining the worst. Kevin would disappear for days at a time, spending large sums of money on crack. Carolyn and Ernie tried to keep his life from falling apart by covering his mortgage and car payments. When Kevin's wife left him, they begged her to give him a second chance. When she refused, Kevin moved in with them. The other children were furious and argued with their parents, accusing them of enabling Kevin. Carolyn and Ernie stopped going to Florida because they couldn't leave Kevin and couldn't take him to the retirement community. Carolyn and Ernie's relationship deteriorated as they argued over what to do. The other children visited less often and wouldn't allow grandchildren to spend the night. Carolyn and Ernie could no longer entertain friends, and they didn't dare leave Kevin alone. They became increasingly isolated, and their health declined. Carolyn couldn't sleep and had frequent headaches. Ernie was put on medication for high blood pressure. When they learned that Kevin had stolen $10,000 from their bank account, Ernie suffered heart failure.

Living with addiction causes unrelenting fear. It's part of our lives whether we recognize it or not, or whether we call it by another name such as anger or indifference. Fear is running the show, and we are reacting to it. Gradually we begin to deteriorate physically and mentally. Changes in our bodies often go unnoticed for long periods of time or are attributed to something other than the addiction. But once we're awakened to the fact that a loved one's addiction compromises the health of the people we love, we can no longer think of it as the addict's problem. It is the entire family's problem, and something needs to be done. It is not acceptable to allow addiction to adversely affect the lives of so many people, especially children, for so long.

How do we overcome pervasive, sometimes unnoticed, fear? We begin by working with other people. When we try to manage the alcoholic one-on-one, we're defeated by the addiction before we begin. Rarely does someone walk away victorious after a little tête-à-tête about the drinking or other drugs. Addiction is challenged successfully when a team of people unites and arms itself with knowledge. However, even building a team can overwhelm us with fear. It's helpful to know that we need fear; fear gives us a sense of urgency and motivates us to act. Fear opens the door to courage. Once we take the first step, the next one is easier. "Courage," said David Ben-Gurion, Israel's first prime minister, "is a special kind of knowledge: the knowledge of how to fear what ought to be feared and how not to fear what ought not to be feared."

We *ought to fear* the disease and the continuing consequences—some tragic—it brings to those we love. We *ought not fear* confronting the disease, taking constructive action with other family members and friends to begin the treatment process. Becoming knowledgeable about the tools needed to be successful—such as how intervention can help—reduces fear and gives us the strength to proceed.

In the Christian gospels, it is promised that when we are strong and do not lose courage, our work will be rewarded. We are asked not to become weary in well-doing, for in due season we reap if we do not lose heart. In the Talmud, a compendium of Jewish teachings, it is said: "Greater is he who acts from love than he who acts from fear." When we act from a place of love, fear loses its power to hold us back. The moment we begin walking forward, fear turns into courage.

ANGER

ANGER IS AN HONEST EMOTION. When we witness cruelty or injustice, we can argue that anger is not only acceptable but also a moral responsibility. Certainly anger in alcoholic families can serve as a protest against unkind and unfair treatment. But there's another kind of anger—one that is destructive, out of control, and disturbing. This anger represents the hurts of the past and the fear of the future, and it immobilizes us in the present. It reveals itself in rage, hostility, and smoldering fire. Hostility is always ready for a fight; rage is retaliation—*I'll make you hurt as much as I hurt;* and smoldering fire is hidden anger, which shows itself passive-aggressively.

These forms of negative anger give us illusions of power and control. When we indulge in them they make us feel strong, but we aren't. Negative anger only adds to the confusion and frustration the alcoholism is already causing. Rather than defeat the problem, we defeat ourselves. The more anger we express, the less effective we become. People stop listening to us and brace themselves against us. As satisfying as it may feel to express anger negatively, it doesn't move us forward. Frederick Buechner, author and theologian, explains:

To lick your wounds, to smack your lips over grievances long past, to roll over your tongue the prospect of bitter confrontations still to come, to savor to the last toothsome morsel both the pain you are given and the pain you are giving back—in many ways it is a feast fit for a king. The chief drawback is that what you are wolfing down is yourself. The skeleton at the feast is you.

In alcoholic families, anger has three main purposes: to instruct the alcoholic, to keep the alcoholic from hurting him- or herself and others, and to make emotional connections. *Instructive anger* points out the many things alcoholics fail to do and emphasizes the necessity of responsible living. It addresses things such as budgeting money, finding a job, getting to places on time, paying bills, taking care of the kids, cleaning house, and fulfilling promises. This anger is about keeping the household running with some normalcy in spite of the addiction.

When alcoholic behavior crosses into a danger zone, *safeguarding anger* is the alarm that sounds a warning. It deals with driving drunk, falling asleep with a cigarette, passing out while food is cooking, forgetting to pick up the kids, drinking on the job, hanging out in undesirable or dangerous places, and any other risky activities. When I receive phone calls from family members asking me what to do about their brother or mother or other relative, it is usually this form of anger that motivates them to call. They now know they cannot control the addiction, and they are gripped with fear that something terrible and irreversible is going to happen.

Addicts aren't emotionally available to other people, and trying to communicate with them is usually a one-sided effort. Families—especially spouses and children—use *relationship anger* to make a connection with their alcoholics. Anger often does a good job of getting an addict's attention for short periods of time, and arguments become the main form of communication in the family. This form of anger is motivated by loneliness, sadness, rejection, frustration, worthlessness, unhappiness, grief, and fear. When it escalates, it can spiral into domestic violence or child abuse.

Connecting emotionally with alcoholics is difficult for a reason. They are unavailable because drugs have altered their brain chemistry. Since it takes time before the brain is restored to normal, when they're not drinking or using other drugs their emotions remain distorted. But anger is something addicts always understand and frequently employ themselves. Therefore, families can rely on anger to get a reaction from an alcoholic. When we successfully engage them in anger, we feel a connection. Children who aren't getting enough quality attention from a parent, for instance, will throw a temper tantrum to attract negative attention. Adults do the same. A wife, lonely in her alcoholic marriage, prefers the emotional stimulation she gets from a knockdown, drag-out fight to no emotional involvement at all. A mother quarreling with her marijuana-addicted son feels a connection she never feels any other time.

We think we accomplish something with anger because we get short-term results. We make threats that get the addict's attention and extract promises that alcohol and other drugs are a thing of the past. These promises last for a few days, a week, or maybe a month. But unless alcoholics get into recovery, they return to where they left off: drinking, drugging, and behaving badly. This sets off another round of family anger.

Alcoholics eventually get used to our rants because we rarely stick to our guns. Wives will say, "I told him I'd leave unless he gets help." But most don't follow through with their threats, and those who do usually back down as soon as promises and pleas of forgiveness are offered. They readily move back into the house—no treatment, no 12-step meetings, and no sobriety, just promises made out of whole cloth. Other threats meet the same fate: we write another check, let her sleep on the couch, buy him beer, give back the car keys. We renege, and by doing so we train addiction to lie to us, manipulate us, and abuse us. We send a clear message to the disease: *You are in charge.* We don't keep our promises to the alcoholic, and the alcoholic doesn't keep his promises to us.

When alcoholics promise things will be different, we want to believe. Faith in the pledge of a new tomorrow eases our fears and melts away our anger. The burden we've been carrying is lifted. Although the past is littered with broken promises, we're willing to grab on to another one in hopes that, finally, lessons are learned. It doesn't occur to us that it's not our beloved husband, wife, son, daughter, father, or mother talking to us; it's the disease negotiating its way out of trouble. We don't realize we're putting our faith in the very thing that is tearing us down—the addiction.

Anger must be positive to be effective. When we are in control of anger, rather than letting it control us, we can use it as a powerful motivator to learn what we need to do to initiate change, to open channels of communication and direct energy toward constructive actions. Positive anger translates into positive energy. It moves us forward and draws people toward us rather than driving them away. Positive anger inspires us to recruit others to join our team and work together to get something done. Sports psychologists tell us that positive anger increases levels of performance on the playing field, but negative anger impairs it. When players use negative anger to retaliate, they take their eyes off the game and focus on the opponent. When families use it, they take their eyes off the solution and focus on the alcoholic. Anger is contagious; we can spread negative or positive energy throughout our families. When we change negative into positive, we influence others for the better.

If we aren't doing something properly, all the effort in the world won't get the job done; as it's been said, a road map to Chicago will never get you to Memphis. If we're angry that things haven't worked out in the past, we need to find out what can be done differently today. We can take heed from Henry Ford: "Failure is simply the opportunity to begin again, this time more intelligently."

PERFECTIONISM

PERFECTIONISM IS NOT THE SAME as excellence. I often hear people confusing the two, praising everyone from surgeons to auto mechanics as perfectionists when they mean to commend them for excellence. Excellence expands our world, whereas perfectionism shrinks it. Excellence gathers valuable information, takes decisive action, pushes beyond self-imposed limitations, and searches for greater possibilities. It expands us emotionally, psychologically, and spiritually, and it commits us to uplifting the lives of others. Perfectionism obsesses over details to the point of paralysis and capitulates to fear by sidestepping challenges. It causes our spirits to shrivel and imposes rigid rules and regulations upon others. Alcoholic families are breeding grounds for perfectionism but offer little sustenance for excellence.

Sandra always made a point of telling her friends how fortunate she was to have been raised in a perfect family. Never mind her father's drinking, carousing, and disappearing acts, let alone his moodiness and running criticism of everyone in the family. Sandra was trained by her perfectionist mother not to see what was really happening. Instead, a fictionalized story of family

harmony and bliss was laid over reality like a fine veneer. When
Sandra tried to talk to her mother about her father's drinking,
her mother reminded her of all the good things in her life. When
Sandra's father was verbally abusive, her mother consoled her
by telling her how much her father really loved her. If Sandra
became angry, her mother quickly reminded her that anger wasn't
a very attractive emotion. Sandra's mother, unable to keep her
alcoholic husband under control, put her energy into keeping
everybody and everything else in perfect order: no clutter, no
mess, no outbursts. Her mother set impossibly high expectations for everyone in the household, assigning value not to people but to their ability to adhere to the rules. Sandra was praised
not for who she was but for how she could improve. Sandra
learned well: keep negative thoughts to herself, never talk about
her father's drinking, and present the world a happy face. When
Sandra reached adulthood, she lived in constant fear of making
mistakes. Paralyzed by the idea that she might step outside the
lines, she avoided trying anything new unless she could do it
perfectly the first time. She lingered in jobs far beneath her abilities because she could do them flawlessly. She couldn't accept
help from others because, to Sandra, admitting the need for
help was the same as admitting failure. She welled up with
shame whenever she gave anyone the slightest indication that
she was less than perfect. The harder Sandra worked to maintain a flawless image, the more her inner world crumbled.

Perfectionists are commonly defined as people who feel that
anything less than perfection is unacceptable, but rarely do
we stop to wonder what exactly they are doing and why.
Perfectionists are working not to improve the world but to keep
it under control. They do everything perfectly not for the satis-
faction of a job well done but as a way of camouflaging addiction's presence in the family. By keeping everything orderly,

they're trying to make the disease less noticeable. They work tirelessly to create a perfect family life but are rarely cognizant of what motivates their obsession. Through their eyes, perfectionism is their finest quality. It's the way they provide the ones they love with the very best. They have no idea that perfectionism is an outgrowth of fear and that it's more about looking happy than being happy. The compulsion to have the cleanest house, cook the best meals, plant the perfect garden, and always look perfectly coiffed is, for the perfectionist, a way to stay safe. After all, when the house is well kept, the children are properly dressed, and everyone has good manners, how can we be an alcoholic family?

Rescuing a family from addiction by making everything look perfect is like rearranging deck chairs on the *Titanic*. We may lull others and ourselves into a false sense of security, but at the end of the day we're still on a sinking ship. Perfectionists desperately want to keep their families from falling apart, but by creating the illusion of a problem-free family, they make it unlikely the alcoholic will seek treatment. Addicts will never find a reason to get sober as long as everything is proceeding smoothly. Furthermore, if family and friends are kept in the dark about the addiction, they have no reason to step in and try to help. Perfectionists, with all their good intentions, only serve to fool everybody, including the alcoholic and themselves, into thinking nothing needs to be done.

Perfectionism leads to spiritual dishonesty. When we act as if addiction doesn't exist or isn't a serious problem, our efforts are co-opted by the addiction for *its* survival. We may not be aware we're helping the alcoholic stay sick, but whenever we attempt to hide the addiction rather than contend with it honestly and openly, and in an educated and proper fashion, we become a pawn and cease being truthful. As perfectionists, we are so busy doing everything "right," we don't notice how we've unwittingly become keepers of the lie. We don't want other people to know the truth, and we don't want to know, either.

Perfectionists don't reach out for help because asking for help is synonymous with failure. It also requires pulling the curtain back and exposing the truth, and perfectionists have maintained the illusion of control for so long they don't necessarily know what's true anymore. They believe their efforts are working. By focusing on keeping the details in order, rather than looking at the big picture, they don't see how addiction is steadily pulling the family downward. As long as they keep doing everything perfectly, they feel that everything is being handled in the best possible way. As Anne Lamott wrote in her book *Bird by Bird*: "Perfectionism means that you try desperately not to leave much mess to clean up. . . . Tidiness suggests that something is as good as it's going to get."

Perfectionists may be devoutly religious, but they usually maintain a vertical relationship with God. They are willing to ask God for help but won't widen the circle to include the people most important to them. By cutting themselves off emotionally from others, they isolate God, too. They deny Him the opportunity to work in their lives *through other people*. Complex situations require an inclusive spirituality. By allowing others to share our burdens, we give God something to work with.

Prevailing over addiction requires challenging the way things have always been done. It involves leaping in and searching around for new answers. We have to trust that by doing the next right thing, we'll eventually end up in a better place. Making changes requires a willingness to take risks, make mistakes, and be vulnerable. Perfectionism paralyzes us, keeps us from trusting or trying, and provides addiction with a place to hide. We must instead refuse to give up our right to be imperfect, because in our imperfection lies our potential and our humanity.

THE WITHERED BRAIN

HOLD A GRAIN OF SAND in your hand and imagine it is a piece of your brain. Neuroscientists tell us that that single grain would be made up of one hundred thousand neurons, two million axons, and one billion synapses. If we were to count the firing of neurons across every synapse that occurs in the brain during the space of one second, we would complete the task in thirty-two million years. Patterns of communication in our brains are complex beyond comprehension. If we were to count the number of possible brain states we can form at any moment, we would have a number greater than the number of particles in outer space. The human brain is thought to be the most complex material object in the universe. Alcohol affects the entire brain, and other drugs target specific regions. Drugs are mind-altering in ways that those who use them never consider—they literally change the brain's anatomy and the way it functions. A healthy brain and an alcoholic brain look frighteningly different; they operate differently, too.

Up until recently we could examine brains of alcoholics only through autopsy, but brain-imaging techniques are so advanced today that we can observe brain function in living, breathing human beings. In this chapter, we're going to look primarily at the work of Daniel G. Amen, M.D., a clinical neuroscientist and psychiatrist who pioneered the use of brain imaging in clinical practice. He has discovered that people who have problems with feelings, thoughts, or behaviors don't have the same access to their brains as healthy people do. This is true of alcoholics and addicts, too. Dr. Amen used SPECT imaging to scan the brains of alcoholics and marijuana, cocaine, heroin, and meth-amphetamine addicts. He also scanned the brains of LSD, PCP, and inhalant users. He describes these brains as having an over-all toxic look, as if someone had poured acid over them. He says they are less active, less healthy, and shriveled compared to nor-mal brains. After years of working with alcoholics and their families, I was stunned, but not surprised, by Dr. Amen's work. Seeing the anatomy of an addict's brain gives one pause. With such extensive withering of the brain, it is no wonder thought patterns and behaviors are so radically altered.

There are several types of brain-imaging techniques that al-low us to gain access to the inner workings of the brain. Dr. Amen's choice, SPECT imaging, uses small doses of radio-isotopes to track the flow of blood and activity patterns within the brain and translates that information into computer-generated, color-coded, 3-D images. SPECT was developed to evaluate brain function in victims of strokes, brain trauma, dementia, and seizures. Dr. Amen expanded the application of SPECT to include attention deficit disorder, anxiety, depression, aggression, and substance abuse.

SPECT images show that consuming alcohol decreases activ-ity throughout the entire brain. The area most affected, how-ever, is the prefrontal cortex, or what we commonly refer to as the seat of consciousness. Our sense of who we are comes from this part of the brain. It controls our thoughts and behaviors, and it tempers impulsiveness and irrational decision making.

When someone tells us to think before we act, they are asking us to use our prefrontal cortex. Success in life is determined by what happens in this part of the brain. It is quite literally the fiber of our moral character. When it is compromised, people begin acting imprudently. They show little forethought or judgment, and proceed without properly considering the consequences of their actions. When prefrontal cortex activity is depressed, as it is in alcoholics, the result is an inability to learn from past mistakes. When experience can no longer teach alcoholics to modify their behaviors, impetuousness takes over.

The prefrontal cortex is the location of our sense of right and wrong. Alcoholics are often unable to behave in ways consistent with their moral beliefs. When someone observes that alcoholics don't seem to have a conscience, they're recognizing that the prefrontal cortex has been adversely affected. The ability to concentrate is also diminished. Alcoholics are easily distracted and have difficulty staying focused on projects, relationships, or their own inner thoughts. An alcoholic who is quite religious, for instance, may find prayer very difficult because alcohol affects the prefrontal cortex's ability to filter out distractions.

The ability to express feelings is also impaired. When I worked in an inpatient treatment setting, we began group therapy by asking each patient to express a feeling. Although alcoholics often don't know how they truly feel until they've had months of sobriety, this exercise can help rebuild a prefrontal cortex that hasn't been properly deciphering feelings for years or decades. The PBS documentary *To Think by Feeling* explains the role of feelings in human life: "We are not thinking machines, we are feeling machines that think." Our thoughts and emotions don't act independently; one is always affecting the other. Emotions aren't an adjunct to human existence; they are necessary for survival.

Human life is governed by emotions, and when alcoholics

lose proper emotional functioning, they have difficulty partici-
pating in healthy relationships, making good decisions, and understanding the world around them. People who have close
relationships with alcoholics often think: *He's just not there for
me. I don't get a good emotional connection anymore.* In addition,
it becomes increasingly clear that addicts can't always think and
reason clearly. This is partly due to their decreased ability to experience healthy emotion. When emotions aren't functioning
properly, neither are our thought systems. It is nearly impossible
to make decisions, plan for the future, or determine what is important.

Addiction stunts the brain's ability to develop emotionally
and socially. The emotional age of alcoholics correlates to the
age when they began using alcohol or other drugs. If they
started drinking at age thirteen and get sober at age forty-five,
they have the emotional maturity of a thirteen-year-old. Working a program of recovery in a 12-step group properly exercises the prefrontal cortex, and recovering alcoholics mature
rapidly and begin experiencing normal emotions. Dry drunks—
alcoholics who stop drinking without an ongoing program of
recovery—don't mature emotionally, continue to have difficulty
with emotion, and return to drinking or live miserably without
alcohol.

In his book *Healing the Hardware of the Soul,* Dr. Amen lists
symptoms of decreased activity in the prefrontal cortex. It is
striking that these symptoms also perfectly describe alcoholic
behavior: decreased attention span, distractibility, impaired
short-term memory, apathy, decreased verbal expression, poor
impulse control, mood control problems, decreased social
skills, and overall decreased control over behaviors. Dr. Amen
explains: "Without proper prefrontal cortex function, impulses
take over, making it difficult to act in consistent, thoughtful

ways. Impulse control issues are one of the main components of . . . doing something that you know is wrong."

Alcoholic drinking has a marked effect on two other important territories of the brain: the temporal lobes and the limbic system. Together, they constitute the *emotional brain*. This is the seat of our spirituality. Our passions, desires, sense of delight, and joy for living are experienced in these regions. When this part of the brain is healthy, it helps us flourish in life. The temporal lobes and the limbic system play a role in forming our personalities and our spiritual experiences. Some think of this area as God's portal into the mind. Antonio Damasio, author of *Looking for Spinoza: Joy, Sorrow and the Feeling Brain,* explains positive spirituality as "an intense experience of harmony . . . the desire to act toward others with kindness and generosity [and] to hold sustained feelings of joy." Once addiction takes hold of the brain, spirituality becomes increasingly negative: addicts live in discord with others, create feelings of sorrow and anger, and behave in selfish and self-centered ways.

The sign of a healthy emotional brain is a stable personality— positive mood, even temper, good memory, bonding with others, and positive spiritual experiences. When unhealthy, the functioning of the brain is quite different, and the characteristics are common descriptors of an alcoholic: easily offended, somewhat paranoid, increasingly malcontent, emotionally unstable, confused, moody, irritable, depressed, and aggressive. By altering their brains with toxins, alcoholics lose the ability to be who they truly are. Families often say to me as we're working together to motivate their loved one to accept help, "She is really such a fantastic person, but in her addiction you'd never know it." They want me to understand that behind this terrible exterior, there is a good person. What they're saying, of course, is they've lost their loved one to addiction. The changes in the temporal lobes and limbic system have transformed her into someone they can't quite recognize.

The addicted brain is changed. We cannot allow ourselves to continue believing that a mind so altered can make good decisions for itself, and certainly not for others. When the health and welfare of so many are at stake, recognizing that our expectations of addicts have been unrealistic gives us the impetus to finally take action. We can no longer pretend the addicted brain is just like yours and mine except for being high. We cannot fool ourselves into thinking we can use logic on a brain that has lost much of its power to reason. When we learn how drugs and alcohol hobble the human mind, we have no choice but to find out what we can do.

Dr. Amen asks how we can judge somebody when the brain that controls behavior isn't operating properly. In *Healing the Hardware of the Soul,* he shares his personal contemplation on this question of morality:

> *"The judgment waters seem murky to me. I trusted that God knew everything I was discovering and that He had the judgment issue figured out. But what about man? We had been operating under erroneous assumptions. We assumed we were all equal and we all have an equal ability to choose between right or wrong, good or evil, and heaven or hell. The brain-imaging work taught me that we are not all equal, and not everyone has the same power to choose."*

DISRUPTED
DECISION MAKING

LBERT EINSTEIN SAID, "The brain that causes the problem cannot solve the problem," yet we still expect alcoholics and addicts to make decisions that reflect normal thinking. Using drugs repetitively changes the brain—both its structure and its function—in ways that can persist long after the drug use has ended. Families often believe that when addicts are sober their thinking is normal, and their brains are altered only when they are actively using drugs. The addicted brain does not return to normal between periods of alcohol or other drug use. Many changes in the brain take months and even years to reverse themselves. Some never do.

Anyone with a close relationship to an alcoholic or addict is repeatedly astounded by what seems to be a disregard for personal responsibility. When I work with concerned families, this is what bewilders them most. Someone in the family invariably asks me, "Can't he see what he's doing to himself? Why doesn't he get his life under control?" Families have tremendous difficulty understanding that addiction is robbing their loved one of the ability to be *consistently* responsible. Understanding addiction as a brain disease helps. When we take a look at other brain diseases, we can see a common thread. Symptoms of loss of control and altered behavior are widespread among these diseases. Schizophrenics can't control their hallucinations and believe the bizarre scenarios appearing in their minds are reality. Parkinson's patients lose control over their bodies and can't stop shaking. People suffering from clinical depression cannot control their moods. Other brain diseases—such as Alzheimer's, stroke, and multiple sclerosis—cause the brain to atrophy, and impair conscious thought. Traumatic brain injury causes a wide variety of symptoms, including excessive sleepiness, lack of judgment, mood outbursts, irritability, slowed thinking, and inattentiveness.

Suffering from any brain disease can lead to financial loss, family problems, inability to maintain employment, loss of status in the community, and inability to preserve friendships. Addiction is only one of the many brain diseases that disrupt lives. Unlike most of these diseases, however, addiction is very treatable. With ongoing recovery, most of the damage to the brain is reversed over time. Unlike sufferers of Alzheimer's or other brain diseases that seal a victim's fate, alcoholics and addicts can achieve sobriety, rebuild their lives, and reestablish healthy relationships.

Researchers have been studying addicts' brains to determine why they seek out and use drugs with no regard for future consequences, even when the drug no longer produces the pleasure it once did. One of these researchers, Dr. Antoine Bechara, of the University of Iowa, notes that the decision-making impairment in addicts' brains is similar to how people with prefrontal cortex injuries make decisions. Like the addict, they too make decisions based on immediate gratification rather than on future consequences. Families think negative consequences will surely turn addicts around, *but their brains are ignoring consequences.* Alcoholics who eventually go into treatment are usually facing extraordinarily negative circumstances too serious to ignore or were intervened upon by their families. This doesn't mean alcoholics aren't intelligent—many are extraordinarily smart. It means their judgment has been severely impaired due to their addiction.

Using brain-imaging techniques, scientists are studying what happens to the brains of addicts while they are engaged in decision-making tasks. The compulsion to use the drug appears to overcome the brain's ability to send out warning signals. In other words, the brain's craving for the drug diminishes the brain's ability to alert itself to the dangers of the drug. Scientists have found that patterns in the brains of addicts differ from those of nonaddicts when making decisions. Addicts are using different systems in the brain, and these systems aren't as efficient and capable of making decisions as those used in healthy brains. Dr. Martin Paulus, of the University of California, after studying methamphetamine addicts, reported that behavior "is not controlled by consideration of what works over what does not." Families often ask addicts: "Why can't you learn from past mistakes?" Science is discovering that the brains of addicts don't always recognize when things are going wrong; therefore addicts don't change their behaviors in an attempt to get different results. Addicts adhere to the same strategies even when they prove to be ineffective. The ability to make better decisions eludes the addicted brain. All the addict can think about is getting high. If he crashes the car while pursuing that goal, he sees it as an unfortunate event, but it doesn't dissuade him from his prime objective—getting more of the drug.

Learning something new, such as knitting, playing an instrument, or riding a bicycle, changes our brain structure. These changes happen very swiftly—within seconds or hours—enabling us to learn new things quickly. Synapses, which are the junctions between brain cells, grow larger and increase cells' abilities to communicate with one another. Research on cocaine and methamphetamine shows that these drugs can inhibit brain cells from growing stronger and building more complex communication networks. As a result, addicts don't learn from their experiences. The capacity to learn is blocked even after the drug use is terminated. In one study, some rats were given cocaine and methamphetamine for twenty days and others were not given any drugs. The researchers then stopped giving the rats drugs and moved all of them into new cages filled with tunnels, climbing chains, toys, bridges, and numerous other stimuli that translated into new learning experiences. After the rats had lived in the enriched environment for three months, researchers found no growth in the brains of rats previously given drugs. The rats not given drugs showed brain growth. Researchers concluded that prior exposure to cocaine or methamphetamine may diminish our ability to learn new things, resulting in cognitive and behavioral disadvantages.

The human brain is not fully developed until age twenty-five. The adolescent prefrontal cortex is not wholly operational, and as a result, teenagers do not always show good judgment or make responsible decisions. They have difficulty determining the future consequences of their actions. Parents say, "Think before you act," but the teenager's brain isn't quite capable of doing that yet. Kids want to be treated like adults, but their brains aren't ready to make adult decisions. Research at the University of California, San Diego, found that alcohol might be more damaging to young brains than to adult brains. Teens who drink heavily—two drinks a day—exhibit worse memory loss than adult alcoholics. In addition, memory problems persist for months after teenagers quit drinking. When it came to performing elementary tasks, such as doing simple math or recalling the location of items, researchers found that adolescent girls who binged on alcohol had "sluggish" brains. Alcohol may be destroying brain cells in the hippocampus—the area responsible for memory—and may block receptors in the brain from forming new memories. Brain development that occurs during adolescence affects us for the rest of our lives. When children use mood-altering substances, they change what happens to their developing brains. Science is just beginning to learn what these changes are, but there are indications that some neurological impairment may persist throughout a lifetime.

Addiction has long been oversimplified as "drinking too much" or doing drugs "you know you shouldn't do." Addiction is a complex disease that is often difficult to understand. Brain-imaging technology, by allowing us to look into the addicted brain and see how it is functioning differently, makes the disease easier to comprehend. We identify it as a disease of the brain, but it doesn't end there. When the brain is affected, the soul is affected, too. Addiction causes a spiritual sickness that can make getting well all the more challenging. In the book *Alcoholics Anonymous,* an alcoholic explains his view of recovery:

> *When I had been in A.A. only a short while, an old-timer told me something that has affected my life ever since. "A.A. does not teach us how to handle our drinking," he said. "It teaches us how to handle sobriety." . . . God willing, we members of A.A. may never again have to deal with drinking, but we have to deal with sobriety every day.*

For addicts, recovery is not simple abstinence. It's about healing the brain, remembering how to feel, learning how to make good decisions, becoming the kind of person who can engage in healthy relationships, cultivating the willingness to accept help from others, daring to be honest, and opening up to doing things differently. Recovery is a spiritual experience that ultimately is about healing the soul.

THE GENETIC FACTOR

SCIENTISTS HAVE SPENT the last eighty years asking whether alcoholism is inherited, learned, or both. After decades of research, science has its answer: alcoholism is an inherited disease.

We don't learn to be alcoholic by watching other alcoholics drink, nor do we become alcoholic because of childhood trauma, low self-esteem, or lack of willpower. The misconception I most commonly hear from people is that addiction is caused by something else. I'm a guest lecturer at a university near my home, and once a semester I speak to graduate-level counseling students about addiction. My greatest challenge is convincing them that addiction is not caused by some other issue in a person's life. I tell students that if they remember only one thing I say, remember this: *the reason why someone drinks is not the reason why he or she becomes an alcoholic.* If it were, everyone who drank for that reason would be at high risk for addiction. For those who are genetically predisposed to addiction, their brains don't care why they drink. The only thing that matters is whether or not alcohol or any other addictive drug enters their bodies.

Grief is often cited, mistakenly, as a cause for addiction. Let's look at two different scenarios to help us better understand that extraneous circumstances don't cause alcoholism. A seventy-three-year-old woman lost her husband to cancer and began drinking nightly to ease her loneliness and grief. One evening after having three glasses of wine, she tripped and fell. She broke her nose and bruised herself quite badly. Frightened, she resolved not to drink again; she also took her daughter's advice and set up an appointment with her pastor for grief counseling. This is an example of what happens when people who are not prone to addiction self-medicate. When the "medicine" starts causing consequences, they stop using it and find a better solution. If the same woman had been genetically wired for addiction, however, the story might have been quite different. The fall, broken nose, and bruises wouldn't have deterred her. Instead, she would continue drinking, eventually developing a tolerance for alcohol and needing to drink more to get the same high. After a while, she'd start drinking earlier in the day, and sometimes she'd pass out in her chair while watching television. When her children expressed concern, she'd react defensively and angrily. She would make excuses why she doesn't spend more time with the grandchildren. Once she uncorked the first bottle of wine she'd stop answering the phone, and she'd hide bottles and lie about her drinking. She long ago ceased self-medicating; now she's drinking because she's an alcoholic.

How is it that scientists are so sure susceptibility to addiction is inherited? To answer this question, we need to go back to the 1930s and the beginning of the long-term studies conducted in Sweden. The studies were designed to determine if alcoholism was caused by nature or nurture. These studies can be divided into the twin studies and the adoption studies.

Twin studies set about to determine whether or not genetics play a role in alcoholism by studying identical and fraternal twins. Identical twins have identical genes, and fraternal twins have some genes that are the same and some that are different. If alcoholism is genetic, identical twin pairs should show the same predisposition to alcoholism. If one becomes alcoholic, so will the other; if one doesn't become alcoholic, neither will the other. Since fraternal twins don't have identical genes, their propensity toward alcoholism would be less likely to match. On the other hand, if alcoholism is caused by environmental influences, the probability that the twin pairs will match shouldn't change depending upon whether they're identical or fraternal, because genetic makeup would be irrelevant. What would matter is whether or not they were having similar environmental experiences. Living in the same environment, not genetic similarities, would determine their risk for becoming alcoholic. After studying twins for decades, researchers found significant differences between identical and fraternal twins. Identical twin pairs were more likely to match each other in their predisposition to becoming alcoholic. Fraternal twin pairs were more likely to differ, one being alcoholic and the other not. This indicates that genes play the defining role, not the environment.

Twins have also been studied to determine if susceptibility to addiction to other drugs is inherited or learned. The outcomes show that for addiction to cocaine, heroin, other opiates, marijuana, and hallucinogens, susceptibility is inherited. Research has also found that addiction to one drug leads to an increased vulnerability to all mood-altering drugs. Harvard Medical School even used twin studies to determine if genetics influence whether or not someone enjoys the effects of smoking marijuana. The research found that genetics do play a significant role in how people experience marijuana, as either a good or bad feeling. If genetics also determine our tendency to find a particular drug pleasurable, some people may be more susceptible to using drugs repeatedly because they find them more enjoyable than other people do. It's long been understood in treatment centers that addicts have a *drug of choice,* the drug they prefer above all others.

Adoption studies further disentangle the questions between genetics and environmental influences. As far back as the 1920s, researchers have studied people born of alcoholic parents and adopted at birth by nonalcoholic couples. These studies are probably the most effective at separating the influences of nature and nurture. If the environment is responsible for alcoholism, then babies born of alcoholic biological parents but raised by nonalcoholic adoptive parents should have a low incidence of alcoholism, because genetics would not be a factor. If alcoholism is inherited, the rate of alcoholism will be high even though the adoptive parents are nonalcoholic. Research has found that babies born of alcoholic parents but raised in nonalcoholic homes are four times more likely to become alcoholic than babies born of nonalcoholic parents and raised by nonalcoholic adoptive parents.

Another Swedish research team combined identical twin and adoption studies, following the lives of twins adopted into separate homes at birth. Even though each twin was raised in a different family, if they were born of alcoholic parents, they had the same propensity for becoming alcoholic. This research further indicates that addiction is a heritable disease, not a learned behavior.

The results of four decades of studies on alcoholism were reviewed, and this forty-year body of work clearly showed that relatives of alcoholics have a higher rate of alcoholism than the general population. Geneticists have determined that a child born of an alcoholic parent has a 50 percent chance of inheriting the genes. Not all alcoholics have alcoholic parents, however. Some have parents who abstain entirely from alcohol and other drugs. Teetotaler families are sometimes anti-alcohol because of a prevalence of alcoholism in previous generations. It is important to note that it is the susceptibility to alcoholism that is inherited, not alcoholism itself. The disease is activated only once alcohol or other drugs are used. Some people report they were alcoholic from their very first drink, while others drank for years before they crossed the line into addiction. Some drugs have a faster addictive cycle than others. Crack cocaine, for instance, creates powerful cravings very quickly. Prolonged exposure to some drugs, such as narcotic pain medications, will cause physical dependency in anyone, but not all people who become physically dependent become addicts. In other words, they don't develop irrational thoughts and drug-seeking behavior. Addiction can progress at different rates in different people. Like cancer, sometimes it is very aggressive and other times it is slow-growing.

Animal studies have also provided invaluable insight into the genetics of addiction. Genetically altered strains of rats have been created that prefer alcohol, as well as others that avoid alcohol. Rats that prefer alcohol choose it over drinking water, but rats that avoid alcohol won't drink it even when deprived of water. The offspring of rats that prefer alcohol also prefer alcohol; the offspring of rats that avoid alcohol also avoid alcohol. Genetics can also affect how rats feel when they drink alcohol. Scientists have altered genetics to create rats that sleep a long time after drinking and those that sleep a short time, rats that have severe withdrawals from alcohol and those that don't, and rats that have a high tolerance to alcohol and those that become intoxicated after drinking small amounts. The ability to breed rats to exhibit specific traits when consuming alcohol proves that these traits are genetic, scientists say.

Alcoholism is caused not by a single gene but by multiple genes. The exact combination of genes can change from family to family. Geneticists tell us that of all genetically based diseases, alcoholism is the most complicated to study. Although science hasn't yet pinpointed the various genes that cause alcoholism, the Washington University School of Medicine has identified one gene that appears to increase the risk of alcoholism. They hope that recent advancements in genetic research will give them more answers in the next five to ten years.

Sometimes I encounter people who become very angry when they are told that alcoholism is a genetic disease. They've often been hurt by an alcoholic and think that saying alcoholism is a disease is the same as saying alcoholics aren't responsible for their behavior. If this book is about anything, it is about responsibility. Every alcoholic and addict is responsible for what he or she does. The illness doesn't give anyone a license for bad behavior. What's more, because addicts and alcoholics have an illness that adversely affects so many, they have a special responsibility to get well. No shortcuts, no excuses. Of course, their illness creates extreme self-centeredness and blocks their willingness to get well, so getting them started almost always requires friends, families, and coworkers who are prepared to take action. No addict wants to get well; they learn to want to get well *while they're getting well*. Sometimes they have false starts, and when they do, they need to pick themselves up and start again. Addiction doesn't have the right to trump the welfare of the family.

PREDICTABLE, PROGRESSIVE, AND CHRONIC

FAMILIES THINK ALCOHOLICS are unpredictable. Alcoholics themselves suffer from what is called *terminal uniqueness*—they believe their circumstances are unlike anyone else's and no one can understand what they are going through. In reality, addiction exhibits very predictable symptoms regardless of the person or her background. Circumstances may be different, but the disease is the same. As addiction intensifies, alcoholics and addicts become increasingly alike. Addiction is a predictable disease with well-defined symptoms.

The disease always gets worse if left untreated. Alcoholics may seem to get better for a while or have periods when things stay about the same, but when we look at the big picture, it becomes clear that the disease is progressive. There are definable stages of addiction: early, middle, and late. It's unlikely anyone is going to notice a drinking problem in the early stages. By middle-stage addiction, the problem is noticeable, but most friends and family resist calling it addiction. Late-stage addiction is hard to ignore by anyone other than those who are suffering from intractable denial.

Many factors determine how rapidly addicts progress from

one stage to the next: an individual's genetics and general health, environmental controls on drinking, and the drug itself. Generally speaking, someone smoking crack will become addicted more quickly than someone smoking marijuana. Someone shooting heroin will reach the late stage of addiction far more quickly than someone drinking alcohol. When different drugs are mixed together, addiction happens more quickly.

The following is a story of how alcoholism typically progresses from the earliest to the latest stages. Of course, the advancement of addiction varies widely from person to person. I've worked with people in their twenties who were already in late-stage addiction and with older adults who didn't cross into addiction until their retirement years. Here's a story of how alcoholism can creep into a family and, over time, undermine everything they worked so hard to build.

When Chad moved his family to Richmond, life was good. His hard work and MBA had led to an executive accounting position in a fast-growing company. At age thirty-one he had a country club membership, drove an expensive car, and owned a beautiful home. His wife, Tanya, was able to leave her marketing job to raise their two-year-old-daughter, Kimberly. They often marveled at how they'd created such a wonderful life for themselves.

Chad had a family history of alcoholism on his father's side and promised himself he'd never let his drinking get out of control. When he was in graduate school and working nights, he swore off drinking entirely. He only allowed it back into his life once his career took off. His golf games began to include a long stretch at the nineteenth hole, dinners with colleagues featured multiple glasses of scotch, and weekend chores began and ended with a cold beer. He looked forward to drinking and preferred social outings that included alcohol. The high stress of his job gave him another reason to have a few drinks—he needed to relax. He never thought twice about driving after drinking because he never considered himself impaired. The few times Tanya suggested she should drive, he agreed but was irritated that she thought he'd had too many. Sometimes he'd tell Tanya he'd drunk less than he really had so she wouldn't question him. When they were going out with friends who didn't drink much, Chad would secretly have a shot of vodka before leaving the house. Tanya viewed Chad as a harmless social drinker who occasionally liked to let loose. His thoughts, however, were increasingly preoccupied with alcohol. Chad was in the early stage of addiction.

Tanya's first scent of trouble came when Chad drove home from a golf tournament extremely drunk. He'd gone to a bar afterward with one of his buddies and returned home quite late. When she questioned him, he snapped at Tanya, telling her that he was out celebrating and to stop her nagging. In the weeks to come, she suspected he was intoxicated on a number of different occasions, but he insisted that he was overly tired and that one drink went straight to his head. Tanya began feeling confused about Chad's drinking, but she believed him.

Chad became fixated on the next drink. He liked taking clients out for lunch because he knew it was an excuse to have a couple of glasses of wine. He wasn't necessarily drinking every day, but he created more and more opportunities to drink, and he usually drank more than he had planned. He rationalized and justified his behavior to himself, never thinking for one instant that he could be triggering a genetic disorder that had afflicted his father and grandfather.

One night Chad came home very late and very drunk. When Tanya asked him where he'd been and how much he'd had to drink, he became enraged and began yelling terrible things. Kimberly woke up and began crying. Tanya sent Chad to bed to defuse the situation. When morning came, Tanya had the distinct impression that Chad didn't remember the night before. She told him what he'd said and that Kimberly had heard him. His face reddened; he muttered a quick apology and then hurried out to mow the lawn. In truth, he didn't remember what happened, but he couldn't admit that to Tanya. He felt terrible and told himself he wasn't going to drink anything all day, but after finishing the yard work he reconsidered: one beer couldn't hurt.

As he drank the beer, he thought about his father and how he used to come home drunk and yell at his mother. Chad assured himself that he was nothing like his dad and that his behavior with Tanya had been a fluke. He'd never do it again. Then Chad decided one more beer would be okay. As he drank the second can, he began thinking about Tanya and how she just didn't seem to appreciate him anymore. He thought about how hard it was to get along with her lately, and he began feeling angry. He went into the house to tell Tanya he was off to the hardware store but instead drove to a neighborhood pub. Chad had moved into middle-stage alcoholism.

Tanya kept her concerns about Chad's drinking a secret. On the surface, their life looked good, and she didn't want to rock the boat. He was up for another promotion, and that meant a substantial pay increase. Kimberly was starting third grade, so Tanya accepted an offer to return to work three days a week. She and Chad were drifting apart, but she didn't let herself think about it. She stayed busy at work, volunteering at Kimberly's school and playing tennis with her friends.

The years passed. Kimberly was heading off to college. Chad was drinking every day. Blackouts occurred regularly, and Tanya threatened divorce many times. Then Chad was arrested for driving under the influence. His blood alcohol content was .18, and because it was so high, he was sentenced to a mandatory five days in jail. Tanya could no longer deny he was an alcoholic. A few months later, Chad was "downsized" and lost his job. He sat at home drinking instead of looking for employment. Tanya started working full time, but with a daughter going away to college, money was tight.

Chad's health was failing. He was forgetful and bloated. He'd gained forty pounds in the last six or seven years. His face was ruddy and his walk unsteady. Tanya made an appointment for him to see a doctor, who informed them that Chad's liver was enlarged and his blood pressure was dangerously high. The doctor told Chad to quit drinking. Once home, Chad ignored the advice and instead restricted his drinking to wine. This, he reasoned, was a sensible compromise. Chad, at age forty-seven, was a late-stage alcoholic.

Tanya learned about intervention and got Chad into treatment. If she had allowed his drinking to continue, he would have quickly moved into end-stage alcoholism—the last stage before death. I've worked with many families concerned about end-stage alcoholics, the point at which all control over alcohol is lost. To avoid becoming sick—with shaking, sweating, fatigue, nervousness, headaches, paleness, rapid heart rate, vomiting, confusion—they need to drink every three or four hours, or they begin to show some or all of these symptoms. They usually have one or more health problems associated with addiction, such as cirrhosis, hypertension, neuropathy, incontinence, memory loss, pancreatitis, or heart disease. Many end-stage alcoholics keep bottles of booze tucked under their beds so when they wake up needing a drink they don't have to get up—they just reach down, grab the bottle, take a couple of swigs, and go back to sleep. One husband told me his wife kept cans of beer under her side of the bed so she could drink during the night. It amazed him that she didn't think he heard her wake up, crack open a beer, and guzzle it down.

Addiction is a chronic disease—there is no cure. Many alcoholics die before reaching the end stage of the disease. Death certificates may say stroke or heart disease or cancer, but the real culprit was alcohol. In Alcoholics Anonymous they have a saying that illustrates the incurable nature of addiction: "Once a cucumber becomes a pickle, it can never be a cucumber again." There is no cure for addiction; therefore, alcoholics cannot successfully return to social drinking. Recovery requires abstinence from all mood-altering drugs. If an alcoholic starts smoking marijuana, she'll either return to drinking or develop a marijuana addiction. Once someone is addicted to one drug, he will have problems with all other drugs. Cocaine addicts almost always insist they can continue drinking alcohol, but alcohol causes cravings for cocaine. The good news is that among chronic diseases, addiction is the most treatable.

Sobriety requires life-altering changes, the most important of which is working a program of recovery. Addicts routinely think they can do it on their own but almost always start drinking or taking other drugs again. Researchers in Finland conducted a study to determine the common denominators among people who remained sober ten years after treatment. They found there was only one: ongoing involvement in a 12-step recovery group. Addicts who do not work a program of recovery almost always relapse, and the tiny number who do not are almost always depressed, difficult to live with, and at high risk of eventually returning to some form of drug use. Are there exceptions? Yes, but among the truly addicted, planning on doing it on your own is as foolish as relying on spontaneous remission when you've been given a diagnosis of cancer.

Compliance is an important issue when treating all chronic illnesses, not just addiction. For example, only 51 percent of patients in the United States adhere to their high blood pressure treatment regimens. The World Health Organization reports that adherence to long-term therapies is low for all chronic diseases, and that only one out of every two people in developing countries complies. This helps us understand that the problem is not unique among alcoholics and addicts.

Chronic diseases aren't cured, they are managed, and this requires a long-term commitment to recovery. Refusing to follow through brings about debilitating consequences: A heart patient who won't stop eating a high-fat diet has another heart attack. A diabetic who won't exercise, change eating habits, or check sugar levels has a foot amputated. A multiple sclerosis patient who doesn't manage stress experiences intensified symptoms. A schizophrenic who stops taking medications begins to hallucinate and lose control of her life. An alcoholic who refuses to go to 12-step meetings begins drinking again. Intervention, according to a study at Brown University, increases the likelihood of success in alcohol and drug treatment by 64 percent. The World Health Organization states that the effectiveness of compliance intervention may have a far greater impact on health than any improvements in specific medical treatments:

> *Poor adherence to long-term therapies severely compromises the*
> *effectiveness of treatment, making this a critical issue in population*
> *health both from the perspective of quality of life and of health*
> *economics. Interventions aimed at improving adherence would*
> *provide a significant positive return on investment through*
> *primary prevention (of risk factors) and secondary prevention of*
> *adverse health outcomes.*

CHOICE AND RESPONSIBILITY

W HEN I TRAVEL around the country and speak to people about addiction, I'm often asked, "But where's the responsibility?" Behind this question is an unspoken question: aren't we letting alcoholics and addicts off the hook when we talk about addiction as a disease? My answer is that alcoholics and addicts are being let off the hook as a matter of course because we don't talk about addiction as a disease that must be treated. When we speak of responsibility it is important to place it where it belongs: *whenever anyone crosses the line into addiction, that person has a moral responsibility to get well.* This has nothing to do with wanting to get well, because we know that the disease keeps alcoholics and addicts from wanting to get well. Consequently, families must participate in defeating the disease. We share in the responsibility.

Where do we direct our focus when a close relative or friend is addicted? Usually it's on the negative behaviors. We exert a great amount of energy trying to manage these behaviors and their consequences. When families try to field all the problems, they exhaust themselves. Addiction creates a stream of negative consequences that doesn't end until we shift our focus onto conquering the disease itself. In *Through the Looking-Glass,* the sequel to *Alice in Wonderland,* Alice has an experience with the Red Queen that compares to what families go through when they're trying to keep one step ahead of addiction:

> *"Now! Now!" cried the Queen. "Faster! Faster!" And they went so fast that at last they seemed to skim through the air, hardly touching the ground with their feet, till suddenly, just as Alice was getting quite exhausted, they stopped. . . . Alice looked round her in great surprise. "Why, I do believe we've been under this tree the entire time! Everything is just as it was! . . . In our country you'd generally get somewhere else—if you ran very fast for a long time, as we've been doing."*
>
> *"A slow sort of country!" said the Queen. "Now, here, you see, it takes all the running you can do, to keep in the same place."*

This is the best analogy I've found for an alcoholic family trying to manage the symptoms of addiction. Like Alice, they continually run as fast as they can just to stay in the same place. Of course, families eventually lose ground no matter how fast they run. The way they will get somewhere else is by getting the addict into treatment and recovery.

The other question I hear is: "How can it be a disease? Isn't drinking a choice?" We've already examined how the disease takes away an addict's capacity to choose, but what about when someone first chooses to drink or take other drugs? Isn't she responsible? Ours is a culture that encourages drinking and, to a lesser extent, other drug use. Ironically, we then blame people when they become addicted to these substances. We seem to say, "Yes, drink! Smoke pot! Take tranquilizers! But if you become addicted, *you* must have done something wrong." How does our thinking change once we know that most addicted people made these choices when they were still children? Joseph Califano Jr., chairman and president of the National Center on Addiction and Substance Abuse at Columbia University, says, "A child who reaches age twenty-one without smoking, abusing alcohol, or using drugs is virtually certain never to do so." Anyone who works in a treatment center can attest to the fact that most addicts start using alcohol while still children. Of the many alcoholics and addicts I've worked with, it's a minuscule number who waited until twenty-one years of age to use mood-altering substances. The overwhelming majority used alcohol or other drugs since childhood.

The average age at which Americans begin drinking is twelve. By age fifteen, they are drinking on a regular basis. Thus, it is children, not adults, who are making the crucial first decision to use alcohol. Can we expect a child to be prepared to make these kinds of choices and fully understand the consequences? Before we answer this question, let's look at the ways society influences our children.

Underage youth are four hundred times more likely to see commercials selling alcohol than ads designed to prevent alcohol use. Children view more commercials for beer and other alcoholic beverages than for products—gum, snacks, juice, jeans, and sneakers—marketed directly to them. Elementary-school-age children trade Absolut vodka ads like baseball cards. Children as young as age six identified Budweiser commercials as their favorites. A four-year study found that the number of beer and liquor advertisements in magazines tends to increase with its youth readership. Another study found that alcohol commercials appeared in every top-rated television show favored by teenagers. By the time teens reach driving age, they've seen an average of seventy-five thousand advertisements for alcoholic beverages. Underage kids drink one out of every four alcoholic beverages consumed in the United States. The alcohol industry has created "alcopops," premixed drinks that are favored by young drinkers for their soda pop taste. One survey reported that 56 percent of drinkers age eleven and twelve preferred alcopops. One out of five children between ages twelve and twenty is a binge drinker. Three million teenagers are alcoholics. The earlier a child begins drinking or using other drugs, the higher the probability of becoming addicted. Children report that they do most of their drinking at friends' homes. Most children who try street drugs first abused alcohol. Alcohol kills six and a half times more kids than all other drugs combined. Most addicted adults start out as children who were influenced to drink at an early age.

Young people's brains aren't ready to make adult decisions, but our culture constantly bombards them with messages that say drinking is a good thing. In her book *Deadly Persuasion*, Jean Kilbourne writes:

> *Most teenagers are sensitive to peer pressure and find it difficult to resist or even to question the dominant cultural messages perpetuated and reinforced by the media. Mass media has made possible a kind of national peer pressure that erodes private and individual values and standards, as well as community values and standards. As Margaret Mead once said, today our children are not brought up by parents, they are brought up by mass media.*

Brains must have their full circuitry before we can expect highly responsible behavior. This occurs at about age twenty-five. When the prefrontal cortex, in charge of judgment and reasoning, is underdeveloped, we can't expect our youth to think like adults. We might remember days gone by when people married young as a matter of course and seemed to handle an early adulthood quite well. But life then was defined more narrowly, and the culture was more restrictive. The extended family was the primary influence, not mass culture and advertisements.

Kids weren't influenced as much by the larger culture as they were by their parents, grandparents, and aunts and uncles.

Although we determine maturity mainly by physical growth and chronological age, the best measure is brain development. As Barbara Strauch writes in her book *The Primal Teen:* "An average teenager gains fifty pounds and grows a foot in the span of four to five years. At the end of that growth spurt, that teenager may outwardly look like a mountain of maturity to us. But it's an illusion." Can we honestly say that any brain can make well-informed decisions about alcohol or other drugs before it's fully formed? Kids drinking their first can of beer don't believe for an instant that addiction could happen to them, and in most cases neither do their parents. Perhaps kids who wait until they are twenty-one are less likely to abuse alcohol or other drugs because they are using a more mature brain—one capable of better judgment—to make these decisions. And since they didn't drink when they were younger, their drug-free brains did a better job of maturing than the alcohol-soaked brains of their peers.

Another way to examine the issue of choice is to discuss *accidental addiction*. These are people who never abused alcohol or any other mood-altering substances but became addicted to a medication after a doctor prescribed it. They use the medication as directed, but over time lose control. They inexplicably begin craving the drug. They start taking more than the prescribed dose and, faced with empty pill bottles, begin lying to get more. They call the doctor and report that a bottle accidentally dropped into the toilet or fell out of a purse, and another prescription is called in to the pharmacy. They begin asking other doctors for the same pills and soon have several doctors writing prescriptions. When doctors catch on and stop prescribing, accidental addicts turn to the Internet or the streets to get their pills. Sometimes, in desperation, they switch to illegal drugs.

Let's not forget, these are people with no prior history of making bad choices with regard to alcohol or drug use. They were simply given a medication and took it as prescribed, which tripped the genetic switch of addiction. They began using the drug not for recreational purposes but for medical reasons.

I lived through the heartbreak of accidental addiction in my own family. It took us all by surprise. She was grace incarnate. She had an indescribable quality that drew people to her. She always prided herself on enjoying life *without* alcohol. When others would drink too much at weddings or family gatherings, she'd sip ginger ale out of a champagne glass. She'd point out to me how alcohol caused people to embarrass themselves and do things they'd never do sober. "That's not having fun," she'd say. Then she developed heart problems, and her cardiologist prescribed Valium. He told her to take one every time she worried—presumably this would prevent stress from harming her heart. Within six months she was addicted. She had bottles of every kind of tranquilizer and sedative imaginable and began experiencing negative consequences. She caused the first car accident of her life and stood in the middle of the street, high on pills, crying. She began calling people late at night, slurring her words and saying irrational things. The pills robbed her of all dignity and cast a shadow over her wonderful spirit. It was hard to spend time with her. We had difficulty recognizing her as the person she once was. She'd talk endlessly about nonsense. Sometimes she'd become maudlin and cry; other times she'd say something cruel. We didn't know what to do. It was the 1970s, and we had no idea you could become addicted to drugs prescribed by doctors. We certainly hadn't heard of treatment even though Hazelden, the pioneer of modern alcohol and drug treatment, was a two-hour drive from our house. So we let things go. She died before she ever found a way back.

Accidental addicts bring the question of "choice" into focus.

Perhaps, when it comes to addiction, choice doesn't play as large a role as we've assigned it. Why someone begins using a particular drug doesn't seem to matter to the brain. It can come from a doctor, the street, or a wine bottle. About half of all adults choose to drink alcohol, for example, and although most won't develop a problem, about 10 percent will be afflicted with alcoholism at some point in their lives. Therefore, it is far more useful to understand that people with a genetic predisposition to addiction will activate the disease by using enough of a drug for a sufficient length of time. We don't have a test that tells us who's inherited the genes and who hasn't. We can't even predict how much drinking it takes to turn someone into an alcoholic or when it will happen. So choice, while important, isn't necessarily the main culprit.

After many years of working with alcoholics, addicts, and their families, and seeing the devastation this disease causes, I have some thoughts about choice, social expectation, and moral responsibility. We have a responsibility to stop our kids from choosing alcohol or other drugs. This requires challenging the messages coming from our culture and the media. We must start talking with our children at an early age and maintain the conversation throughout high school and college. Parents need to give kids clear expectations about abstaining from mood-altering substances and spell out the consequences for breaking the rules. If alcoholism runs in our family, it is our moral responsibility to avoid addictive drugs. We have a fifty-fifty chance of having inherited the genes. If someone we love becomes addicted, we are morally responsible for learning appropriate and effective ways to intervene. Anyone who becomes an alcoholic or addict himself has a moral responsibility to get well. The person may not want to get well, *but not wanting to do something has never been a reason not to do what we are morally obliged to do.* As a society, we are morally responsible for supporting and applauding the people who have the courage to overcome addiction and live life in sobriety. We are also called upon to support families who are striving to motivate a beloved alcoholic to embrace recovery.

In the words of Dr. Seuss, the well-loved author of children's books: "Unless someone like you cares a whole awful lot, nothing is going to get better. It's not."

HOW THE BRAIN MAKES
SENSE OF THE SENSELESS

T HE BRAIN *CONFABULATES*. It associates diverse sensations, defies contradictions, and creates coherence. It even seeks explanations for its own unfathomable behavior." Those are the words of Dr. Gerald M. Edelman, Nobel laureate in physiology and medicine and author of *Wider Than the Sky,* talking about the human brain. He tells us that our brains confabulate—unconsciously replacing fact with fantasy when necessary. The brain also defies contradictions—it won't simultaneously believe two ideas that are in direct opposition to each other. The brain even goes so far as to come up with explanations for behaviors that are beyond understanding. All of this is necessary if we're to maintain a sense of coherence, because when the mind isn't logical and orderly and consistent, we can't function. Without a mechanism to correct incoherence, we would plummet into mental disorder. Our brains literally fill in the gaps for us—even when they have to make things up—so we don't lose equilibrium.

Addiction is not a mental illness (many brain diseases, such as Alzheimer's and Parkinson's, are not mental illnesses), but there was a time when some medical researchers wondered whether alcoholism was related to schizophrenia. Both demonstrate a thought impairment that results in an abnormal interpretation of reality. Like schizophrenics, alcoholics eventually withdraw into delusions and a reality separate from other people. Both disorders appear slowly and affect only some behaviors some of the time. Schizophrenics may continue to appear normal to family and friends well into the earlier stages of the disease, and even once the disease is quite advanced, schizophrenics can seem quite lucid at times. Symptoms aren't consistent and they can change quite radically. Things are very bad and then they get better. Alcoholism has similarly confusing patterns.

A friend of mine was schizophrenic. She resisted treatment, as do alcoholics, and refused medications. She was raised in a family of considerable wealth and fame, and would frequently hallucinate visits with famous friends of her grandfather's who had long since been dead. She'd tell me of these visits in such a sensible and intelligent manner that I would believe her until my brain caught up with the fact that her visitors were no longer living. She once engaged in a knowledgeable discourse on drug trafficking, and her arguments were quite well thought out until she ended with an assertion that Rose Kennedy was the head of the worldwide drug trade. I once tried to evacuate her during a hurricane and she adamantly refused. She believed it was a trick—the CIA was plotting against her. When I turned on the television to show her the weather report, she pointed out that she couldn't trust broadcasters. I telephoned another good friend to try to convince her. She turned and said to me with authority and incredulity, "You know the rules. I can't trust anyone on television or over the phone. Maybe they're really who they say they are, maybe they're not." She was explaining to me how her schizophrenia worked, yet she was still tightly wrapped up in the delusions of the disease. It reminded me of addicts who talk about addiction yet are completely convinced by their altered reality. When I said to my schizophrenic friend, "But you know you can trust me," she replied, "*You* can't see the truth. You don't know what is really happening." The disease was much more powerful than my relationship with her. Much like the alcoholic, she was quite sure everyone else was wrong. She was incapable of questioning herself. She couldn't say, "A lot of people are telling me something is wrong. Maybe I need to reevaluate my own beliefs." She never agreed to treatment on her own, but family and friends finally took it upon themselves to have her committed to two months of inpatient treatment. She now takes medication and lives a full and normal life.

Even though alcoholism isn't a mental illness and is not related in any way to schizophrenia, it is very helpful to see the similarities between brain diseases and how confusing the symptoms can be. We know addiction hijacks the brain. We've already discussed how it co-opts the survival instinct for its own benefit. But I also think it takes over this mechanism of confabulation for its own purposes. The alcoholic mind makes sense of a disease that doesn't make sense. It seeks out explanations for the unfathomable. When things are going terribly wrong, the disease uses the brain to create alternative realities. The addicted person, like the schizophrenic, can't see beyond the false reality the brain is presenting. The disease tells the alcoholic, *You are still in control. You still have more time.* Alcoholics, even in the end stage of addiction, believe these thoughts. When we try getting through to the addicted brain, it responds as did my schizophrenic friend: "*You* don't know what's going on." That's why, one-on-one, we rarely succeed in talking sense to an alcoholic or addict.

Another example of how the brain confabulates is written in the book *A Brief Tour of Human Consciousness,* by neuroscientist V. S. Ramachandran, M.D., Ph.D. The author tells us about a rare brain disorder called Cotard's syndrome. Patients with this disorder believe they are dead even though they are fully functional human beings. What happens is that all senses become detached from the emotional centers of the brain. As a result, nothing in the person's life has any emotional impact—someone with this syndrome is totally devoid of any emotional response to anything, even the people and things he loves most. These patients' minds translate this emotional emptiness into the belief that they are dead. Dr. Ramachandran explains: "However bizarre, this is the only interpretation that makes sense to them; the reasoning gets distorted to accommodate the emotions . . . [and] is notoriously resistant to intellectual correction." Ramachandran goes on to explain that if you reason with a Cotard's patient that dead people do not bleed, he will agree that that is true. Then when you prick his arm with a needle and he bleeds, the patient will change his mind and say that dead people do bleed after all. Dr. Ramachandran notes that "once a delusional fixation develops, all contrary evidence is warped to accommodate it." This is also what we experience with addiction. Even when presented with indisputable evidence, the addicted mind will dispute the veracity of the evidence, much to the amazement of family and friends.

Bill Wilson, cofounder of Alcoholics Anonymous, wrote about this phenomenon of the alcoholic mind in 1953 in *Twelve Steps and Twelve Traditions:*

> *"Few indeed are the practicing alcoholics who have any idea how irrational they are, or seeing their irrationality, can bear to face it. . . . 'Sanity' is defined as 'soundness of mind.' Yet, no alcoholic, soberly analyzing his destructive behavior, whether the destruction fell on the dining-room furniture or his own moral fiber, can claim soundness of mind for himself."*

Addicts cannot identify their own delusional thinking. The identification—and the motivation to get help—must come from outside the addicted brain.

THE MANTRAS OF THE ADDICTED BRAIN

A MANTRA IS a sacred word, chant, or hymn endowed with the power to transform and protect whoever repeats it. It is thought to be a condensed essence of reality, or a spiritual power in the form of sound. When repeated, it activates a certain state of consciousness and achieves peace of mind. While mantras are usually associated with Hinduism and Buddhism, formal prayer and chanting are practiced in virtually all religions. For instance, the Maranatha mantra is an ancient mantra of the Christian tradition. Rosary prayers or praying without ceasing are other forms of Christian mantras. The literal translation of *mantra* is "mind protection": mantras protect the mind from harmful manifestations.

I use the word *mantra* quite deliberately to describe the words alcoholics repeat to themselves and to others. You will hear these same words come from the mouths of alcoholics of great wealth and those of little means, alcoholics who are well educated and those who are illiterate, alcoholics from every corner of the world and those of every profession. It matters not who the person is, because it is essentially the disease that repeats the mantras with the express purpose of protecting the addiction. If mantras used in prayer and meditation are mind protectors, mantras used by the addicted mind are addiction protectors.

These mantras ease the addicted mind. Through repetition, alcoholics and addicts are reassured that everything is normal, that the drug is a powerful solution in their lives, and that the problems they experience are caused by someone or something else. Sometimes mantras are repeated silently to themselves and sometimes openly to others.

◆ *Alcohol and other drugs don't cause my problems.* This is the principal mantra of the alcoholic mind. It is the cornerstone of denial. Regardless of how bad life becomes and how much pain is inflicted on family members and friends, this mantra beats on like a drum. Even once alcoholics are admitted into treatment, this mantra continues to pound through their heads. The idea that the *drug* is the problem is hard for them to hang on to—it keeps slipping away. Ongoing recovery groups play an important role in reminding addicts of an important fact: "Yes, alcohol and cocaine and pot and all other drugs are a problem for us."

◆ *Alcohol and other drugs are a solution.* It's not enough to say drugs aren't a problem; this mantra takes it a step higher. Drugs are solutions to problems, even those caused by the drugs. Jeff was a National Merit Scholar, an excellent student, and an alcoholic. One semester, he drank his way through finals week and skipped every exam. When his friends asked him how he could possibly have done such a thing, Jeff became confused and upset. His behavior wasn't making sense, and he knew there was trouble ahead since he wouldn't pass any of his classes. He didn't know what to do. Then it occurred to him: *have a drink*. He left the dorms, went to a bar, and got drunk. That was the solution.

◆ *I'm so special, so unique, and so smart, I don't fit into normal society.* Alcoholics suffer from *terminal uniqueness,* which means they believe they are so unique that the usual rules of life do not apply to them. They believe their problems are fundamentally different than the problems of others, so no one can help them. Terminal uniqueness is easy to spot in newcomers to Alcoholics Anonymous. They quickly indicate that they have nothing in common with people in the meetings. They focus on one or two people they find to be most unlike them and generalize that all people in AA are far worse off than they are and that they can't possibly identify with anyone. Addicts claim they are *different* from recovering people in the meetings, when what they really mean is that they are *better*. This is another way of avoiding recovery. An old joke in AA illustrates addicts' predisposition to set themselves apart from others: "The definition of an alcoholic is *somebody worse off than me*. When I had a wife and a house and a job, the alcoholic was the guy who had a wife and a house, but lost his job. When I lost my job, the alcoholic was the guy who lost his job and his house. When I lost my job and house, the alcoholic was a guy who lost his job, his house, and his wife. When I finally lost everything and was living under a bridge, the alcoholic was the guy who was sleeping in the rain on the street."

◆ *I am in control and I have more time.* From the earliest stages of the disease to the very last, alcoholics and addicts always believe they are in control. They often say, "I could quit anytime, but I choose to drink because I enjoy it." Of course, no one chooses to self-destruct and put family members through misery just to have a beer unless they have lost control. Addicts also believe they have more time—and don't need treatment—even when they are quite literally on their deathbeds. I'll sometimes say to an addict who is having trouble making the decision to accept help, "The disease will always tell you that you have more time and that you're still in control." Many addicts reply in astonishment: "That's exactly what I was just thinking."

◆ *I'm a better person when I drink or drug.* Alcoholics and addicts think they are sexier, funnier, smarter, more creative, better-looking, and more fun to be around when they're high. Many worry that if they get sober, they'll lose their finest qualities. A friend of mine, when she began treatment for alcoholism, said to me: "I'm afraid I won't be funny when I'm sober." She had no idea how unfunny she was when she was drunk. Steve Tyler, the lead singer of Aerosmith, discussing his recovery during a televised interview, said he had worried he wouldn't be able to write music sober. Of course, the band made its biggest comeback after Tyler's recovery. Alcoholics and addicts can't see themselves clearly. They think they are at their best when they're taking drugs or drinking, whereas families and friends see them as being at their worst.

Alcoholics are so convinced they are managing everything, despite clear evidence of loss of control, that even when their physical world falls into shambles, they're not alarmed. Disarray, filth, even living in their car—everything is converted into a normal part of their addicted life. I've walked through homes of alcoholics and addicts that defy description, yet people lived in them without thought to the degradation. Augusten Burroughs, in his memoir *Dry,* describes seeing his apartment for the first time after returning home from a rehab program:

> *I am not prepared for what I see when I unlock the door to my apartment. Although I have obviously seen it before, lived with it even, I have never encountered it through the lens of thirty days of sobriety. My apartment is filled with empty Dewar's bottles, hundreds of empty Dewar's bottles. They cover all surfaces. . . . There appears to be far more bottles than I remember, as though they multiplied while I was gone.*
>
> *The air seems moist and putrid. And then I see them: fruit flies hovering at the mouths of the bottles. They form dark clouds at the ceiling above the kitchen sink. And dead fruit flies cover everything, like dust.*
>
> *Clothing is strewn around the room, carpeting the floors, covering the chairs, sofa and bed. It looks like the home of Raving Insanity. It does not look like the home of somebody who makes TV commercials. . . . The only word is* squalor.

SPIRITUAL AWAKENING CHANGES THE BRAIN

AFTER JEFF MISSED ALL HIS EXAMS, he dropped out of college. His alcoholism had reached a new level. He began hitch-hiking around the country, fancying himself the new Jack Kerouac. He kept his mind occupied with ideas of becoming a great writer or musician, but his alcoholism kept him from seriously pursuing either dream. He landed a job as a writer for a large Chicago firm, but he couldn't stay sober. He'd leave for lunch, get drunk, and upon returning to work pass out on his office floor. The president of the company, impressed with his talent, gave Jeff second and third chances to get his drinking under control, but no one ever mentioned treatment. Jeff didn't know he was an alcoholic but he knew he couldn't quit drinking. Finally, Jeff was asked to come to the president's home for a private discussion about his future employment, but along the way Jeff stopped at a bar and got drunk. He desperately wanted to keep his job, but he *needed* to drink. Finally arriving at his boss's house hours late, he was told, "I have no use for you any longer," and the door was shut in his face. Jeff had lost all control of his drinking—he couldn't curb it even when the stakes were so high. At age twenty-six, he was a late-stage alcoholic.

Jeff's family talked to him endlessly about getting his drinking under control. They paid for him to go back to school, found him jobs, and gave him money. All their efforts fell away as alcohol demanded Jeff's full attention. He tried smoking pot so he wouldn't have to drink, but even that wouldn't suffice. Jeff found one girlfriend after another, with apartments and jobs and the willingness to let him move in, but they all became exasperated and kicked him out. In the end, he was living on the streets in San Francisco. At night he slept under bushes or on the benches in city parks. By day he'd panhandle money so he could buy enough wine to get him through. He couldn't hold down a job or eat solid food. He had a bleeding ulcer and a bleeding colon. He walked the streets as another homeless, faceless alcoholic.

Jeff knew he had problems, but he thought he had a cash flow problem. With an extra twenty dollars he would be all right. Then he heard about his friend Rickie's suicide. *That's the solution for me,* he thought. Jeff learned how Rickie had killed himself, and set about gathering the necessary accoutrements: large plastic bag, rubber bands, Valium, and vodka. He panhandled enough money to rent a four-dollar-a-night-room in a flophouse. He had it all planned out: he'd take the Valium, drink the vodka, put the plastic bag over his head, secure it around his neck with rubber bands, lie down, and breathe normally. As he was preparing everything, an idea occurred to him: *I should give myself a one-man going-away party.* He proceeded to get drunk and, in a blackout, called an old girlfriend to tell her of his brilliant plan. She called his parents in Michigan.

Jeff's parents hadn't seen or heard from him in months. In the past, they had tried finding him by hiring a private investigator. When they received the phone call, they went into full action to find out how they could save their son. They talked to a doctor who knew about intervention, and early the next morning they called the flophouse and intervened on Jeff over the phone. The tone was different from anything Jeff had heard in a long time—calm and loving. He listened to his father and agreed to go straight to the airport and fly home. Jeff's parents arranged to take him directly to the hospital. After a ten-day hospital stay, he was healthy enough to enter a thirty-day rehab program.

Jeff wanted to leave treatment every day, but every day his counselors convinced him to stay. After three weeks in treatment, he became paralyzed with fear. He knew he would drink again and he knew he would die. Alcohol-free for twenty-one days, his brain was now clear enough to understand the terrible nature of what he was facing. He was tormented day and night with thoughts of drinking and dying. In desperation—and even though he was a self-avowed atheist—he sank to his knees in the wee hours of the morning and cried out: "God, help me!"

Suddenly, like the morning sun rising above the horizon, heaven opened up and poured down upon him a waterfall of love. It was pure rapture, and it went on and on. Jeff, still on his knees, felt a divine love coming down around him that was beyond any earthly love. He then fell back with his arms spread wide open, and love continued washing over him. For thirty minutes he was overcome not only by the love of God but also by a powerful enlightenment: *he could stay sober.* It was suddenly clear that the power to stay sober wouldn't come from within him; it would come from a Power greater than him. He didn't need super-human willpower. It was as if he were a drowning man and this tremendous ship came out of nowhere to his complete and obvious rescue. "All I had to do was open my heart and allow myself to be lifted to safety," he says.

The next night, being an alcoholic and always looking for a high, Jeff got on his knees again and said, "God, help me." He waited and waited for that powerful feeling of love to descend upon him again, but nothing happened. It was at that moment he realized he would have to walk forward on faith. He'd have to follow the directions, go to his 12-step meetings, and live his new life in sobriety one day at a time. But he also knew, no matter how many angry seas he encountered in the future, that safety—in the love of God—would always be there, if he ascended to it.

Jeff had what recovering people call a *spiritual awakening*. Many people believe it is divine intervention. Robert Coleman, author and evangelical Christian, defines it as an awakening of God's people to their true nature and purpose. The book *World Scripture* says: "The true self . . . is suddenly revealed. The inner eye, which was blinded by defilements of worldly living, opens to a vision of the true Reality. From that moment life can never be the same, as the enlightened person begins to live by the knowledge he has acquired." Psychologist William R. Miller defines it as a quantum change: "a vivid, surprising, benevolent, and enduring personal transformation." Writer and editor Stephen Kiesling says: "It seemed to me a moment of grace." William D. Silkworth, M.D., who began treating alcoholics in the 1920s and supported Alcoholics Anonymous in its earliest days, characterizes spiritual awakenings, which he called "vital spiritual experiences," in the following way:

> *They appear to be in the nature of huge emotional displacements and rearrangements. Ideas, emotions, and attitudes which were once the guiding force of the lives of these [alcoholics] are suddenly cast to one side, and a completely new set of conceptions and motives begin to dominate them.*

Spiritual awakenings can happen very suddenly, as in Jeff's story, or are achieved slowly, over time, by working a 12-step program. Jeff's experience was an epiphany—it came on suddenly and without expectation, and he knew immediately that it changed him in a profound and lasting way. Most alcoholics achieve spiritual awakenings through a learning process—they realize that there is a different way of doing things and that it works. This type of spiritual awakening is a string of insights that, cumulatively, has a profound, life-altering effect. The twelve steps of Alcoholics Anonymous are a practical path to a spiritual awakening. The steps do not conflict with anyone's religious beliefs and can be worked by those who are agnostic or atheist. They are the best-known method for staying sober. Dr. Silkworth noted that prior to the existence of the twelve steps of Alcoholics Anonymous his success rate with alcoholics was only 2 percent. After his epiphany, Jeff knew he had to work the twelve steps to stay sober because God was not going to do it for him. God was going to provide the fuel for him to *do it for himself*. So, like many other successfully recovering people, he dedicated himself to a program of recovery, which he maintains today after over twenty-four years of sobriety.

We know that some experiences, such as trauma, can sear memories into the brain instantaneously. Primitive parts of the brain can record memories before events are perceived by our senses. In other words, before we see it, hear it, touch it, taste it, or smell it, our brains remember it. Our brains have plasticity—they can change, adapt, and improve in relationship to our experiences. It's possible for brain cells to grow new connections and receptors in seconds. When an experience is exceptionally powerful, connections between brain cells become stronger and communication is enhanced. Knowing these things, one can imagine that a powerful spiritual awakening could radically reformat the brain by sparking a tremendous growth spurt in synapses, dendrites, and axons, and it could all happen in seconds or minutes. This would explain how an immediate and fundamental transformation in attitude and behavior could take place after an epiphany.

There is a natural rhythm to the brain—called theta waves—that consolidates our memories, making them permanent. The more periods of theta waves we experience, the more we remember and learn. Theta waves occur during deep relaxation such as meditation, prayer, spiritual awareness, and sleep. Could it be that there is a drastic increase in theta waves during spiritual awakenings, facilitating the formation of vibrant and lasting memories? We also know that when we experience a powerful emotion, our brains release chemicals that strengthen the storage of that particular memory. The sheer power of the emotion is telling the brain: *This is important. You need to work extra hard at remembering it.* Is it possible that the intensity of emotion during a spiritual awakening releases an inordinate amount of these chemicals, creating deep-seated memories that remain vivid even decades later? Once someone has a spiritual awakening, he does not forget it. The transformation is so life-altering that people who experience it cannot go back to who they were before. Dr. William Miller, in his book *Quantum Change,* describes the experience: "Everything, or at least it seems like everything in the person's inner world has changed: emotions; values; spirituality; sense of self and personal growth; significant relationships; understanding of the past, present, and future . . . all of it had changed, and continued to change, for the better." A spiritual awakening doesn't make life perfect or easy, but it bathes everything in the light of promise and hope and possibility.

John Newton, a sea captain working in the slave trade, had a spiritual awakening on March 10, 1748—a date he never forgot—aboard his ship as it was being battered by a raging storm on the Atlantic Ocean. He gave up slave trading, and as a prayer of gratitude to God for having saved his soul, John Newton wrote

the famous hymn "Amazing Grace," a song sung by recovering
alcoholics worldwide:

> *Amazing grace! How sweet the sound*
> *That saved a wretch like me!*
> *I once was lost, but now am found;*
> *Was blind, but now I see.*

PART FOUR

Spiritual Negotiation

GETTING READY REQUIRES AN ACT OF FAITH

The way out into the light often looks dark,
The way that goes ahead often looks as if it went back.
The way that is least hilly often looks as if it went up and down,
The virtue that is really loftiness looks like an abyss,
What is sheerest white looks sullied.

—LAO TZU

THESE WORDS, written in the *Tao Te Ching*, perfectly describe the upside-down sensation families feel when changing their old ways of approaching addiction. Undoing the rules put in place by the disease can cause emotional vertigo. It's a journey out of accordance with what we have learned to expect. We feel as if we're falling back when we're moving ahead, losing ground as we begin to prevail, weakening while we're finding our strength. We interpret these feelings as meaning that we are not ready to take action, but they are a normal response when we are getting ready to make change.

When our spirits have collapsed under the weight of a loved one's addiction, the world appears inhospitable. Addiction repeatedly threatens our sense of security. In a world rich with solutions and ideas, we pull our heads into our shells and stop looking for a better way. We don't feel ready to do anything. But believing that *feeling ready* is a prerequisite to *getting ready* is one of the greatest blocks to taking action. Feeling ready is a myth. We go to kindergarten whether we feel ready or not; we learn to dive into water by doing it regardless of how frightening it seems; we learn to ride a bike in spite of the possibility of landing

squarely on the concrete. If everyone waited until they felt
ready, very little would get done in this world. As a recovering
friend of mine frequently proclaims, "Action before motivation!"

Feeling ready is illusive. We can be ready one minute and not
the next. We may feel ready to take action when our alcoholic is
out on a binge, but when he begs for forgiveness, we stop feeling
ready. The need to feel ready holds us back from taking action.
But the willingness to get ready moves us forward. Getting
ready is tangible and real. It requires taking practical steps.
How we *feel* about taking these steps is irrelevant—it's only
once we begin the journey that we truly understand the journey.
When we step out on faith, a wealth of knowledge and experience opens up to support us.

Taking action is an act of faith. As Helen Keller so beautifully
said: "Faith is the strength by which a shattered world shall
emerge into the light." We must rely upon faith—trusting that
life can get better, that other people will help, that there is an alternative to the breakdown of the family, and that there are ways
to take action that get results. Faith is what gets our feet moving.
We must step away from what *feels* right and toward what *is*
right. Getting ready calls for acquiring rock-solid information
on how to proceed. We must follow the directions even when it
goes against what we believe will work. When it comes to addiction, doing the right thing usually feels wrong. It's not unusual
to feel emotional discomfort and uncertainty as we proceed.
This is when we must rely on faith.

The original meaning of *faith* was "trust and vision." When
facing the tough stuff in life, the ability to trust and our capacity
for vision supply us with the fortitude to hurdle ourselves
through fear. As Thoreau put it, "We must walk consciously
only part way toward our goal, and then leap in the dark to our
success." When we don't trust and we've lost our vision, faith

falters. Without faith, we can't take the leap. We continue acting in accordance with old beliefs that have been influenced by the addiction: *You can't help an alcoholic until he wants help. We've tried everything. It's none of our business. It's her choice if she wants to drink. Treatment won't work unless he wants it. She has to hit bottom.* When these beliefs define our faith, we are placing our trust in the disease. Only by taking a leap of faith do we begin to see the possibilities.

As I was searching for the perfect metaphor for faith in action—the type of faith upon which we, as families of alcoholics, must depend—I thought about the final scenes of the movie *Indiana Jones and the Last Crusade.* Indiana Jones and the duplicitous multimillionaire Walter Donovan are searching for the Holy Grail—the cup Jesus used at the Last Supper. When they finally find the temple where the Holy Grail is hidden, Donovan says to Indiana: "Time to ask yourself what you believe," and then turns and shoots Indiana's father. Donovan knows that since only the Grail can save Indiana's father from an otherwise certain death, Indiana will traverse the series of deadly traps protecting the Grail. Indiana begins with only a book of secret codes to guide him. After successfully using the codes to pass through the first two deadly traps, he reaches the third and last challenge. Standing on a stone ledge overlooking an expansive abyss, he reads the final code: *Only he who leaps from the lion's head will prove his worth.* Indiana, gazing in disbelief at the vast divide below, says: "Impossible. Nobody can jump this." Then it occurs to him that he is being asked to take a leap of faith. Without being given any reason to *believe* he can walk through midair, Indiana extends his foot out into the nothingness. He literally steps out on faith, and it's not until then that the bridge becomes visible.

Everyone who has seen the movie knows Indiana Jones didn't

plummet to his death, but I'm quite sure he didn't feel ready when he took that first step into the abyss. His common sense would have told him that he surely was about to die. It was only through faith that he was able to find the courage to do what he needed to do. If Indiana had waited until he believed he could do it, he never would have taken the step. In alcoholic families, we believe our lives will collapse if we take the first step toward change. But unless we step out on faith, we never see the bridge that will take us safely to the other side. Feeling ready is not the key; we won't start feeling ready until we begin.

Getting ready often requires acquiring new information that diverges from our beliefs. If we won't make room for new information, we become paralyzed. Our old belief systems aren't getting the job done, yet we won't entertain ideas other than our own. As a result, we begin chasing our tails. Time passes, the addiction gets worse, and we get nowhere. If we hope to save our families from addiction, we must allow faith to take us places we can't yet see.

There are many ways to intervene on addiction successfully, but they all require forethought, preparation, and perseverance. Families already exert tremendous effort in an attempt to cope, but their efforts rarely lead to long-term change. Intervention requires effort, too, but it's an endeavor that leads to solutions. As long as our loved ones still live and breathe, the disease of addiction always gives us another chance to step in and take action. But first we must know what to do. This requires getting ready. In the following chapters, I will cover the many ways we can intervene on alcoholics and addicts. When we know our options, we can come together with our families to make the best decisions on how to proceed under the circumstances we are facing.

Getting ready always begins with one step in the right direction. Taking this step is an act of faith. Former president Jimmy

Carter's personal convictions demonstrate faith in action: "I have one life and one chance to make it count for something. . . . I'm free to choose what that something is, and the something I've chosen is my faith. Now, my faith goes beyond theology and religion and requires considerable work and effort. My faith demands—this is not optional—my faith demands that I do whatever I can, wherever I am, whenever I can, for as long as I can with whatever I have to try to make a difference."

INTERVENTION:
THE ROAD TO INTEGRITY

ADDICTION CHIPS AWAY at our integrity. We behave in ways counter to our deeply held convictions. We give money to addicts and tell ourselves it's going toward the rent when we know it pays for cocaine; we watch as someone gets behind the wheel drunk, but consider it excessive to call the police; we allow children to fend for themselves in alcoholic homes by professing that youngsters don't notice the problem. We allow things to happen in our families we once believed we would never tolerate. By failing to take proper action—whether by ignoring the addiction, attacking it with unproductive anger, or appeasing it by giving it whatever it wants—we damage *our* integrity.

Integrity is defined as taking action in accordance with our principles and commitments. It is living honestly and with an uprightness of character even when faced with challenging circumstances. The word *integrity* originates from the Latin word *integritas,* which means "untouched, whole, entire." Our inner and outer worlds are consistent with our values; we stand up for our moral convictions even when they're unpopular and we treat others with care. Jeffrey Blustein, author of *Care and Commitment,* describes what it means to act on principle: "A person acting on principle is also naturally standing *for* something, and not just being willing to stand *by* what has been done." Much like pilots flying in zero visibility, those of us who belong to families of alcoholics easily lose our bearings. We think we're on the right course while we're headed for a nosedive. Misdirected by the addiction, our moral compass is no longer reliable—we're doing the opposite of what we stand for and then standing by and letting it happen.

Intervention is our road map back to integrity. It is a journey back to our deepest commitments and convictions. We no longer bend to the will of addiction, but instead take a firm stand for recovery. Once we have made the decision to intervene, we strongly identify with the words of Mahatma Gandhi: "A 'no' uttered from deepest conviction is better and greater than a 'yes' merely uttered to please, or what is worse, to avoid trouble." Gandhi believed that how people behave is more important than what they achieve. In alcoholic homes, families often excuse how they behave by declaring the situation hopeless. Many people have told me they don't intervene because "it's no use trying." They allow alcoholism to define what is worth doing and quit before finding out what is possible. If we value integrity, then, like Gandhi, we believe our behavior is valuable regardless of what alcoholics do or don't do.

Intervention changes our thinking patterns. It is *thought realignment*. It moves us toward a sense of purpose, productive behavior, accurate thinking, and clear goals. Intervention requires that we connect with knowledgeable people and communicate on a meaningful level. We focus on what we want from our lives rather than what we don't want. These types of thinking activities and behaviors strengthen *our* brain and improve *our* health. Neuroscientist Daniel Amen explains: "Most people do not understand how important thoughts are and leave the development of thought patterns to chance. Did you know that every thought you have sends an electrical impulse throughout your brain? Thoughts have actual physical properties. They are real. They have significant influence on every cell in your body." Every experience in life has a thought behind it. When our lives are in chaos, it indicates that our thinking is in turmoil. When our thinking is straightened out, our lives return to order. Intervention is not just for the benefit of addicts; it's a way of thinking that helps everyone who participates. Intervention puts the entire family back on course.

It is often said that our future is determined not by our past but by what we do today. To transform each day into one that holds promise for a better future, ask yourself this question every morning: "Who do I want to be today?" When we ask this of ourselves, it's hard not to stand a little straighter and hold our head a little higher. This simple question puts us in the powerful position of decision maker rather than rudderless bystander. We can choose the words we want to use to describe ourselves: *authentic, curious, energetic, hopeful, considerate, persistent, proactive, respectful, generous, loving.* We can decide what virtues we want to convey: wisdom, courage, humanity, justice, patience. These virtues are often lost in alcoholic homes, but I truly believe that when we commit ourselves to intervening on the disease rather than enabling it, we bring these virtues back into our families.

This isn't always easy, however. Families often establish rules and expectations that are given more importance than intervening on addiction. For example, a woman named Gwendolyn called me about her husband, Steve, whom she described as her "soul mate" until he discovered cocaine. Now he had a girlfriend and didn't come home most nights. Gwendolyn would sometimes go to his girlfriend's house in the middle of the night, stand in the street, and scream for Steve to come out. "I realized I was losing my mind and my dignity," she said. "I decided it was time for a family intervention." Working together, we assembled a strong team: Steve's parents, his brother, two uncles, three friends, and his thirteen- and fifteen-year-old sons. Steve had tremendous respect for his family, and I was confident he would go to treatment rather than disappoint them. On the day of the intervention, Steve said yes when his mother asked him if he'd accept help. One week later, however, Steve wanted to leave treatment. When I spoke with Gwendolyn, I told her this was a critical moment in Steve's recovery. I explained that his urge to leave treatment was the addiction reasserting itself; he wanted to use drugs again. I recommended that she tell Steve he couldn't come home before completing the entire program. Gwendolyn encouraged him to stay, but she didn't tell him he couldn't come home if he decided to leave. When I made it clear that leaving treatment was a guarantee he'd return to cocaine, she said: "He'll go to his girlfriend if I don't let him come back to me." Steve called Gwendolyn the next day and promised he was ready to quit drugs forever, and she let him come home. Within two days, Steve was smoking crack with his girlfriend again.

Gwendolyn was acting out of fear, not love. She chose to re-align herself with the disease rather than stand by her commitment to recovery. Gwendolyn wasn't willing to risk anything for recovery even though everything was on the line for the addiction. She feared *she* might lose something if she didn't give the disease what it wanted. What families don't understand is that without sobriety, addiction always wins. Whatever we think we are saving by avoiding the rigors of treatment and recovery, we eventually lose to the addiction. In Gwendolyn's case, she thought she could save her marriage by letting her husband come home early. Her efforts helped bring about the opposite results.

When families don't do the right thing, we cannot expect alcoholics to act with moral fortitude. By taking the easy way out, we always give the addict permission to do the same. When we abandon integrity, we invite addiction back into the family. Intervention always asks us to return to our integrity. We must be willing to leave behind our old ways, learn what actions need to be taken, and persevere even when it becomes difficult. In other words, we need to do exactly what we are asking alcoholics to do: follow the directions and go to any length for recovery.

A few years ago, I consulted with a couple whose twenty-seven-year-old daughter was addicted to alcohol and marijuana. When I asked how their daughter was supporting herself, they told me they paid her rent, covered her car payments, and provided her with a monthly allowance. As a way of explaining, they told me Cathy was a student. I learned that she had already completed her undergraduate work and a master's degree in hospital administration. But upon graduation, Cathy announced she was no longer interested in her chosen field. She wanted to become a masseuse. When her parents suggested she get a job and take night classes, she threw a fit. She accused them of not understanding her needs and of being uncaring. They quickly relented and agreed to continue supporting her until she completed the six hundred hours of training she needed to be a licensed massage therapist. Two years passed, but Cathy still hadn't completed her coursework. She was spending nights drinking and smoking pot. She slept long into the day and often skipped class. Cathy was being *paid* by her parents to continue in her alcoholism. She had no reason to get sober.

It wasn't until Cathy was rushed to the hospital with alcohol poisoning that her parents decided to take action. When they called me, they asked about doing a structured family intervention. They had never before set limits or penalized Cathy's unacceptable behavior, even as addiction invaded her life. They wanted to turn that trend around and save their daughter. But Cathy was conditioned to expect her parents to roll over and cave in at her every demand. I warned them that Cathy might test their resolve by refusing treatment. I asked both parents if they were prepared to end her financial support, giving Cathy a reason to get sober. They readily agreed. Based on this understanding, we built an intervention plan.

We assembled a team of eight people, including Cathy's best friend from high school, both of her grandmothers, two cousins, an aunt, and her parents. When the intervention team asked Cathy to accept help, she began bargaining with her parents. These were well-practiced tactics that had worked for Cathy throughout her life. She was skilled at negotiating and began by saying that she wouldn't go to treatment, but she would see a counselor on an outpatient basis. When we told her that seeing a counselor was insufficient for treating her addiction, she shifted her strategy. She promised to go to treatment, but not until she finished her coursework. When we said waiting for several months was unacceptable because it would endanger her safety, she became obstinate. She denied she had a problem and flatly refused treatment. She tried to intimidate the team, but they maintained a composed, loving demeanor.

When it became clear that Cathy wouldn't budge from her position, her father calmly told her that he was only willing to support recovery. He went on to explain that he and her mother would no longer provide her rent, car payments, or allowance. He ended by saying that he loved her too much to continue making it easy for addiction to thrive in her life and asked her again if she would accept help. Cathy's rent was due the next day, and we knew she had very little money left in her checking account. Her car payment was due in two weeks. She couldn't last long without her parents' support. Cathy, however, didn't believe her parents would follow through with their promises. They never had before. She decided to test them by saying she didn't need their help. Everyone on the team was prepared for this result and understood that the intervention was going to be a process lasting several days or weeks. It wasn't easy for her parents to endure this period of uncertainty, but they didn't waver. When Cathy called them, yelling and threatening, her father told her he wasn't willing to talk to her while she was verbally abusive. If she wanted to have a conversation, he said, she needed to communicate in a respectful manner. This made Cathy even angrier, at which point her father told her he loved her but he had to end the phone call. Cathy's parents understood that her anger was a symptom of her addiction, and they weren't going to allow a symptom of the disease to stop them from helping their daughter. Five days later, when Cathy's landlord called her about her overdue rent, she went to her parents' house begging them for money. When they lovingly but firmly denied her request, she broke down crying and agreed to treatment. Cathy completed a twenty-eight-day inpatient program and then went into an extended program for recovering women for an additional three months. She now has almost two years of sobriety, she has an excellent job in hospital administration, and she's supporting herself.

There are several different ways we can intervene on alcoholics and addicts, but all have one common principle: zero tolerance for untreated addiction. When a family unites behind this principle and takes action accordingly, it becomes exceedingly difficult for alcoholics to continue in their disease. Families have tremendous power to either support the disease or support recovery. We need to make a choice. In the words of entrepreneur W. Clement Stone: "Have the courage to say 'no.' Have the courage to face the truth. Do the right thing because it is right. These are the magic keys to living your life with integrity."

SPIRITUAL NEGOTIATION

INTERVENTION BECOMES A SPIRITUAL NEGOTIATION when founded upon empathetic family relationships and a pledge to act with virtue and dignity. We do not battle addiction with anger, judgment, or blame; instead we reach out to the true person behind the addiction using love, compassionate honesty, and a vision for the future. Every life has a purpose, and intervention is a negotiation for *life* and the fulfillment of its purpose. Somewhere far beneath the addiction, inside the captive heart, the true spirit hears the voice of love calling and experiences a moment of clarity. In that moment, our loved ones cease to listen to the voice of addiction. They instead listen to our voice and trust us. Addiction loses its power and the true spirit asserts itself and says yes. In that moment, we open the door and move the person we love into the first stage of recovery.

It goes without saying that God works through people more often than lightning bolts. God rarely jumps in until we first start moving our feet; then all previously unforeseen assistance becomes visible to us. For those who are agnostic or don't believe in God, love provides a commanding universal guide for action. Regardless of individual beliefs, love has the power to transcend the greatest difficulties in life. It gives us the courage to persevere and the patience to wait. Spiritual negotiation creates hope for those who have none by putting love into action. Where there is hope, we can envision triumph. As writer Mignon McLaughlin said: "Love unlocks doors and opens windows that weren't even there before."

Whether we acknowledge it or not, we are always negotiating with the alcoholics in our lives. Negotiation is simply a discussion intended to bring about an agreement or resolve a problem. But most families are ill prepared to negotiate with addiction. Consequently, they are locked into a win-lose approach: the addiction wins and the family loses. Spiritual negotiation generates a win-win-lose approach: the family wins, our loved one wins, and addiction loses. Up until now, we've been rewarding alcoholism. We reward it by believing that all we have to do is let go and everything will work out for the best. We reward it by believing we're helpless or that loving someone means abdicating our authority. We reward it by imagining that a breakthrough will magically appear around the next corner. We reward it by ignoring it, making excuses for it, or denying it exists. Even family members who are outwardly angry and confrontational are playing into addiction's hand. Unproductive anger fuels chaos and weakens the family by pitting individuals against one another. By rewarding addiction, we've given it the dominant role in the family. Spiritual negotiation takes the authority away from the addiction by putting the family into a leadership position.

Spiritual negotiation uses *loving assertiveness.* Timidity and aggression no longer have a place at the negotiation table. Aggression only serves to incite addiction. Timidity or submissiveness gives it free reign. Calm, collected, and consistent assertiveness takes control. It changes the rules. Addiction quickly senses that the family has established a new position: they are making the decisions. By tempering assertiveness with love, we preserve the alcoholic's dignity while overpowering the addiction.

Spiritual negotiation begins with a new mind-set, but before we can achieve a shift in our thinking, we must identify how we currently negotiate with the addiction. What are our negotiation styles, and what do they tell us about our *true* goals? Are we negotiating for recovery or for something else? How do we have to change ourselves before we can change our results?

There are five types of negotiation styles found in alcoholic families: *adversary, aggressor, appeaser, avoider,* and *analyst.* Each negotiation style unwittingly supports the addiction. None of the negotiators is aware of this fact, however. They are quite certain that their efforts are geared to the betterment of the family. In spite of this, they're usually able to recognize how others are enabling the disease. A sixth negotiation style is available to families, but it does not occur spontaneously. It must be sought out purposely, with a willingness to learn a new way. I call this style the *ambassador.* The goal of spiritual negotiation is to transform all family members into ambassadors.

Adversaries are the alcoholics and addicts in our families. To be more precise, we can define the adversary as the addiction itself, because it not only controls the family but also controls the person who is addicted. Adversaries need to win at all costs. Since they believe alcohol and other drugs are required for their survival, every negotiation is perceived as a fight for their lives. As a result, they are hostile, inflexible, aggressive, and secretive. They use threats to intimidate their opponents or lies to pacify them. They manage their addiction by managing the family. Addiction is a taskmaster that doesn't allow for concessions. There is no middle ground. Agreements are made to be broken. The goal is to protect the addiction and avoid pain. Solutions are seen as threats. Over time, adversaries lower the quality of life for themselves and everyone close to them.

Aggressors deflect input from other people. They want to deal with the alcoholic in their own way. Once taking a position, aggressors stubbornly refuse to alter their thinking. They are more invested in protecting their stance than exploring effective solutions. The goal is to bully others into submission. Over time, aggressors become increasingly hostile, facilitating a breakdown in family communication.

Appeasers fluctuate between playing the rescuer and the victim. Their world is one of scarcity. They don't believe they can win, so their best efforts are reserved for not losing. This is why appeasers work so hard at resolving the problems of alcoholics— they think they won't lose if the alcoholic doesn't lose. Appeasers are always busy "helping" but back away from making meaningful change. They submit to the alcoholic's threats and use them as excuses for not taking action. Easily intimidated, they prefer to resolve negotiations by giving up or giving in. Appeasers don't strive for a good life; they settle for a life that's not too unpleasant. Good times are defined as times that don't cause much pain. The goal is to protect what they have, rather than work toward solutions. Over time, appeasers lose the respect of others and end up with less and less in life.

Avoiders don't like conflict. They ignore problems by hiding, stalling, or delaying. They resolve negotiations by getting out. They choose flight over fight when faced with a challenge. This leads to self-imposed isolation. Without access to cooperative efforts, avoiders are at a greater disadvantage than other negotiators. They live without whatever communication and support their families can offer. Avoiders believe they have no choice but to withdraw. The goal is survival. They define solutions as intrusions into a person's right to self-determination. Over time, avoiders are increasingly lonely, unfulfilled, and fearful.

Analysts are always seeking to understand. They often displace primary problems onto something else, redirecting emotion from a threatening situation to a safer one. For instance, analysts often identify low self-esteem or depression as the key issue rather than addiction. They search for solutions to the wrong problems. Analysts' negotiation style is to always need more information. They systematically pick apart ideas to avoid taking action. The chaos and confusion caused by adversaries feeds into analysts' need to scrutinize problems, break things down into essential elements, and consider all possible angles. Analysts tie themselves up in logic. The goal is not to feel. Over time, they increasingly detach from others emotionally.

Ambassadors are ideal negotiators. They can be described as Mother Teresa meets Donald Trump. They are motivated by love of family and zero tolerance for untreated addiction. Ambassadors know how to approach adversaries from a position of strength. They ingeniously leverage resources, change strategies, consider possibilities, think effectively, and maintain a state of loving assertiveness. They differentiate between the disease of addiction and the person suffering from it. They rely on cooperation and trust, but when provoked by an adversary they respond quickly and firmly. They draw a clear line between working for recovery and supporting addiction. Ambassadors do more with less. Over time, they spend the least amount of energy contending with addiction, as compared to other negotiators, because their efforts generate results. They keep their eye on the big picture, understanding that failures are stepping-stones to success. All actions are designed to send a strong message: *We will not give in to the disease.* At the same time, relationships with adversaries are preserved as a way of keeping the door open to future negotiations. Becoming an ambassador is a conscious choice. It requires obtaining instruction from a professional interventionist or learning new skills with the help of an intervention guidebook. The goal is to eradicate addiction and improve the quality of life for the entire family. Over time, ambassadors build trust and rapport. They are the people for whom recovering alcoholics and addicts have the most gratitude.

The aim of spiritual negotiation is to transform all family members into ambassadors. This is the most effective way to disempower the disease and, since alcoholics resolutely resist treatment, is supremely necessary for the health of the family. Alcoholic souls are locked down by addiction. The disease changes their personalities in ways that elicit dislike and distrust. But the person with the disease *is not the disease*. A friend of mine recently said to her sister, in asking her to accept treatment, "It's important that you know that I do not confuse *who you are* with what the disease does. I am your sister and I love you and I know you. The disease is not you, but it hurts you and it hurts me." I often hear people say of alcoholics, "That's just how she is." But it is not how she is; *it is how the disease is.* Differentiating between our loved ones and the disease is the first step in a spiritual negotiation.

Even the most recalcitrant addicts have difficulty standing up against a family of ambassadors. Recently I consulted on a case involving a thirty-two-year-old alcohol and cocaine addict. His parents reported their son had repeatedly told them that if they ever intervened on him, he'd never speak to them again. "I know all about intervention," he said, "and it'll never work on me." The parents, having heard this many times, acquiesced. They didn't understand that it was the addiction saying *Intervention won't work* as a way of protecting itself. Fortunately, their other children insisted on an intervention. Throughout the training process, the parents remained convinced we would not succeed. But they loved their son and agreed to do everything recommended. Every family member and several of their son's friends learned how to be an ambassador for recovery. At the conclusion of the intervention, when the father turned to his son and said, "Will you accept the help we are offering you?" the son looked up at his father and asked only one question: "Where do you want me to go?"

The power of spiritual negotiation is not to be underestimated. There are many different ways to proceed. Some interventions achieve results quickly, and others require a longer process. But when done properly, intervention works in most cases. Love, when harnessed by the most significant people in an addict's life, becomes a powerful foe to addiction. In Judaism we are told: "All men are responsible for one another." Traditional African religions teach us about God's benevolence: "God drives away flies for a cow that has no tail," meaning, of course, that God's love reaches out to help those who cannot help themselves. Christianity says: "We who are strong ought to bear with the failings of the weak." Confucianism speaks of a similar wisdom:

Those who are morally well-adjusted look after those who are not; those who are talented look after those who are not. That is why people are glad to have good fathers and elder brothers. If those who are morally well-adjusted and talented abandon those who are not, then scarcely an inch will separate the good from the depraved.

COMING TOGETHER:
FAMILY INTERVENTION

STRUCTURED FAMILY INTERVENTION is ideal for those who want to take action swiftly and precisely. Using the power of the group, this form of intervention is designed to get immediate results. About 85 percent of family interventions motivate the addicted loved one to accept treatment that same day. Of the remaining 15 percent, most eventually admit themselves into treatment within a few days or weeks. It's only the smallest minority that refuses treatment entirely. One fellow I intervened on resisted for a full year, but once he was in treatment he excelled. His family cherished every day they spent with him thereafter. He passed away in his late seventies but died sober with a loving, grateful family surrounding him. His daughter said, "Being able to remember him sober is the greatest gift he could have left us."

Family intervention starts with the basic premise that working together works. Great accomplishments are not achieved alone. Climbing Mount Everest requires a vast team and impeccable planning, along with the shared knowledge from teams who have gone before. A choir is a team that creates beautiful music. The finished product requires assembling the best voices, planning performances, and devoting long hours to rehearsal. Paul McCartney once said, "I love to hear a choir. I love the humanity to see the faces of real people devoting themselves to a piece of music. I like the teamwork. It makes me feel optimistic about the human race when I see them cooperating like that." Vince Lombardi, the famous football coach, pointed out that individual commitment to a group effort is what makes a team work, a company work, a society work, a civilization work. It's also what makes a family intervention work. By reaching out to one another and building a team, families can change the direction of their future. The group wields more power than any individual. Helen Keller perfectly describes the power of coming together: "Alone we can do so little; together we can do so much."

Some family members resist a team effort. I've seen many cases when one family member hinders the rest of the family's plans to intervene by insisting on confronting the alcoholic single-handedly. In one particular case, a brother was more interested in playing hero than helping his brother. He stood in firm opposition to family intervention and insisted that, unaided, he could convince his older brother, Bill, to accept treatment. He arrived at Bill's house alone and without a plan. He tried initiating a heart-to-heart talk, but when it became clear that Bill wasn't going to cooperate, he blurted out, "I'm doing you a favor here. If you don't get your act together, the whole family is going to show up and do an intervention." He not only failed to get Bill into treatment, but he also sabotaged the family's plans. Rather than move things forward, he set everyone back.

Working with a team is not a sign of weakness or defeat. We may have romanticized ideas of going it alone—like John Wayne or James Bond—but loners don't accomplish much outside of the movies. It is widely understood that our greatest strength is found in numbers. African religions use parables to teach the importance of working together: "The pebbles are the strength in the wall." The Buddhists also understand the power of collective efforts: "A drop of water is a little thing, but when will it dry away if united to a lake?" Even Jesus didn't work alone. The first thing He did was bring together a team of disciples, and then He instructed others to build teams: "For where two or three are gathered in my name, there I am in the midst of them." Build a team and you will produce a formidable opponent to addiction.

Some want to tell the alcoholic beforehand about the family's plans to do an intervention. This is not a good strategy when negotiating with an adversarial opponent such as addiction. By laying our cards on the table before the intervention, we give the alcoholic time to prepare for a fight. As a result, we begin the negotiation process at a disadvantage, because addiction doesn't want to cooperate. Family intervention is designed to mollify this ruthless adversary. We use the element of surprise not as a deception but as an effective way to disarm the disease. When families digress from this tried-and-true method, they reduce their chance of success. As negotiation specialist Charles Carver explains, "If [families] behave in their usually open and cooperative manner with adversaries, they'll fare poorly in negotiations. They give adversarial opponents an edge due to the fact that they disclose more salient information than do manipulative adversaries." If we announce our arrival with trumpets blaring, the disease will pull up the drawbridge and lock all the gates. There will be no way in. It is far wiser to catch the disease off guard. By using defensive tactics, we have a good chance of neutralizing our adversary—the addiction—long enough to reach the heart and soul of our loved one.

The disease may be our adversary, but the person who has it is not. I always imagine the alcoholic or addict as a hostage who has been brainwashed by his captors. He no longer knows the good guys from the bad guys. He's confused when the rescue party arrives. He doesn't know where his loyalties lie. We are calling out to him, but he doesn't know he needs saving. Intervention is a strategic plan designed to subdue the addiction long enough to allow us to convince alcoholics that we are the good guys. Once that's accomplished, it's relatively easy to move them into treatment.

Love is one of the most powerful intervention tools I've found. Interventions have always included a few caring and loving thoughts, but when love becomes the heart and soul of an intervention, it not only becomes the force that breaks through denial, it preserves the alcoholic's dignity and thus the relationships within the family. Even the angriest alcoholics soften as they listen to the most important people in their lives tell them how much they are loved. Alcoholics and addicts expect family members to be angry, not loving. A strong and sincere message of love catches them off guard. Their hearts open up and, as a result, they are able to listen to what their families have to say. Many people, after intervening on a loved one, say to me, "Even though I don't have a drug problem, I wish my family would intervene on me just so I could experience that tremendous outpouring of love. Most of us live and die without ever knowing, in such detail, how our families and friends feel about us. That's usually reserved for our eulogies."

Before anyone attempts an intervention, they need to learn how it's done. It's not unusual for some families to resist new information. They prefer to think up solutions on their own. This is a sign that the family is underestimating the power of addiction. They want to get their loved one sober, but they don't have the necessary skills and aren't willing to acquire them. While reading an article about Tiger Woods, I was struck by the important role humility plays in achieving our goals. We sometimes need to put pride aside and admit we need someone to show us the way. Tiger Woods could have easily assumed he was at the top of his game after winning the Masters in 1997, at only twenty years of age. Instead, after watching videos of his game, he came to the conclusion that his golf swing wasn't good enough to reach his goal of winning more titles than Jack Nicklaus. So he picked up the phone and called one of the most respected coaches in golf, Butch Harmon. The coach warned Tiger that reinventing his swing would cause his game to get worse before it got better. But Tiger wasn't dissuaded. He put his ego aside and began to relearn everything—his grip, his stance, and his swing. He hit hundreds of balls a day. It was only after a year of intense training that he finally hit the first shot that accomplished what he wanted. Then he went on to win six consecutive pro tour events. By 2001, he was the first golfer to hold all four major titles simultaneously. If Tiger Woods can ask for help, so can we.

The first question to ask ourselves is: *What kind of help do I need?* Most families work with professional interventionists, but some do not. Some educate themselves using a guidebook on intervention. The founder of intervention, Dr. Vernon Johnson, says: "Anyone who sincerely wants to help, can help. Chances are you're quite able to do an intervention without the assistance of a qualified professional. However, if you feel the need for such assistance, you should seek it." Families who dedicate themselves to completing all necessary preparations are often capable of intervening on their own. I receive many e-mails from families reporting that they intervened without a professional after following the instructions from Hazelden's guidebook *Love First,* which I coauthored several years ago. I received the following e-mail as I was writing this chapter:

> *Thank you, thank you for detailing and explaining intervention so*
> *well in your book. We succeeded in doing an intervention on my*

twenty-five-year-old son yesterday. Today is his first day in treatment. The intervention team was comprised of family members, my son's friends, and his boss. We weren't able to afford to hire an interventionist, since we were using our resources to pay for treatment, so we asked a recovering alcoholic who has been sober in Alcoholics Anonymous for over twenty years to serve as a chairperson for our team. Although she had no experience with this type of intervention, she read your book along with the rest of the family and learned what to do. She was recommended to us as someone who could answer our son's questions about treatment and recovery. These were questions the rest of us couldn't answer. We planned thoroughly and worked out all the details. Everything on your checklist was attended to in advance. We dedicated ourselves to turning my son's life around. Of course, I know that getting him into treatment is the first of many important steps. I consider the entire intervention experience as being right up there with the two or three most powerful moments of my life. One of my son's friends said to me this morning that he was more proud of his participation in the intervention than most anything else he has accomplished in his young life. I will share what I've learned about intervention with my Al-Anon Parent Group and anyone else who will listen or read. God bless.

Although many families are fully capable of proceeding with intervention on their own, other families face complications that require professional help. Whenever an alcoholic's problems exceed a family's ability to manage them, hiring an interventionist is highly recommended. Threats of suicide, history of mental illness, violent or abusive behavior, severe depression, or prior treatments followed by relapse all signal the need for professional help. Families who don't have enough time to prepare for an intervention on their own—such as when facing an imminent crisis—also need to rely upon the expertise of a specialist. If family relationships are badly deteriorated or it's difficult to bring a team together, working with a skilled interventionist can unite family members who otherwise wouldn't cooperate with one another. Many families decide to work with interventionists simply because they prefer the security a seasoned professional can offer. If you decide you need help but it's not possible to hire a professional, ask your pastor, priest, or rabbi to participate. If you don't have a relationship with clergy, ask a former teacher or coach, a recovering person in your community, an esteemed family member, a colleague, or a highly respected friend. Someone from outside the immediate family can command a level of respect from the addict that perhaps closer family members cannot.

Family intervention, above all else, is an act of love and a rare opportunity to save another life. It is both profoundly spiritual and eminently practical. It begins as a way to release a loved one from addiction and ends by bringing people together in ways they never expected. It's a spiritual realignment, because by doing an intervention we are making the kinds of spiritual changes we're asking the alcoholic to make. We first must admit that we need to change before we can expect the alcoholic to change; we must recognize our need for help before we can ask the alcoholic to accept help; we must be willing to work together before we can invite the alcoholic to work with us. The family and the addict must put aside their well-worn ways and begin to trust a process that is unfamiliar. Like the addict, we will be called on to do things that are diametrically opposed to how we've done them in the past. Intervening is a concrete demonstration of trust. We set aside our ideas and expectations and put our faith in what others, who have come before us, have discovered. Alcoholics must walk in the footsteps of other recovering people if they hope to stay sober. We must walk the path trodden by families who've triumphed over addiction by committing themselves to go to any length for recovery. Settling for half measures never works. Addiction will always prevail when we stop short. As Harriet Beecher Stowe so wisely said: "When you get in a tight place and everything goes against you, till it seems as though you could not hold on a minute longer, never give up then, for that is just the place and time that the tide will turn."

A CHECKLIST:
PREPARING FOR FAMILY INTERVENTION

ABRAHAM LINCOLN SAID, "If I had six hours to chop down a tree, I'd spend the first hour sharpening the ax." He was speaking of preparation. Any job is easier when we have the right tools. Intervention, like most everything in life, depends more upon our willingness to prepare than our desire to succeed. The following checklist presents an overview of the groundwork necessary to complete before doing an intervention. This is not meant to be a training course for intervention. Use these guidelines as a companion resource when working with a professional or reading a book on structured family intervention.

1. *Build a team.* Start by compiling a list of every significant person in the alcoholic's life. Include relatives, friends, coworkers, employers, teachers, clergy, and medical professionals. Don't overlook anyone even if you think they're not right for the team or you don't believe they'll participate. Include former friends who've drifted away, people who live out of town, and close relatives outside of the immediate family. Take an inventory of everyone in the addict's life. You'll use this list to select the people who will produce the strongest intervention team. If you're

tempted to reject important people because you don't want to tell them about the addiction, you have to ask yourself what is more important, keeping secrets or defeating addiction. Keep in mind that by the time families decide to intervene, the problem is usually serious enough to have attracted outside attention. Even those who don't suspect a problem are almost always very supportive when they are told. After all, this is a common problem today—one in three Americans is living with or related to someone with an alcohol or other drug problem. Once the inventory is complete, determine if any candidates are unsuitable. Cross off those who can't keep a confidence and are likely to inform the alcoholic of the intervention plans. Anyone the alcoholic *deeply* mistrusts or dislikes should be eliminated. Do not cross off people simply because the alcoholic is angry with them from time to time, or you'd be left with very few people. Someone suffering from an addiction is usually not included, because that person's own obsession for alcohol or other drugs can cause him to sabotage the intervention. When it's nearly impossible to leave someone who is addicted off the team, such as an alcoholic parent, consult with a professional interventionist. Most teams include between three and eight people, but I've worked with teams as large as fifteen. If your team is large, write shorter letters so the intervention doesn't last longer than the alcoholic's attention span. If your team is small—two or three people—it's wise to use an interventionist for added leverage.

2. Set up a planning meeting. Once you've assembled your team, schedule an initial meeting to decide how the family wants to handle the intervention training. Are you going to hire a professional, or will the team train themselves using a book on intervention? If you decide on a book, everyone should read the text in its entirety before proceeding. If the team prefers to work with an interventionist, call a treatment center for a referral.

Interview three interventionists before deciding which one is best for your family. Select a date for the intervention. Is everyone on your team available that day? If so, work backward from that date as you plan. The intervention rehearsal, for instance, is usually scheduled the day before the intervention. Appoint a detail person to collect all information pertinent to the planning process. When working with an interventionist, he or she will oversee the preparations. Consult the Resources section of this book for intervention resources.

3. Choose a team chairperson. This is important when you're not working with an interventionist. The chairperson acts as the spokesperson during the intervention. The best person for the job is someone the alcoholic respects and won't want to disappoint. Those who are emotionally entangled with the alcoholic aren't good choices. A revered uncle or a well-regarded friend is a better choice than a mother or spouse, for instance. The chairperson must be capable of remaining calm and steady during the intervention. Anyone with a quick temper or high anxiety shouldn't be considered. If no one in the family is prepared to act as chairperson, then it's best to work with an interventionist or a clergyperson. The chairperson must actively participate in the training sessions and be ready to handle the alcoholic's objections.

4. Discuss the negative consequences addiction has caused. The team needs to understand the scope of the problem before intervening. Each team member holds a different piece of the puzzle. As a team, review how the disease is disrupting the addict's life. When did the problem first begin and what types of drugs are used? When the team openly discusses what they know, it's usually the first time the family realizes the full extent of the problem. If the team is poorly informed, alcoholics who insist they don't have a problem can easily sway them. But the well-informed remain firm in their convictions. Knowing the alcohol and drug use history is also vital when arranging for admission into a treatment center. Write down all the negative consequences witnessed by team members. Keep in mind that you are cataloging the symptoms of a disease and how it has manifested itself in your loved one's life. Examine the alcoholic's family life, friendships, career, finances, emotions, and spirituality.

5. *List ways you have unwittingly enabled the addiction.* Enabling behaviors are responsible for the longevity of addiction. They provide addicts with resources, opportunities, and permission to continue using alcohol and other drugs. Every addict needs enablers and usually has no trouble finding them. One of the most important components of an intervention is recognizing how love and fear are transformed into enabling behaviors. Write down how you've enabled addiction in the past and what you hoped your enabling would accomplish. Share your list with at least one member of the intervention team. Make a vow not to help the disease in the future. Many family members have enabled the addiction for so long, they find it difficult to stop. Al-Anon, Nar-Anon, and Families Anonymous are 12-step groups that help families change these behaviors. When enabling ends, alcoholics more readily accept help.

6. *Write an intervention letter.* Letters bring predictability, order, and control to an intervention. Alcoholics and addicts usually politely listen and rarely interrupt as letters are read. Free-for-all discussions, on the other hand, invite pandemonium. Someone says the wrong thing, anger is sparked, an argument breaks out, and control is lost. It is far better to have each

member of the team prepare a one- or two-page letter, which is then read to the alcoholic during the intervention. Letters consist of three sections: *love, honesty,* and *hope for the future.*

The longest part of the letter is the *love section.* We tell our alcoholic, very specifically and from the heart, how much he or she is loved. We recount favorite memories, past accomplishments, funny experiences, and ways the alcoholic has helped us. We speak of their character and personality. Is he big-hearted? Does she have a great sense of humor? Sometimes we need to go back in time to find happier memories, especially if the alcoholic has caused us pain for many years. If a marriage is badly damaged due to alcoholism, for instance, a spouse may have difficulty writing the love section of the letter. In such cases, I ask questions that help bring up past memories: *Why did you marry your husband in the first place? What were the qualities that drew you to him when you were dating? What dreams did you share when you began your life together? Describe the day when you learned you were expecting your first baby or bought your first house. What sacrifices did he make for you and your family? Has he accomplished things in his career or in the community that make you proud?* In the love section, we celebrate the true person hidden behind the addiction.

The *honesty section* of the letter identifies addiction as the enemy. This is accomplished without anger, judgment, or blame. We avoid saying things such as "I can't believe you are doing this to yourself." Alcoholics translate these types of statements as "You are a weak, disgusting, and bad person." Shame and defensiveness result, and our negotiations are more likely to fail. It is far better to reduce shame by differentiating between our loved one and the disease by saying: "Alcohol has turned against you. It is robbing you of your best qualities and your greatest achievements. It's no longer your friend." Then give two or three examples of the damage caused by alcohol. The goal is to bring the problem into the light without alienating our loved one. This section of the letter is always kept short. Long lists of transgressions are unnecessarily humiliating. We want to use a loving honesty, not a punishing one.

The *hope for the future section* presents alcoholics with a sense of who they can be in sobriety. As an alcoholic, our loved one's overriding purpose in life has been drinking and getting away with it. A recovering friend of mine provides a glimpse into the alcoholic's thinking by describing how this single-minded pursuit—*drinking*—consumed his thoughts:

> *It was a summer backyard family get-together. I remember being very close to finishing my second beer, and trying to figure out the logistics and posture I would need to adopt as I oh-so-casually went to the cooler for the third one; everyone else was just on their first. Did they notice I was already one up on them and, if I pulled this off right, two ahead of them? Should I say, "Hey Mom, need another one while I'm up?" You know—no big deal, "Just grabbing another beer, want me to fetch you one as well?" Would it be less conspicuous if I went to the bathroom first and then circled around for the beer, as opposed to making the straight shot from lawn chair to cooler? Hey, is there maybe a portion of the twelve-pack still in the refrigerator inside, and I can bypass the cooler altogether? Now that would be the ideal scenario.*

He went on to say that it was incredible, in retrospect, how much worrying and planning of diversionary tactics and emotional energy he spent on his drinking. It also shows how much power families have in the minds of alcoholics. We may believe they don't care what we think, but they do.

Alcoholics need a higher purpose in life than finagling the

next drink. Change requires a reason. Therefore, our letters include a new vision for the future. We remind the alcoholic of
their dreams. We tell them of their strengths and the good they
can do for others. We speak of future milestones—graduations,
weddings, grandchildren. We paint a picture of the alcoholic's
place in the family. We tell them why we need them and what it
would be like without them. Our intervention message is that
recovery is about saving the family. Each team member pledges
to do his or her part. The letter ends with a simple call to action:
"Will you please accept the help we are offering you today?"

7. *Brainstorming objections.* During an intervention, alcoholics
are searching for escape routes to avoid treatment. They present
their escape routes to us in the form of objections. When alcoholics refuse treatment, they come up with reasons why they
can't go: *I'm too busy at work. I can't leave my dog. My best
friend's wedding is in two weeks. I've volunteered to be on the
steering committee for a community project. I have an important
doctor's appointment coming up. My friends and neighbors will
wonder where I've gone. I can't leave my house unattended. I
will stop drinking on my own. I don't have a problem . . .* and the
list goes on. Some objections are legitimate. A mother won't go
into treatment without knowing her children will be well cared
for by someone she trusts. Others are irrational, such as the
alcoholic who told me he was too important to be away from
his job even though he missed work on a regular basis and was
close to being fired. Intervention teams need to prepare for
all possible objections, large and small. If an objection is too big
to overcome—a daughter's wedding or college graduation, for
instance—the team needs to consider intervening after the
event unless the alcoholic is in imminent danger. Other objections require satisfactory answers. Can someone take care of the
dog, someone else pick up the mail, and yet another person pay

the bills? When the family has a solution for every objection, the alcoholic knows they are prepared and serious. This alone can convince alcoholics to accept help.

8. Determine bottom lines. When determining bottom lines, we ask two questions: *What have I done in the past to enable the disease and am willing to stop? What do I need to do to take care of myself if the alcoholic refuses treatment?* Bottom lines are read only if, after reading the letters and answering all objections, the alcoholic still refuses treatment. When this happens, addiction is telling our loved ones: *You're still in control and you still have more time.* Bottom lines are designed to counter that message by letting alcoholics know that time is up and the family is taking control. Upon reading bottom lines, the interventionist or the chairperson will turn to the alcoholic and say: "We respect your right to make this decision and ask that you respect our right to make some decisions for ourselves. We'd like to share those decisions with you now." Then each member of the team reads his or her bottom line and, again, asks the alcoholic to accept help. Here's an example of a bottom line written by a woman whose husband's addiction was destroying her marriage and family life: "Tom, we've been married for fifteen years and my hope is that we'll celebrate our fiftieth wedding anniversary surrounded by children and grandchildren. But if we don't make major changes, our life together is in jeopardy. I've learned how I've helped your addiction in so many ways, and I apologize to you. But today I promise I will only contribute to your recovery and your health. I will no longer make excuses for the drinking. I won't lie to our children and tell them you are sick when you are intoxicated. If you choose not to get well, I must also begin taking care of myself. As much as I love you, I can't expose our children to this problem any longer. We are unhappy and we hurt. I know you hurt, too. But until you embrace recovery, we cannot live together. It breaks my heart to tell you this, but a lawyer has drawn up papers for a legal separation that he will file today if you don't accept help. I'd prefer to avoid such a drastic step and instead work on rebuilding our marriage. I love you very much, and I believe you love me. So won't you please accept the help we are offering you today?" After Tom listened to the bottom lines from everyone on the team, including his parents and his best friend, he changed his mind and agreed to treatment.

9. Rehearse the intervention. We always rehearse interventions. This gives everyone a chance to experience the intervention before they actually do it. Everyone sits in their assigned places, reads their letters, reviews possible objections, and shares bottom lines. It's not unusual for rehearsals to be more emotional than interventions. People break down and say they can't possibly finish reading their letters. I remind them to breathe and continue reading when they're ready. By experiencing these intense feelings during rehearsal, emotions are moderated during interventions and reading letters is easier. This is also a time to review details. Has everything been completed? Is a suitcase packed, are travel plans finalized, did someone buy a phone card, do we need to confirm our reservation at the treatment center? Go over everything a final time to prevent any last-minute delays or confusion. Hitting a snag can give alcoholics a reason to change their minds.

10. Intervention day. Everyone arrives thirty minutes before the alcoholic. Cars are parked somewhere out of sight. Everyone take their places. Cigarettes, food, and drinks are put away. Phone ringers and cell phones are turned off. Pets are put outside or in another room in the house. A box of tissues is available. When the alcoholic arrives, the interventionist or chairperson greets him or her at the door. Once the alcoholic is

seated, the first letter commences. Intervention, properly executed, appears deceptively simple. What makes it look simple is
behind-the-scenes dedication and hard work. As poet Marcus
Annaeus Lucanus said: "The conditions of conquest are always
easy. We have but to toil awhile, endure awhile, believe always,
and never turn back."

INTERVENTION:
A DRAMATIZATION

Characters

David, a forty-three-year-old with an alcohol and cocaine
   problem
Barbara, his seventy-two-year-old mother
Bill, his seventy-nine-year-old uncle
Susan, his forty-eight-year-old sister
Mark, his forty-six-year-old brother
Brian, his best friend since high school
Amanda, his twenty-year-old daughter
Richard, his employer

THE INTERVENTION IS TAKING PLACE *at David's mother's house on
Saturday morning. Barbara asked David if he'd help her with
some odd jobs. Since David's father passed away two years ago, he
and his brother, Mark, have taken over many responsibilities
around their mother's house. Mark told David he'd help out and
said he'd pick him up at 8:00 a.m. so they could drive over together. The other family members arrived at Barbara's house at
7:30 a.m. so they'd have time to assemble before David's arrival.*

*Richard has been David's employer for ten years. He was
unable to attend the intervention but wrote a letter supporting
treatment. Uncle Bill will read Richard's letter during the intervention.*

*David is not expecting anyone but his mother to be at the house,
so all cars are parked two blocks away in a church parking lot.*

*The team previously drew up a seating chart, determining
where each person will sit. When David walks through the door*

with his brother, Uncle Bill will greet him and ask David to take a seat. The team decided to position David on the couch between his mother and Uncle Bill. David has tremendous respect for both his mother and his uncle and will have difficulty saying no to either one. If David tries to leave the intervention, he'll have to walk by his uncle, his best friend, his daughter, and his brother to get to the door. Everyone agrees it is unlikely he'll leave because the people in the room create a strong emotional force in his life. But if he does leave, his brother and uncle will follow him outside and gently coax him back into the house.

David and his brother are expected in fifteen minutes. All food, beverages, and cigarettes are put away. Pets are confined to another room and telephone ringers, cell phones, and pagers are turned off. Distractions interfere with the emotional impact of the intervention.

The team listens for Mark's car to pull up in the driveway. Everyone is feeling apprehensive. When they hear the car arrive, Uncle Bill prepares to greet Mark and David at the door.

DAVID [*surprised*]: Uncle Bill, how are you? Mom didn't tell me you were coming by. What brings you here so early on a Saturday morning?

Mark walks past David and goes into the living room to take his seat.

UNCLE BILL [*warmly*]: David, your family loves you very much, and we've all come together today to share something important with you. Come on in and take a seat next to me and your dear mother.

Uncle Bill puts his hand on David's back and gently guides him toward the living room couch. David takes a seat next to his mother and Uncle Bill sits down next to David. David looks around the room. Everyone is silent. He looks at his mother.

DAVID *[quizzically]:* So, Mom, what's up? What's everyone doing here?

Barbara smiles at her son and gives his hand a reassuring squeeze but says nothing. Uncle Bill answers his question instead.

UNCLE BILL *[reassuringly]:* David, we are all here today because we've each taken time to write you a letter and we'd like to share our letters with you. Your sister, Susan, would like to begin.

Susan and David have always been close, and he loves being an uncle to her three teenage sons. Susan makes eye contact with her brother, gives him a little smile and a wink, and begins to read her letter.

SUSAN *[takes a deep breath]:* Dear David: You are my baby brother, and I still remember the day Mom and Dad brought you home from the hospital. Mom sat me in that green over-stuffed chair and put you in my arms. You were only three days old, but you looked right into my eyes and I fell in love with you instantly. When you got bigger and Mom let me take you outside to play, I loved it. You were the best little kid in the world. You had the biggest heart. If we had ice cream and I finished mine first, you'd try to give me yours. You have that same generous heart today. After Dad died, you spent so much extra time with my boys while they were grieving for their grandpa. I can't tell you how much that meant to me. They love when you show up to play basketball or take them out on the boat fishing. You remind me so much of Dad in that way, always taking time with the kids. You know how to talk to them and how to listen, and they love you.

Susan continues reading her letter, sharing concerns about David's problem with alcohol and cocaine. She gives three examples of how it is hurting him and the family. Susan is loving and nonjudgmental as she talks about the addiction. She finishes her letter by asking David to accept the help they are offering him today, and then begins to cry. David stares down at the floor, biting his bottom lip. Uncle Bill glances at Brian, indicating that it's his turn to read.

BRIAN *[choking up]:* Dear David: We've been best friends since the tenth grade. That's twenty-eight years. My mother often said to me, "If you have one good friend throughout life, that's a greater treasure than all the riches in the world." You've been that friend to me. You were my best man when I married Wendy, you are the godfather to my son, and you gave me so much support when my mom had cancer. You've stood by me in the best times and through the worst. We never talk about these things, but I can't imagine what my life would have been like without you as my friend.

Brian breaks down crying and can't go on with his letter. He gives himself time to breathe and begins to read again. He tells David that he can't stand by without trying to help him, because he knows David would do the same for him. He ends his letter by asking David to accept the help they are offering him. Uncle Bill nods to Mark to let him know it's his turn.

MARK *[calmly]:* Dear David: I know I've been hard on you lately and we've had a few blowups. We haven't gotten along so well in the last couple of years, but I want to say that I've only been

angry because you're my brother and I haven't known what to
do. I've always been proud of you, whether I've told you that or
not—and maybe a little envious, too. You were the athlete in the
family, and when you went to State for basketball, it was the
greatest experience for all of us. Dad was thrilled. I was the kid
with his nose in a book, and you were the one who was good at
any sport you tried. We were a good pair, though. I helped you
with math, and you taught me how to pitch a baseball. We were
lucky growing up. We were close as kids. Mom and Dad would
have it no other way. I miss that closeness now.

*Mark finishes his letter by telling David that he has known
about the cocaine for over two years. He gives one example when
David showed up at his house late at night and very high. Without
any recrimination or blame, he explains that addiction requires
professional treatment. He asks David to please accept the help
that they are offering him today. Uncle Bill glances at Amanda, indicating that it's her turn.*

AMANDA [*looking at her dad with a smile and then down at her
letter*]: Dear Dad: It was hard when you and Mom divorced. I
was only twelve and afraid you'd forget about me. But you never
did. You've been a great dad. Our weekends together were always a blast. You always thought of fun things to do. Remember
the time we went camping and it poured rain the entire weekend? We sat in the tent and sang songs, played cards, and told
each other stories. I think that was one of the best times we ever
had together. I love you so much, Dad. Lately, though, things
have been different. [*starts to cry and takes a moment to compose
herself*] When you came to visit me at college, you seemed too
happy and too talkative. When we went out to dinner, you had a
lot to drink and you tried to get me to have a drink, too. It didn't
seem like you, and it scared me. When you wanted to visit again

I told you I had too much studying to do, but that was a lie. I was afraid to have you back. I wasn't sure how you'd act. I know this isn't my dad. This is a drug that has taken over the person my dad used to be. I miss you, Dad, and I want you back. I'm growing up, and I need a dad for when I get married and have kids of my own. Please, won't you accept the help we're offering you today?

David begins to cry. Uncle Bill turns to David and begins to read his letter.

UNCLE BILL *[kindly]:* Dear David: I'm here today because I'm your uncle, your father's brother. I think I know a few things he might have wanted to say if he could've been here himself. Throughout the years your father kept me abreast of your many accomplishments. He had such pride in all the things you did. Not just when you succeeded, mind you, but when you gave it your best, win or lose. Your dad said to me just a couple years before he died, "My children are my greatest accomplishment. When my time comes, it's the best thing I have to leave this world." When you get as old as I am, David, it comes as no surprise that life, with its many joys, also knocks us around quite a bit. You're facing some tough stuff right now, but it's nothing you won't beat with the right assistance. Your aunt Ruth faced severe depression after our Amy was born, and at first we thought she could get over it on her own. But it only got worse, so we found some help. It was a hard thing to face up to back then, because no one understood depression. But it wasn't her fault. We know now that it's a brain chemistry problem. You have a problem, and science says it's genetic. That doesn't surprise me. Your great-grandfather was an alcoholic, and so was my cousin Al. Both died from alcoholism, but you won't be defeated because you can get the help they never had. We're going to see to that. All you have to do is trust us and accept the help we're offering you.

David hangs his head and puts his hands over his face. Uncle Bill turns to him, holding the letter from his employer. He tells David that Richard wrote him this letter, and then proceeds to read it. In the letter, Richard assures David that his job will be waiting for him when he completes treatment. He encourages David to do as his family asks and go into treatment immediately. Then Uncle Bill nods at Barbara, David's mother.

BARBARA *[takes David's hand and looks at him before reading her letter]:* Dear David: When your father and I were married, we decided we wanted three children, so when you were born he told everyone, "Three's a charm!" He should have said, "The third's a charmer," because from the moment you were old enough to talk, you could charm the socks off anyone. You were born with quite a personality. Your dad and I enjoyed your zest for life. As your mother, you have given me so much joy. You can make me laugh like no one else. I am so lucky to have you for a son. Now that your father is gone, you are a great comfort to me. You have done so many thoughtful things for me. Of course, you always help around the house, and I thank you for that. But you also make life fun. You stop by and surprise me with a bouquet of flowers, or you insist I get changed and go out with you for lunch. You always have something delightful up your sleeve. David, I love you more than my very life. I know that you are having a tough time, even though you've tried mighty hard to hide it from me. I'm your mother. I've seen the changes in you. Alcohol isn't your friend, that I know. And now the cocaine. Son, I'm here today to tell you that this is an illness. It's not something you wanted for yourself, but it's happened. You're not the first person in the world to have a problem with addiction, and you won't be the last. However, we live in a time when we can do something about it. We've done a great deal of research to find the very best treatment for you. I need you in my life and cannot sit by idly as your life slips away. You have too much life to live and many wonderful things to experience as a son, a brother, a father, and a friend. When my time comes to leave this world, I want to know that you are healthy and strong. None of us knows how much time we have left together. We must make the very best of each and every day. Let's start with today. Please accept the help that we are offering you—that I am offering you.

David reaches over to his mother and hugs her. They both start crying. Barbara looks him in the eye and asks him again if he's willing to accept help.

DAVID *[taking his mother's hand]:* Yes, Mom, I'll go.

Everybody on the team gets up and gives David a hug and thanks him. Uncle Bill tells him that his mother packed a suitcase for him and it's already in the trunk of the car. Everybody drives to the treatment center together, and David is admitted into a thirty-day inpatient program.

David agreed to treatment immediately because the family had all the elements for an ideal intervention in place. Including a letter from David's boss almost guaranteed that David would agree to treatment immediately. He couldn't use work as an objection to treatment; instead, he felt obliged to accept help if he wanted to keep his job. His uncle Bill's presence made it unlikely David would become angry. He had far too much respect for his uncle to behave badly in his presence. His friend Brian represented the concerns of David's peer group. With his best friend on the team, David couldn't accuse his family of overreacting. David's mother is the most important person in his life, so the team decided Barbara should read her letter last because David would have difficulty saying no to her.

Not all families can put together a perfect intervention team. Circumstances vary widely, but interventions can accommodate most situations. If David's uncle wasn't present, his boss didn't write a letter, and he'd been estranged from his family, he probably would not have agreed so readily. It's more likely he would have voiced numerous objections and resisted treatment. The family would have been prepared for these objections and could negotiate with him until he agreed.

If David refused treatment, his family was prepared to share their bottom lines: how they would stop supporting the addiction and support only recovery, and how they planned to take care of themselves if he chose to stay in his addiction. This is how they would have presented their bottom lines:

UNCLE BILL *[calmly]:* David, although we are not happy that you've decided not to accept treatment today, we have great faith in you and know you will make the right choice before long. We are all committed to you and your health. Each of us would like to share with you the decisions we've made. We will not do anything to help you stay sick, but we will do all we can to help you get well. Your addiction hurts us, too, so until you get into recovery we must take care of ourselves, and we want to tell you how we plan to do that. I think Susan would like to begin.

SUSAN *[composing herself before reading her bottom line]:* David, I love you too much to do anything to make it easier for you to stay sick. I have pretended not to notice things in the past. A couple of weeks ago you called the house sounding intoxicated, and one of the boys answered the phone. He asked me afterward what was wrong with you. I lied to my own son, telling him you must have been overly tired. I didn't want him to know the truth. But I can't lie to my children anymore. I think he knows I was lying anyway. So I promise that from now on I will be honest about your disease and will no longer ignore it. If you change your mind, however, you can call me anytime, and I will help you get into treatment. But as long as you are still drinking and doing cocaine, you can't take the boys out with you anymore. It's just not right. I know you would never want to hurt them, but the addiction can't be trusted. I wish we didn't have to go down this unpleasant road, because this will be hard on them. Instead, won't you please accept the help we're offering you?

The team members read their bottom lines in the same order as the intervention letters, and David's mother reads hers last.

BARBARA *[deep sigh]:* David, I've nursed you through more than a few illnesses and some scrapes, bumps, and broken bones. If I could fix this one, I would. But you need professional help. I've helped you out financially lately, thinking I was doing the right thing. But I wasn't. I was helping your addiction, not you. If you aren't going to accept treatment, I cannot give you any more money. This is going to be hard on me, but I know it's the right decision. I will only help you get well, and you can always come to me for that. As a matter of fact, I expect you to come to your senses and make the right decision. You are always welcome in my home and that won't change, but there won't be beer or anything else. If I sense you've been drinking or something's not right, I'm going to drive you home. If you try to get in your own car drunk, I'll call the police. I won't have you killing yourself or someone else. When you come to my house, I want you sober. But what I really want is to put this behind us and begin a new day. We are a family, and we're not going to let this get between us. I am asking you, again, won't you accept the help we're offering you today?

Most people agree to treatment after hearing the bottom lines. Some do not, however, and test their family's resolve. When alcoholics are accustomed to empty threats, they may not believe their families will follow through with what they say. Once it becomes apparent that families are sticking to their promises, most alcoholics enter treatment within a relatively short time. Those who don't will face future crisis due to alcohol or other drug use, giving families another chance to step in and recommend treatment.

INTERVENTION IN THE WORKPLACE

A MANUFACTURING BUSINESS with one thousand employees can expect to lose approximately $450,000 a year due to lost days and medical costs related to problem drinking. A wholesale company with five hundred employees can expect to lose 772 workdays to alcohol problems and almost $300,000. American businesses lose a total of $140 billion a year to employee alcohol and drug problems. Yet, most companies have trouble recognizing addiction and even more difficulty knowing what to do about it.

The Kimberly-Clark Corporation, with sixty thousand employees, could expect to lose almost thirty thousand workdays every year and $26.5 million to problem drinking. Instead, they developed an education and intervention program to encourage employees to access treatment. The vice president of medical affairs at Kimberly-Clark reports that recovering employees come back to work better than ever. The Chevron Corporation reduces employee turnover, saves on training expenses, cuts health care costs, and reduces the number of lost days by encouraging employee participation in treatment programs. The company contributes the first $5,000 for treatment, and the rest is covered by health insurance. A General Motors plant in Michigan saw the following results after its alcoholic employees underwent treatment: lost man-hours declined by 49 percent, health care benefit costs fell by 29 percent, leaves dropped by 56 percent, grievances fell by 78 percent, disciplinary problems declined by 63 percent, and accidents dropped by 82 percent. Programs supporting treatment save companies $10 for every $1 spent, according to one corporate cost analysis.

Whenever an employee's work performance declines, the workplace has the right to intervene. Supervisors do not have to be experts in the field of addiction to take action. Workplace interventions, with or without a professional interventionist present, are almost always successful given that most people want to save their job. Since 80 percent of alcoholics and 76 percent of illicit drug users are employed, the workplace can be a powerful force in moving large numbers of addicted Americans into treatment.

There are four types of workplace intervention: *informal, structured, executive,* and *peer.* The *informal intervention* is simply a discussion between a supervisor and an employee. The supervisor must have well-documented evidence of the problem. Common workplace symptoms include absenteeism, arriving late or leaving early, long lunch hours, frequent complaints of not feeling well, missed deadlines, concerns voiced by other employees, complaints from clients, poor work quality or quantity, evidence of intoxication, repeated hangovers, short attention span, marital problems, repetitive lying, and changes in personality. Based on the documentation and company policies, the supervisor can suggest that the employee seek treatment on his or her own or ask an employee assistance professional (EAP) for a referral. Supervisors can also participate in structured family interventions. Families are sometimes reluctant to notify a supervisor, but this fear is unwarranted. Supervisors want healthy, reliable employees. Most have seen problems at work and are willing to collaborate with the family. But if the family decides that contacting the supervisor is not an option, they can take an intermediate step. Call the human resources department anonymously. Explain that the family is intervening on one of their employees and hopes to get him or her into treatment for alcoholism. Ask about the company's policies regarding treatment and about job security. During the intervention, this information can be relayed to the alcoholic. The combination of workplace and family is highly effective. In my experience, nearly 100 percent of interventions result in treatment when an employer is involved.

I was working on an intervention for a thirty-two-year-old man who was employed in a tool-and-die shop. His dad was friendly with his boss and said he'd inform him of our plans. Just before the intervention, I learned the family had decided not to call the boss. During the intervention, their son objected to treatment, saying, "I absolutely cannot go to treatment because I'll lose my job." His dad immediately picked up the phone and called his boss, who said, "I've been wondering what to do with him. Truthfully, I've been considering letting him go. You tell him to get himself into treatment, and he'll keep his job. If not, I can't make any promises." The son immediately agreed to treatment.

A *structured workplace intervention* is very similar to a family intervention. The intervention team is composed of several coworkers, supervisors, and members of management. Sometimes a spouse or parents of the alcoholic are invited to participate. The intervention might take place during a performance review or at another regularly scheduled meeting. Most of the time, the alcoholic doesn't know his drinking is on the agenda, but occasionally he'll be told in advance. If he's told ahead of time, management should feel quite confident that they have enough influence to overcome his defensiveness or inclination to avoid the meeting. Someone who highly values his job is likely to show up, whereas an employee who thinks he can easily get a job somewhere else may turn in his resignation. Interventions are positive and supportive, and when the employee attends, he almost always agrees to accept help. Therefore, using the surprise method is preferable when there is any chance the alcoholic will leave his job rather than attend the intervention. The goal of workplace intervention, after all, is to avoid losing employees, not frighten them out the door.

Executive interventions are designed specifically for chief executive officers, high-level executives, senior partners in law firms, doctors, and other professionals. These are complex interventions for two reasons. Power and money can insulate top executives from the consequences of their addiction and therefore make it more difficult to convince them to go to treatment. When they agree, the company may need to know how to handle sensitive issues with subordinates, customers, shareholders, and the public. For instance, James Fearing, in his book *Workplace Intervention,* says it is sometimes necessary to include very few individuals on the intervention team to avoid panic in the executive ranks. When the alcoholic is the president of the company, board members should serve on the team because they are the only people with the power to request a resignation. Using a professional is recommended when intervening at the executive level. There are many nationally known interventionists who are experienced at working with executives and other professionals. These interventionists can recommend treatment centers experienced at treating impaired professionals, ensure that sensitive information is kept strictly confidential even during the intervention itself, advise the company on public relations issues or internal communications, and act as a liaison between treatment staff and members of the intervention team. Interventionists are often in communication with the board of directors and corporate attorneys. They are responsible for guiding the entire process without mistakes or oversights.

Peer intervention occurs primarily among colleagues who have a great deal invested in the well-being of their coworkers. This form of intervention most frequently occurs among doctors, dentists, psychologists, attorneys, and airline pilots. When drinking crosses the line into addiction, it becomes apparent to peers long before supervisors recognize the problem. Coworkers take it upon themselves to intervene without involving higher-ups. They offer their colleague treatment with the understanding that if he or she refuses, they will report the problem to the licensing board or their superiors. The peer group usually consults with a professional interventionist, sometimes invites the family to participate, and is effective at moving impaired professionals into treatment.

Some companies do not have policies in place for handling alcohol and drug problems. Smaller companies wrongly believe addiction won't affect their bottom line because they have so few employees. However, if a business has two people working in their sales department and one is alcoholic, the bottom line is affected to a much greater extent than would be the case in a large corporation with thousands of employees. Until a company clearly defines its policies, supervisors may be reluctant to intervene on employees. There are many organizations that help employers set up a drug-free workplace. Ordering the free materials offered by the National Clearinghouse for Alcohol and Drug Information, *Making Your Workplace Drug Free: A Kit for Employers,* is a good starting point.

When the workplace is involved in the treatment and ongoing recovery of an employee, the employee has a greater sense of accountability. Knowing his job is on the line, he is more likely to complete treatment, follow aftercare recommendations given to him by his counselor, and attend his 12-step meetings. The more accountability, the more likely someone will stay sober. Pilots, for example, are closely monitored and must complete three to five years of aftercare programs after being released from treatment. To the extent they are required to account for their actions, alcoholics and addicts who must answer to employers have greater success in recovery than those who have no sense of accountability to others.

MEDICAL INTERVENTION

THE ADVICE MOST COMMONLY OFFERED to people looking for help for an addiction problem is to contact their family physician. I read it in magazine articles, hear it on public service announcements, and even find it in publications printed by reputable treatment centers. It is not the best advice, however. Few doctors are well educated about addiction, and some studies suggest they are less knowledgeable on this topic than the general public. Thomas R. Hobbs, Ph.D., M.D., medical director of Physicians Health Programs, describes the scope of the problem:

> *Based on my experiences working in the addiction field for the past ten years, I believe many, if not most, health professionals still view alcohol addiction as a willpower or conduct problem and are resistant to look at it as a disease. Part of the problem is that medical schools provide little time to study alcoholism or addiction and post-graduate training usually deals only with the end result of addiction or alcohol/drug-related diseases. Several studies conducted in the late 1980s give evidence that medical students and practitioners have inadequate knowledge about alcohol and alcohol problems. Also, recent studies published in the* Journal of

Studies on Alcoholism *indicate that physicians perform poorly in the detection, prevention, and treatment of alcohol abuse.*

Yet physicians can serve as important allies when intervening on an alcoholic or addict. There are three types of medical interventions: *physician referral intervention, hospital-based intervention,* and *brief intervention. Physician referral intervention* occurs when a patient's addiction could seriously complicate surgery or other medical treatments. When doctors are astute enough to recognize this danger, they may require a patient to complete a drug and alcohol rehabilitation program *prior* to surgery. For instance, Rosa was a seventy-three-year-old mother and grandmother with a twenty-five-year addiction to Valium, sleeping pills, and various pain medications. She also drank three or four glasses of wine a day. Rosa needed bypass surgery, but her doctor wouldn't schedule surgery until she was treated for her prescription drug addiction and alcoholism. He understood the risk of anesthetizing her: she could come out of the anesthesia during surgery or even lose her life. Alcohol and drug use can contribute to a condition called *anesthesia awareness,* when patients wake up during surgery but are unable to tell the surgeon they are conscious. In addition, alcoholics and addicts can experience delirium tremens or other potentially fatal withdrawal symptoms after surgery, which are not always correctly diagnosed by the medical staff and therefore may be improperly treated.

Hospital-based intervention is a structured family intervention that takes place in the hospital with a doctor present. When an alcoholic is hospitalized, it's the perfect opportunity to step in and intervene. Faced with a health crisis, most alcoholics become frightened and are more willing to examine the adverse effects alcohol is having on them. To leverage this crisis, it is important that we intervene before they begin feeling better or we lose our advantage. In addition, hospital stays are shorter than they were in the past, so the window of opportunity is smaller. Since families must act quickly, working with a professional interventionist is crucial. Families don't have time to train themselves. An interventionist is also experienced at coordinating doctors and other hospital staff. Although most doctors are willing to participate, many are more receptive when an addiction specialist is guiding the process.

The goal of a hospital-based intervention is to transfer alcoholics directly from the hospital into treatment once the doctor determines they're medically stable. I've experienced different levels of doctor participation when working toward this goal. Some will participate for only five to ten minutes and then leave the family to complete the intervention. Others participate throughout the entire intervention to learn how the process works. Occasionally a physician will refuse to attend or is unable to do so. In this case, ask for a letter recommending treatment and request that the hospital social worker be present to read the letter.

Never assume that doctors have a working understanding of intervention or treatment. Most do not. Without proper guidance, their inexperience can be a detriment. I once worked with a doctor who sabotaged an intervention by deciding he should confront the alcoholic on his own, even though he was aware of the upcoming intervention and had been asked not to discuss it with the patient. By the time we intervened, the doctor had created a high level of defensiveness in the patient, making it very difficult for the rest of us to negotiate with him. On another occasion, a family informed their father's physician of his advanced alcoholism and discussed the possibility of doing an intervention at the hospital. The doctor took it upon himself to tell their father about the intervention plans, and then told him he could continue drinking if he was willing to cut back to one or two drinks a day. Once the doctor gave the father permission to drink, it was nearly impossible for the family to intervene. In contrast, I've worked with doctors who demonstrated a thorough understanding of addiction and recovery. These are often doctors who are in recovery themselves or have a family member in recovery. They are a powerful ally to the family and exhibit brilliance during interventions. But even if a doctor lacks experience, most perform quite well during interventions when guided by an addiction specialist and gladly make recommendations for alcohol and drug treatment.

Brief intervention occurs during routine office visits when doctors suspect a patient is an at-risk drinker. This method of intervention is most effective with heavy drinkers who are not alcoholic. For alcoholics, it is a preliminary step. Most will not seek treatment as a result of brief intervention. Doctors trained in this approach are warm, empathic, and direct. They begin with an opening statement of concern: "I'd like to take a few minutes to talk with you about your alcohol use." The doctor then explains that his screening indicates that the patient's level of alcohol consumption is unhealthy and could lead to alcohol-related illness, accidents, or death. The doctor will ask the patient: "On a scale of one to ten, how willing are you to change your drinking patterns?" If the patient indicates little willingness to change, the doctor initiates a discussion to find out why. When the patient's willingness is high, the doctor will make recommendations. If the patient doesn't appear to be dependent on alcohol, the doctor will suggest limiting alcohol intake to no more than one or two drinks a day. If it isn't clear whether or not the patient is dependent, the doctor will recommend abstinence. If the patient appears to be alcoholic, the doctor will recommend abstinence, an evaluation at a treatment center, and Alcoholics Anonymous meetings. The doctor will attempt to elicit a commitment from the patient by asking, "How does this sound to you? I'd like to call and set up an appointment for you right now. What do you think?" Brief intervention is highly effective at modifying the habits of nonalcoholic drinkers. Most will follow through with a doctor's recommendations once they are educated about alcohol's adverse effects on their health. Alcoholics, however, are more resistant. They may promise to stop drinking or go to Alcoholics Anonymous, but they are unlikely to follow through. However, when their doctor tells them they are exhibiting signs of alcoholism, a seed is planted in their mind. They may refuse help, but now it's harder to deny their problem *to themselves*. Even if they dismiss the doctor as "not knowing what he's talking about," the conversation continues to resound in their head.

There is nothing more frustrating than when an alcoholic announces she's been given a clean bill of health by her physician. Families often wonder why doctors can't see what is so obvious. But doctors have little time with patients and rarely have access to information from the family. Patient privacy laws make it difficult for doctors to communicate with families without the alcoholic's permission. Privacy laws, however, do not prohibit families from supplying physicians with information. When a doctor is treating the symptoms of alcoholism but not the alcoholism itself, it is perfectly acceptable to send the alcoholic's physician a letter providing specific information about how much and how often the patient is drinking or using other drugs. Here is an example of a letter two daughters wrote to their mother's primary care physician:

Dear Dr. _____:

Our mother, Mrs. Irene ____, has been your patient for over five years. She has been suffering from various ailments we believe

*are caused or exacerbated by alcoholism and addiction to mood-
altering prescription drugs. We are aware of our mother's dishonesty about her alcohol and drug use, and we realize this puts you at
a disadvantage as her health care provider.*

*We have consulted with an addiction specialist and have
learned that several of our mother's medical issues are affected by
her addiction: hypertension, arrhythmia, osteoporosis, insomnia,
anxiety, edema, and diarrhea. The following medications produce
adverse reactions when mixed with alcohol: beta-blockers,
loperamide, calcium channel blockers, Ambien, Xanax, and
Librium. She is receiving prescriptions for Xanax and Librium
from three doctors. She takes multiple doses daily.*

*She drinks wine and vodka. We suspect that she consumes a
liter of wine daily and approximately a pint of vodka. She drinks
wine openly but conceals her vodka consumption. She often keeps
a tumbler of vodka hidden in a kitchen cabinet or a closet and "visits" her drink throughout the day. She has suffered falls, burns, and
memory loss due to alcoholism. Her personal hygiene is suffering
as well as her ability to take care of her home, pay bills, and socialize with family and friends. We have found her passed out on several occasions.*

*We are conducting a family intervention on July 3. It is impera-
tive that our mother not be told about the intervention in advance.
After the intervention, we will tell our mother that we sent you
this letter. We ask that you decline from prescribing any mood-
altering medications to our mother in the future. We also hope that
if she rejects treatment, you will make a recommendation that she
seek help during her next office visit.*

We've included two publications for your benefit. The first is
Alcoholism in the Elderly, *published by the American Medical
Association, and the other is* The Physicians Guide to Helping
Patients with Alcohol Problems, *developed by the National*

Institute on Alcohol Abuse and Alcoholism. We found both very informative.

We will call your office after our family intervention and notify you of our mother's decision.

Sincerely yours,

Anne P. _____

Carol R. _____

LEGAL INTERVENTION

I'S BEEN SAID THAT LAWS are felt only when individuals are in conflict with them. It's the nature of addiction to lead many into the long arm of the law. Sometimes the results are devastating. Families watch as their loved ones are sentenced to long prison terms for vehicular manslaughter or drug dealing. But most legal entanglements are not as dire. Nonetheless, when alcoholics face minor offenses, families scramble to hire the best lawyers, hopeful the alcoholic will be let off the hook. It would be far wiser to leverage the law, using it to move alcoholics into treatment and recovery.

I'm going to recount how several families I've worked with have used legal resources to move a loved one into treatment. The first is the story of Clara. She was raising her grandchildren because her daughter, Leigh, was addicted to heroin. Clara didn't think family intervention would work because Leigh lived with a grandfather who refused to believe she had a drug problem. He blocked Clara's every effort to get her help. Grandpa gave Leigh a free place to live, plenty of money, and a car. Leigh had been convicted of heroin possession the year before and was assigned to a probation officer. Clara decided to ask the probation officer to leverage the law and force her daughter into treatment. Even if Leigh had to spend time in jail, Clara thought, she'd be safer than she was now, shooting heroin every day. Clara went to the probation officer and informed her that Leigh was still using drugs. The overloaded court system had ignored the fact that Leigh wasn't following through with her required drug screens. Due to Clara's insistence, the probation officer requested a warrant for Leigh's arrest. At the hearing, the probation officer asked the court to mandate long-term treatment for Leigh in a county-funded facility.

Marsha and Clark's thirty-five-year-old son, Clayton, avoided them as his alcoholism progressed. He eventually cut them off entirely. He lived in a small apartment, drove a twelve-year-old car, and worked at a low-paying job for a man who was a known alcoholic. The parents considered a family intervention, but they felt their hands were tied. First of all, it was unlikely they could successfully contact Clayton, and they knew they couldn't approach his boss. When they talked to his old friends, they all said the same thing: "I haven't seen or heard from Clayton in several years." When I consulted with them, I expressed concerns that Clayton might also be suffering from a mental illness. Our chances of intervening were bleak, so I suggested they wait for a crisis and then step in. I warned them it could be a long wait. A few months later, Marsha read in the paper that Clayton had been arrested for driving under the influence. She knew this was his second drunk driving arrest. I advised them to contact the court and find out when Clayton's hearing was scheduled and the name of the presiding judge. I then had them write a letter to the judge. Here's a copy of that letter:

Dear Judge _____:

   It has come to our attention that our son, Clayton Michael _____ , is appearing before your court on the twenty-second of

September, facing his second charge for driving while under the influence of alcohol.

Although our son is presently estranged from us, we are aware of his long history of alcoholism. We are also concerned that he may be suffering from an undiagnosed mental illness. We are concerned that he will eventually kill himself or someone else while driving intoxicated.

While we are supportive of justice being served, we do not believe punishment alone will deter our son from drinking in the future. After consulting with an addiction specialist, we are convinced our son needs treatment for alcoholism. We ask the court to mandate our son into ninety days of residential treatment. As his parents, we are willing to pay for these services.

If the bench would care to speak with us directly, we will be present at Clayton's hearing. Thank you for any help the court can offer us in our attempt to help our son.

> *Yours truly,*
> *Clark and Marsha _____*

The judge ordered an alcohol and drug assessment for Clayton at a local treatment center and scheduled a second hearing to evaluate the results. Clayton's parents were not invited to participate in the assessment process, so I recommended they fax the treatment center a letter documenting Clayton's alcohol use as well as the negative consequences caused by his drinking. Clayton was assessed as alcohol-dependent, and the court ordered him into a treatment program.

Darryl's wife, Lynn, was a chronic alcoholic and a stay-at-home mom. Darryl didn't want to divorce Lynn because they had two children. But he worried about the impact her drinking was having on them. Their daughter suffered from nightmares, and their son's performance in school was suffering. Darryl consulted with me about a structured family intervention, but we didn't have much to work with. Both of Lynn's parents were late-stage alcoholics. One brother used marijuana and cocaine on a regular basis, and Lynn hadn't talked to her other brother and his wife in over five years. Lynn's girlfriends were all drinking buddies. She'd stay out at the bars with them until two o'clock in the morning. Lynn had as little to do with Darryl's family as possible. Without an intervention team, we decided that Darryl and I would meet with Lynn together. We waited until she had a bad drinking night, so we could approach her when she was hungover and remorseful. We talked to her about treatment, but she insisted she could stop on her own. We told her she needed medical detoxification to withdraw from alcohol safely, but she adamantly refused. When it became apparent she was not going to accept help, we said that she could try quitting on her own with the understanding that if she failed, she would admit herself into treatment immediately. She quickly agreed.

Thirty-six hours later, Lynn was feeling nauseous and her skin was clammy. She was withdrawing from alcohol. I recommended she go to the hospital, but she refused. Instead, she started drinking. Darryl and I met with her the following morning and told her we had arranged for her admission into treatment, based on our agreement. Not surprisingly, she went back on her word. She had long since lost any sense of honor, so breaking her promise didn't trouble her. But we were prepared. Darryl told her that he had made some important decisions. He had arranged for their children to go to his sister's house every day after school. He would pick them up after he got off work. He explained that he was no longer willing to leave them alone with her. In addition, he was prepared to call the police if Lynn attempted to get behind the wheel drunk. He told her she would have to face a judge, who would then deal with her drinking problem. For the next three weeks Lynn didn't drive. She had her girlfriends pick her up and drop her off. Then one day she tested Darryl's resolve. She got into her car after binge-drinking all afternoon. Darryl immediately called the police. Lynn was arrested with a blood alcohol content of .26. Darryl went to the jail and told Lynn he would pay her bail only if she agreed to go directly into treatment. Darryl was prepared to file for divorce and sue for custody of the children if his wife didn't complete treatment and remain sober. She sensed his serious-ness and completed her treatment program. When she returned home, she joined Alcoholics Anonymous. She had one small re-lapse, which convinced her to go to more AA meetings. She's re-mained sober since.

Another family asked me to fly down to Boca Raton, Florida, to help them intervene on their sixty-four-year-old mother, Patsy, after she had a bad fall and broke her arm while intoxi-cated. Their father had died the year before, and now their mother, who'd been an alcoholic for years, was drinking around the clock. To complicate matters, Patsy was very wealthy and ac-customed to always getting her way. Her children said she had never been interested in motherhood even though she had five children. She rarely visited her grandchildren and was more concerned with social status than family. Her friends were all big drinkers, so the children couldn't ask any of them to partici-pate. I suggested that the children call the doctor who had been treating the family for thirty years. He was also a family friend. I felt certain he'd talk with the children about their mother. He told them he'd been concerned about her drinking for years and had repeatedly recommended she quit. They asked the doctor if he would attend an intervention, and he agreed. I then directed the family to go to the courthouse to get paperwork for the Marchman Act, which is a Florida law that permits families, doctors, and others to ask the courts to mandate alcoholics and drug addicts into treatment. With papers in hand, we were ready for the intervention. We expected Patsy would refuse treatment, and she did. She even threatened to throw us out of her house. But everyone remained calm and focused on our mission. The family doctor told Patsy that if she did not choose to go to treatment of her own free will, he and the children were prepared to use the Marchman Act to have the court order her into treatment. He explained that they were willing to go to any lengths to save her life. He added: "We've arranged for you to go to a lovely program in West Palm Beach for adults over the age of fifty-five. You'll be with people in your own age group, not with young drug addicts. It looks like a resort, not a hospital. You can even have your hair done there. I think this is a much better option than having the courts send you away." She stubbornly refused for another twenty minutes, but finally agreed to go.

Unfortunately, not all states have laws that allow families to have courts order alcoholics and addicts into treatment. Call your courthouse and ask to speak with someone in probate. They can usually tell you what your legal options are, although in some states you'll find that you have none. However, if an alcoholic threatens suicide, you can have him or her committed to a psychiatric hospital. You might then be able to intervene and convince the alcoholic to transfer to a treatment center.

When we are forced to rely on legal interventions, we are facing tough situations with our alcoholics and addicts. We want to help, but we have few options. It's difficult for families to engage in legal interventions, but we must remember two things: it is far more difficult when loved ones die or lives are ruined, and it is far easier to leverage a minor legal offense than experience a tragedy. I once worked with a mother who waited too long. She talked about intervention but kept putting it off. Then her son was arrested for selling cocaine and sentenced to fifteen years in prison.

The following letter was written by a recovering alcoholic
and has been widely circulated among recovering people for
years. It has given many families the courage to do what they
must do to help a beloved alcoholic.

To my family and friends:
    *I am an alcoholic and I need help. Don't allow me to lie to you
and accept it as the truth. For in so doing, you encourage me to lie.
The truth may be painful, but get at it. Don't let me outsmart you.
This only teaches me to avoid responsibility and to lose respect for
you at the same time. Don't let me exploit you or take advantage
of you. In doing so, you become an accomplice to my evasion of responsibility. Don't lecture me or argue with me when I'm intoxicated. And don't pour out my liquor. You may feel better, but the
situation will be worse. Don't accept my promises. This is only my
method of postponing pain. And don't keep switching agreements.
If an agreement is made, stick to it. Don't lose your temper with
me. It will destroy you, and any possibility of you helping me.
Don't allow your anxiety for me to compel you to do for me what I
must do for myself. Don't cover up or abort the consequences of my
drinking. It reduces the crisis but perpetuates the illness. Above
all, don't run away from reality as I do. Alcoholism, my illness,
gets worse as my drinking continues. Start now to learn, to understand, and to plan for my recovery. I need help from professionals
and other recovering alcoholics like me. I cannot help myself. I
hate myself, but I care about you. To do nothing is the worst choice
you can make for me.*

                                              Sincerely,
                                              Your alcoholic

SOFT INTERVENTION

*S*OFT INTERVENTION is a slower, indirect approach for motivating alcoholics into sobriety. This approach focuses on dismantling the enabling system rather than directly asking the alcoholic to accept treatment. By doing so, negative consequences mount over time and the alcoholic's life becomes increasingly unmanageable. Eventually the alcoholic may decide to reach out for help out of desperation. Some alcoholics respond well to this method of intervention, whereas others need a more structured approach. The one requirement of soft intervention is that family members attend 12-step programs—such as Al-Anon, Alateen, Nar-Anon, or Families Anonymous—and practice recovery principles in their daily affairs.

Soft intervention transforms us into an example of *recovery in action*. We're not promoting recovery in the style of a used-car salesperson; instead we promote it through *attraction*. Our action step is initiating change in ourselves. Napoleon Hill, the motivational writer who studied the traits of America's most successful people, said: "The world pays you for what you do and not for what you know." As family members, we're constantly telling alcoholics what we know, and the payoff is slim to none. Soft intervention focuses us on what we do. Following Hill's advice, everyone involved in soft intervention—and those who are not—will do well to keep a sign on their desk or bathroom mirror that reads, "Do not tell others how to live—show them!"

When we're affected by someone else's alcoholism, their disease begins to define how we live. Addiction controls our every thought and deed, and most of the time we're not even aware of it. Below is a list of the most common ways we get tied up in alcoholism. Take a pen and cross each one off the list after you've read it aloud. As you do this, imagine each unwanted behavior leaving you and flying away. I imagine a ghostly bat out of hell, swiftly winging its way out of my sight. Then read the corresponding italicized affirmation. In doing this, we are establishing the right to determine who we are and how we are going to live.

◆ Preoccupation with the alcoholic. *I choose to focus on myself.*

◆ Reacting to the alcoholic. *I choose to act.*

◆ Blaming the alcoholic. *I choose recovery.*

◆ Worrying about the alcoholic. *I choose serenity.*

◆ Controlling the alcoholic. *I choose to change my behaviors.*

◆ Raging at the alcoholic. *I choose respect and dignity.*

◆ Enabling the alcoholic. *I allow others to have their consequences.*

◆ Hitting bottom with the alcoholic. *I choose life.*

Soft intervention requires that we once again recognize that we are people in our own right. As it says in the book *Al-Anon Faces Alcoholism:* "Most Al-Anon members come to realize they themselves have been forgotten in the midst of alcohol turmoil and confusion." We must reclaim our happiness and peace. Simply making this decision, however, doesn't magically cause it to happen. Like alcoholics, we need a program of recovery. By working a 12-step program, we heal ourselves and initiate a soft intervention.

Alcoholics underestimate how hard it is to get sober, and families underestimate how hard it is to stop enabling the addiction. Both think they can do it on their own, and failure is the usual outcome. It doesn't matter whether we think Al-Anon is right for us; what matters is that *we are right for Al-Anon.* Our exposure to another person's alcoholism has changed us, and Al-Anon is still our best way to rescue ourselves. Once we begin to truly understand the Al-Anon program, we begin to think we're the luckiest people in the world because alcoholism pushed us toward this great gift. Abraham Twerski, M.D., writes in *Al-Anon Faces Alcoholism:* "Sometimes I feel sorry for people who never had a drinking problem because they cannot benefit from the personal growth provided by AA. I feel even sorrier for the people who are living with an alcoholic and who could benefit from the personal growth available in Al-Anon as nowhere else, but are somehow unable to take advantage of it."

Soft intervention is synonymous with ending the enabling process. It isn't easy, but it's necessary if we hope to make the drinking and drugging life so arduous that the alcoholic can't take it anymore and recovery begins looking good. Here are ten ways to intervene by ending enabling practices:

1. *Stop reacting to what alcoholics do.* When we react, they focus on our reactions rather than their actions. In other words, our reactions become a vehicle for them to escape thinking about their own behavior.

2. Don't lie, cover up, or make excuses. Each time we do this, we are sacrificing our integrity while helping addiction exist more comfortably in our families.

3. Do not argue with, plead with, or lecture alcoholics. When we do this, the alcoholic views us as the problem and nothing is resolved.

4. Stop making empty threats. Set boundaries instead. Every time we set boundaries, we make a promise to the alcoholic and ourselves. Do not break promises.

5. Stop taking on responsibilities that belong to alcoholics. By doing this, we give alcoholics permission to become chronically irresponsible.

6. Do not give or loan money to alcoholics. This includes mortgage and car payments.

7. Don't bail alcoholics out of jail, pay fines, or hire lawyers.

8. Don't drink with alcoholics.

9. Don't try to control someone's drinking by dispensing a daily supply of alcohol or other drugs.

10. Do not do for alcoholics anything they would be capable of doing if they were sober. When we break this rule, we only succeed in convincing alcoholics that alcohol isn't causing them any problems.

Locating an Al-Anon meeting is easy. They are everywhere. Meeting lists are available online or by calling your local Al-Anon chapter. Churches provide space for Al-Anon meetings, so call neighborhood churches and ask. You will quickly come across several meetings. Meetings are free. A donation basket is passed around to cover expenses. Most people contribute a dollar. You are not required to speak. There is no pressure. When it's your turn, you can simply say, "I pass." But let people know you're new to Al-Anon. They'll welcome you and give you a newcomers' information packet. Don't make up your mind about Al-Anon based on one meeting. Go to at least six. If you don't like a particular meeting, try a different one. Stick with it and you'll begin to see why the twelve steps have been hailed as one of the most important spiritual movements of the twentieth century. As they say in Al-Anon, "It works if you work it."

Al-Anon helps us change, but it doesn't give advice about how to change alcoholics. It doesn't invite talk about outside therapies, books other than Al-Anon literature, intervention techniques, or other 12-step programs, such as Alcoholics Anonymous. Some people are frustrated by these rules and choose to break them. These rules are not in place because Al-Anon begrudges the advances made elsewhere in the recovery field. It certainly doesn't advise against other ways of finding help. To the contrary, *Al-Anon Faces Alcoholism* salutes the successes from the professional arena: "Much has been accomplished in helping alcoholics toward recovery in the last 20 years. The success rate has been raised by early intervention, motivation into treatment and continuous follow-up. It has been proven that alcoholics don't have to 'hit bottom' to get well." Al-Anon asks us not to talk about outside therapies for only one reason—to keep Al-Anon pure. We don't want to spoil the program by adding everything to the pot.

Soft intervention begins in Al-Anon. We change ourselves, then our world changes. With time, these transformations in ourselves might raise the curiosity of our alcoholic, and maybe

he or she will try Alcoholics Anonymous. We cannot predict
when or if this will happen. If it doesn't happen within a period
of time we're comfortable with, we can look to other forms of
intervention for help. But in the meantime, Al-Anon has given
us our lives back. Apart from how we choose to help our
addicted loved ones, as family members, this is our path to recovery. It's a spiritual journey. It revives our true selves. I whole-
heartedly believe that anyone who sincerely works a 12-step
program will become a far better person than he or she ever
could have imagined.

I'd like to share an excerpt from an English professor's description of her experience as a member of a 12-step program:

> By now, I've met people who bring to [meetings] a variety of
> spiritual paths, as well as atheists who use [12-step] philosophy as
> a way of life. I still go to meetings where many people appeal to a
> masculine, Christian, personal deity; but others at those meetings
> are interested in Buddhism or a more eclectic, nondenominational
> power. For me, that higher power is ethics and morality, the voice
> that points to compassion, courage, and goodwill each time I
> would like to succumb to pettiness, passivity, and impatience. . . .
> In the same way, I look forward to [12-step] meetings as a
> comforting alternative to committee and professional meetings at
> the university. Yes, there are occasional clods and bores in both
> groups, but at [12-step] assemblies, there are no pressures or
> agendas except figuring out how to live decently, honestly. . . . I'm
> relieved that several times a week I can go to a room where hope
> prevails.
> Asking for help is the turning point. After that, the story
> changes tone, from anxiety to hope, from tragedy to laughter. That
> story is called recovery. And that is where it gets good.

INFORMAL INTERVENTION

YOGI BERRA ONCE SAID, "It was impossible to get a conversation going; everybody was talking too much." There's a lot of talking in alcoholic families but not too many conversations. Our words don't make connections. A wife says to her alcoholic husband, "I won't take this for another minute." But she's been taking it for years and gives no true indication she intends to stop anytime soon. Her husband doesn't hear her words because they have no meaning. Only by giving our words meaning can we have a conversation.

Informal intervention is a carefully executed conversation. It begins with two relatives or friends who still have credibility with the alcoholic. Even the sickest alcoholics will listen to those they admire and respect. A thirty-seven-year-old alcoholic man, for example, still held his father and older brother's opinions in high regard. He knew they both lived with integrity and their words had value. They were the perfect pair to engage in an informal intervention. On the other hand, the alcoholic's wife was not an ideal candidate. She spent a great deal of energy yelling and threatening but never followed through on her word. She

didn't back up what she *said* with what she *did*. This wife depleted
her words of their value, and as a result, her husband no longer
found reason to listen.

Informal intervention adheres to the 12-step slogan "Easy
does it." We don't say too much. We rely on the meaning we
bring to what we say. We let alcoholics know we've noticed they
need help and aren't forgotten. We offer solutions. We don't debate or push. We may not experience the high success rate of a
structured family intervention, but this is a worthwhile first step
for families who prefer to have a conversation before launching
a full-scale intervention. Sometimes the addict surprises us and
says, "Yes, I'll go to treatment."

A father called me a few years ago. He told me right away
that he'd been a member of Alcoholics Anonymous for almost
twenty years. Now his daughter Jill was an alcoholic. Her thirti-
eth birthday was coming up in a couple of months. He had en-
tered treatment when he was thirty, and he wanted the same for
her. He asked me if I thought he could try talking to her first,
before doing a family intervention. I asked him to tell me about
his relationship with his daughter. He said they had always been
close, but now she was hiding her drinking, so he didn't see
much of her. He went on to say that his brother, Joe, also played
a major role in Jill's life. Joe had taken his niece under his wing
when she was a little girl and her dad was still drinking. I helped
them script a nonthreatening conversation they could have with
Jill. I used what I learned about their relationships to tailor their
words to their shared experiences.

I suggested that Uncle Joe ask Jill to stop by for a Saturday
morning get-together. He called her and said, "We haven't
talked in a while, and I found myself missing you. How about
drinking a pot of coffee together on Saturday morning?" When
she arrived, her dad was sitting in the kitchen. He gave her a big
hug. She could smell the coffee brewing and spotted a plate of

cheese Danish—her favorite breakfast indulgence—sitting in the middle of the table. This was a place she loved—sitting at her uncle's kitchen table, talking the morning away. It made her feel good just being there. They spent some time catching up and laughing. Then her uncle said, "Your dad and I haven't been seeing you much lately, and we miss you. We think maybe something's pulling you away from us, and we think it might be that unwanted guest that always seems to descend upon the best people in our family." Jill got quiet. She knew what her uncle was talking about. Her grandmother—Joe and her dad's mother—had died of alcoholism. Two cousins were recovering drug addicts. Another uncle, estranged from the family, was called a "functioning alcoholic," which meant he managed to drink and keep a job. He didn't function well in the family, however. An aunt married and divorced two alcoholics. The "unwanted guest" was ever present in their family. Her dad reached over and took her hand but didn't speak. They sat silently. Finally Jill started to cry. Then her dad said, "You know, my twentieth anniversary in AA is coming up in two weeks. I thought maybe you'd help me celebrate by checking into our favorite treatment center. It's becoming a family tradition, after all." Jill got up and went out into the backyard. They didn't chase after her, but took a look out the window. She was smoking a cigarette. They left her alone, and she came back in after a few minutes. "I'm not going to treatment," she said. "But Dad, I'll go to one AA meeting with you. I can't make any promises after that." Jill's dad took her to her first Alcoholics Anonymous meeting that night, and she kept going to meetings ever after. She got a sponsor and found a meeting for women she called her "home group." Jill never had to go to treatment because she never drank again.

This intervention led to an immediate action step—going to an Alcoholics Anonymous meeting—owing to the particular circumstances in this family. Jill still had a strong emotional connection with her father and uncle. Her uncle had been her rescuer and best friend when her father's alcoholism was raging. Her father had demonstrated his own recovery to her since she was ten years old. We had an excellent foundation for an informal intervention.

The execution of the intervention appeared deceptively simple. But every detail was thoroughly considered beforehand. Dad, Joe, and I had a brainstorming session. First I wanted to discover the best location for the conversation to occur. It had to be a place where Jill felt safe, and preferably one that was associated with good memories. Her uncle's kitchen, it was decided, was the perfect place. His house had been a retreat for her since childhood. I wanted her dad and uncle to add something extra to the meeting that would tell Jill she was loved. What about food? I asked. What did she like? Giving someone food, after all, has always been equated with giving love. Both her dad and her uncle chimed in: "Coffee and cheese Danish from the local bakery." By having these Danish piled high on the kitchen table, her dad and uncle were telling her: *We remember what you love and went out of our way to get it for you.* It seems like a small detail, but it's not. It conveys more than words. It tells her she's important.

We scheduled the get-together in the morning because we knew Jill would be sober. By afternoon or evening, she could be drinking. Then she wouldn't show up or wouldn't be responsive. I didn't want Joe to tell Jill that her dad was going to be there. Shame was keeping Jill away from her father, and I was afraid she'd come up with an excuse not to come. On Saturday morning, her dad arrived at Joe's house thirty minutes early and parked his car in the garage, so Jill wouldn't see it. When Jill came in, her dad and uncle hugged her. They sat around the table, engaging in small talk and telling jokes. Everyone was relaxed and having fun before Joe approached her about her drinking. His words were designed to keep her shame low. He never said the word *alcoholism*. He made reference to the long history the family had with this disease, and by doing so he sent Jill a message: *You're not alone. This is common in our family. It happens to the best of us.*

Her dad and uncle knew not to push Jill, so when she went outside, they remained calm and waited for her to come back. They also knew not to draw her into a debate; when she refused treatment, they did not attempt to convince her otherwise. When Jill agreed to attend one Alcoholics Anonymous meeting, they knew she was compromising with them, and they readily agreed. When they decided to do the informal intervention, their only goal was to be *heard* by Jill. When she agreed to go to an AA meeting, that was a bonus. Dad and Joe were hoping for a little miracle, but they knew not to expect it. When the miracle showed up, however, they ran with it. Her dad said, "Let's make it a date for tonight. We'll go to my regular AA meeting and then out to dinner." Since it was an open AA meeting—meaning nonalcoholics are welcome to attend—Joe went with them. Dad and Joe knew if they waited until later in the week, Jill might change her mind.

Most informal interventions serve as a lead-in to a more structured form of intervention, such as family intervention. They don't often result in immediate treatment or attendance at a 12-step group. But they play an important role for some families and some addicts. A family may need, for their own peace of mind, to do an informal intervention first. They may want to give the addict a chance to do something on his or her own. Most addicts do not take this opportunity, though, and don't agree to treatment. Once the family is satisfied the addict is incapable of making a healthy decision, they move forward with a structured intervention. Sometimes during interventions addicts

say, "Why didn't you talk to me first?" The family who has done
an informal intervention won't hear that question from the addict. Instead, they can say: "After we talked to you, we realized
that the disease has gripped you so tightly, it won't let you help
yourself."

Many families don't need to do an informal intervention first.
They've had many conversations with the addict and now they
need to move forward more definitively. But for those who wish
to take this step first and have a conversation with the addict,
here are a few guidelines:

◆ *Don't go it alone.* Select one other person to go with you
  when meeting with the addict.

◆ *Stay calm.* Even if the addict becomes defensive or argumentative, never follow suit. Anger will derail the conversation,
  and the addict will win.

◆ *Choose the place and time carefully.* The addict's home turf
  should be avoided when possible, because this is where he or
  she is in control. Don't have this conversation if you suspect
  the addict is high. Some people are never sober. When this is
  the case, select a time they are the least intoxicated.

◆ *Don't tell the addict what he or she is thinking.* Use "I" statements. For example, avoid saying, "You were so drunk last
  Friday night you made a complete fool of yourself. I was
  never so embarrassed." In two sentences, the addict has
  stopped listening. By stirring up shame, we've slammed the
  door shut. We want to keep the door open by reducing
  shame. This is a much better way to talk to an addict: "I see
  how alcohol is hurting you, and it won't let go. It's taken
  over without your permission, that much I know. I've been

wondering if you're feeling somewhat uncomfortable about it, too."

◆ *Have an action plan in place.* If the miracle happens and the addict agrees to accept help, have the telephone number of a treatment center in your pocket. Be prepared with the name of somebody in admissions whom you've already contacted. In addition, know the times and locations of several Alcoholics Anonymous or Narcotics Anonymous meetings.

◆ *If the addict becomes angry, remain calm and loving.* Breathe steadily and calmly. Keep your voice low and steady. Say: "I can understand this is a sensitive topic. I know I could be risking our relationship by sitting down with you today. It's only out of my love for you that I am willing to take that risk. I'm your biggest fan. I love you. I want you to know I'm here for you if you change your mind." Then ask for a hug. End by making some plans to socialize, and choose a time the addict isn't likely to be high. You might say, "Let's go out for breakfast next week, okay? I'll call you and we'll pick a day." You're telling the addict the door to the relationship is still open.

Informal intervention can be included in a course of action when working with an interventionist. With professional help, families can sketch out a multilevel approach. This requires looking at the big picture and committing to a *process* of intervention. It takes into account the addict's needs, the family's preferences, and the interventionist's recommendations. When family teams commit to the process and follow through every step of the way, very few addicts refuse help.

BEHAVIORAL INTERVENTION

ANOTHER FORM OF INTERVENTION requiring a long-term approach is the Community Reinforcement and Family Training (CRAFT) model of *behavioral mapping*. The thrust behind this technique is to encourage family members to change their behavior as a way of changing the behavior of alcoholics. Although similar in attitude to the Al-Anon approach of soft intervention, this program is designed with a framework of goals, activities, and exercises. Families learn new behaviors called *alternatives,* which eventually steer the behaviors of alcoholics into more positive directions. We are, in essence, leading by example. A relatively new intervention program, behavioral mapping helps us learn how we affect the alcoholic and how the alcoholic affects us. Then we modify our pattern of communication and wait for the alcoholic to respond in kind. Once the alcoholic softens and becomes receptive, we can broach the topic of treatment and recovery.

Behavioral mapping has two goals. First, we are asked to improve the quality of our own lives. This is something we do separately from our alcoholic's decision to get sober, which is in alignment with the purpose of Al-Anon. As we calm down, we can begin interacting differently with our alcoholic. We control what we say and do, rather than reacting blindly to alcoholic behaviors. The CRAFT model teaches us alternatives to our old behaviors. For instance, when an alcoholic comes home two hours late, his wife ordinarily gives him the third degree: "Where have you been? Were you out drinking with Bob again? I put a lot of time and effort into preparing dinner. The least you could do is show up." Her husband then says, "Get off my back. I've had a hard day. Why do you think I don't come home? All you do is nag." The CRAFT model suggests another way for the wife to respond: "I'm glad you're home. I was a little concerned. Do you want to eat?" Then the alcoholic responds differently as well: "No, I just want to watch the ball game." It is obvious he's been drinking, and his wife knows not to start an argument when he's intoxicated. The psychologist who created this program, Robert Meyers, says: "Achieving your ultimate goal might require sacrificing a little for now." Even when we want to lash out, we resist the urge in favor of the greater goal: slowly initiating a shift in our alcoholic's frame of mind so he'll be more receptive to talking about treatment.

The program provides many activities and exercises geared to changing our thinking. We're asked to visualize a better life and write our goals in a notebook. We also list activities we enjoy doing with our alcoholic, those things we don't enjoy, what we can do to make it more likely our alcoholic will do what we find pleasurable and stop doing what is troublesome. The CRAFT model recommends doing a series of exercises to better understand our choices when dealing with alcoholics. Here's an example adapted from the book on behavioral mapping, *Get Your Loved One Sober,* by Meyers and Brenda Wolfe:

STEP 1: Describe an activity your drinker currently does that you would like him or her to stop doing.

ANSWER: *My alcoholic makes fun of me when I ask her not to drink.*

STEP 2: Describe what you would do to make it more likely your drinker would do the behavior you just described or make the situation worse.

ANSWER: *If I get defensive or try to argue with her. If I try to explain that someone has to keep it together and take care of the house. Sometimes I tell her I just want to do something to help her, and then she really gets mad. If I start to cry, she picks on me more.*

STEP 3: Describe what you might do that would make it less likely your drinker would do the behavior you just described or make the situation better.

ANSWER: *Sometimes when I get angry, I just walk away. She usually doesn't follow me; she just stops belittling me. I could try saying, "If you choose to continue drinking, that's up to you. But I don't have to sit and watch. I'm going out to a movie. When you're sober, maybe we can discuss this."*

The entire program comprises twenty-three activities as well as checklists, charts, and examples, all designed to help family members remap their behaviors. This is essentially a behavior modification program designed for alcoholic families. For those who dedicate themselves to the CRAFT model, studies conducted by Meyers show a 58 to 76 percent success rate. Families experiencing higher levels of success participated in an expanded version of CRAFT, which includes attending aftercare sessions. The amount of time it takes before an addicted person will agree to accept help is unspecified and varies from family to family. The program works best for people who live in the same house as the alcoholic or who have a very close relationship and see the alcoholic on a regular basis. It's not a good choice for families who are rarely in the company of the alcoholic or live in another city. When a family wants to intervene quickly or an alcoholic is in crisis and needs immediate attention, structured intervention is a better choice. Approximately 85 to 90 percent of structured family interventions lead to treatment, according to the Hazelden Foundation.

CRAFT is a good choice for someone who wants to do an intervention but cannot build an intervention team. I often talk to people who describe themselves as the only sober person in their family. They want to know how to help a husband or mother or other close relative. CRAFT is a workable option for them if they stay in close contact with the alcoholic. This form of intervention requires patience and dedication. It is not something we can do for a week or two and then give up. I highly recommend pairing the CRAFT program with involvement in Al-Anon or other 12-step meetings for families. The twelve steps will greatly accelerate the family's progress.

If an alcoholic never responds and doesn't get sober, the CRAFT program asks us to ask ourselves when enough is enough: "When you have done everything you can to improve your life with your drinker and nothing has improved, it may be time to consider life without him. We know the pain that comes with thinking of giving up this relationship you have worked so very hard to preserve, but we also know the pain that comes with continuing to beat your head against a brick wall." The authors recommend that we turn our focus toward ourselves and other family members.

I'd like to offer another option for families who work the CRAFT model and aren't ready to give up on a loved one who isn't responding. After carrying out this program, you are in the perfect position to implement another form of intervention. Your alcoholic may simply need a little more organization and structure to her intervention. Without you knowing it, she may be teetering toward recovery and a little push is all she needs.

Giving up doesn't always end the problem. A wife can divorce her husband, but the kids still have an addicted dad. He might even get weekend visitations. I've talked to many mothers and fathers who have divorced their alcoholic spouses only to find the court granting visitation or shared custody. One judge said, "If I refused to give every alcoholic father visitation rights, most divorced men wouldn't see their kids." Suddenly the non-alcoholic parent is forced to turn children over to the alcoholic unsupervised. Because few of us can walk away from the consequences of addiction entirely, I am an advocate of doing whatever we can to get our loved ones into treatment. Sometimes we do come to the end of the road, but more often we mistake a bend in the road for the end. As the old adage goes: "The bend in the road is not the end of the road unless you refuse to take the turn."

IMPAIRED PROFESSIONAL INTERVENTION

SINCE IT IS OFTEN WRONGLY ASSUMED that addiction is caused by weakness of character, we also mistakenly think people in exalted professions are less likely to become dependent on alcohol or other drugs. Doctors, for instance, are sometimes thought to be immune from such problems. Physicians would certainly know better, the reasoning goes. Let's remember that the cofounder of Alcoholics Anonymous was a doctor. This is what Dr. Bob Smith, who was a surgeon, had to say about his alcoholism: "I knew if I did not stay sober enough to earn money, I would run out of liquor. Most of the time, therefore, I did not take the morning drink I craved so badly, but instead would fill up on large doses of sedatives to quiet the jitters." Not only do we find alcoholics in every profession, but studies indicate that doctors and lawyers are more vulnerable to alcohol problems than the average citizen.

There are many reasons why we might avoid intervening on addicted professionals in our family. We fear damaging a career that required years of schooling and untold sacrifices and hard work. We fear tearing down a professional reputation that took years to build. We're intimidated by the doctor or lawyer in our family. We enjoy a nice lifestyle and don't want to jeopardize the paycheck that maintains it. So we ignore the addiction and hope for the best, thinking that maybe no one will notice.

Ignoring the problem can lead to career-destroying consequences, lawsuits, and criminal charges. For example, two pilots who smelled of alcohol were pulled from the cockpit of a commercial airliner filled with 124 passengers. Their blood alcohol content was tested, and both had levels higher than the law allows for operating automobiles. The pilots were fired, lost their licenses, and were charged with a crime by the state of Florida. Both face up to five years in prison. I counseled professionals in treatment who described blood-chilling examples of how their addiction endangered the lives of others: a doctor showed up for surgery drunk; a pilot flew a commercial jet from New York to Los Angeles in a blackout; a lawyer ruined a man financially by negligently losing his case. When someone is responsible for the lives of other people, we must not turn a blind eye to the signs of addiction. The consequences are far too costly.

Fortunately, there are excellent organizations that help impaired professionals get sober while preserving their careers. Families who want to intervene can access these organizations. The purpose is to treat impaired professionals compassionately, recognize they have a disease, and arrange for treatment, not punishment. These programs are called *monitoring organizations, diversion programs,* or *peer assistance programs.* While they differ from state to state, the goal remains the same: provide advocacy, referral, and monitoring services to professionals impaired by substance abuse, and provide an alternative to licensure disciplinary action. If impaired professionals turn themselves in to these organizations—or are turned in by someone else—before the problem is brought before the licensing board, their chemical dependency is not reported to the board and their license is not affected. Colleagues, employers, friends, family, or members of the public can report professionals to monitoring organizations.

Whenever we intervene on a professional, we can make use of the services offered by monitoring organizations. For example, I facilitated a structured family intervention on a forty-three-year-old emergency room physician. She was addicted to prescription medications and alcohol. When she was on the job, she took pills; when she was home she mixed alcohol with her pills. She promised her husband several times that she would detox herself and quit, but she always started again. During the intervention, she told her family she didn't need treatment. She was a doctor, she said, and she knew what to do. Her husband reminded her of the times she'd tried to quit and failed, but she continued to insist she could do it on her own. Unable to change her mind, the team read their bottom lines and explained what they planned to do if she did not accept help. Each family member told her they planned to report her to the physician's monitoring organization. Upon hearing this, she quickly changed her mind and checked into treatment that day. While she was in treatment, her family worked with her and her counselor to formulate a relapse agreement. If she started drinking or using drugs again, the family would immediately involve the monitoring organization.

Interventions can also be left entirely to a monitoring organization. I consulted with a wife who didn't want to tell friends and family that her husband, Albert, was an alcoholic. He was a wealthy and successful surgeon. She was worried she'd ruin his professional reputation if too many people knew about his drinking. Yet she understood she had to help him. She could see his hands tremble in the mornings and feared for his career. She talked with Albert on several occasions about his drinking, but the most he would promise was to cut down, which only lasted a week or two. She asked me what she could do that would effectively motivate her husband to accept treatment without doing a family intervention. I put her in touch with the Health Professional Recovery Program (HPRP), a monitoring organization in Michigan. She leveraged the power of HPRP to get her husband into recovery. These are the steps they took:

◆ Albert's wife filed a report with HPRP stating that her husband was suffering from alcoholism. She did not want to be identified as the person who reported him and was assured all information would be held in strict confidence.

◆ HPRP began an information-gathering process. They launched an investigation and determined that Albert showed symptoms of alcohol dependency.

◆ HPRP asked Albert if he was willing to participate in the monitoring program. If so, his confidentiality would be protected. If he refused, they would be required to notify the state licensure board. Albert agreed to enter the monitoring program.

◆ Albert was referred to a treatment program that specializes in working with addicted medical professionals. When he completed treatment he was given an aftercare plan to follow and was told that HPRP would monitor his recovery for three years.

◆ It was explained to Albert that once he successfully completed the monitoring program, his record would be maintained by HPRP for five more years. If he remained sober, his record would be expunged.

◆ If Albert had a relapse, HPRP might require him to withdraw from or limit his practice while he received more treatment and reestablished his sobriety. If he refused to comply, HPRP would notify the state licensure board.

These are examples of health professions typically covered by state monitoring organizations:

Audiologist	Physician's assistant
Physician (M.D.)	Podiatric physician
Chiropractor	Marriage and family therapist
Nursing home administrator	Optometrist
Osteopathic physician and surgeon	Professional counselor
Pharmacist	Physical therapist
Psychologist	Respiratory therapist
Social worker	Social worker assistant
Veterinarian	Veterinary technician
Registered nurse	Licensed practical nurse
Dentist	Dental hygienist
Dental assistant	Sanitarian

Lawyers Assistance Programs (LAPs) offer help to addicted judges, attorneys, law students, and support staff. The programs recognize addiction as a treatable illness, and the only stigma attached to the illness is the refusal to accept help. Family members, friends, and colleagues can seek support from a LAP. Confidentiality is ensured, and the addicted will not be reported to the state bar, the board of bar examiners, or their employers. LAPs help arrange and implement formal interventions, identify appropriate treatment programs, and provide monitoring and aftercare services. A network of recovering attorneys offers ongoing support to lawyers newly in recovery. Since services vary from state to state, call the Lawyers Assistance Program in your home area for specific information. The American Bar Association maintains a directory of state programs. Contact them at 800-285-2221 or www.abanet.org. The Commission on Lawyers Assistance Programs national directory is available on the Web site.

Major airlines and most regional carriers offer confidential services for addicted pilots and crew. If the airline has a union, families can report addiction problems without threatening a loved one's career. When impaired pilots are caught through random drug testing or are observed intoxicated on the job, they will be terminated. It is far more prudent for families, friends, or colleagues to step in before this happens. A wife who wants to help her husband, for example, can call the union. She will be referred to the Professional Standards Committee or the Aeromedical Committee. Her husband's job is safe while the union helps him begin the recovery process. The wife can also call her husband's boss, the chief pilot, who would then contact the union. Once it is determined that the pilot shows signs of addiction, he'll be professionally assessed by a doctor or addiction specialist. If he is diagnosed as chemically dependent, he is asked to check into treatment. The airline will dictate where he goes and for how long. The usual requirement is a twenty-eight-day inpatient program. After treatment, the airline stipulates a full psychiatric evaluation, and the pilot begins aftercare and enters a five-year monitoring program. In addition, he's required to attend monthly meetings with his supervisor, doctor, employee assistance professional, and union representative. Alcoholics Anonymous attendance is highly recommended. This entire recovery process takes place without ever breaching the wife's confidentiality. Her husband will never know she made the call unless she tells him herself.

In addition to employee assistance programs, there are numerous recovery groups helping people in a range of professions.

For instance, Birds of a Feather is a 12-step self-help group for recovering pilots and crew. Other self-help groups include International Lawyers in AA and International Doctors in AA. For a full list, see the Resources section.

For those concerned about an impaired professional, we are very fortunate to have the irreplaceable support of professional organizations that respectfully demand recovery. Very few professionals will abandon careers by refusing help from their peers. Since professionals are monitored closely and for a number of years after treatment, they must demonstrate a high level of accountability to others. This is the key to greater success in recovery. One study investigated one hundred doctors twenty-one years after they completed treatment and found a success rate of 73 percent.

CRISIS AS INTERVENTION

ADDICTION WILL ALWAYS LEAD TO CRISIS. All crises are opportunities for interventions. Most families, however, put their efforts into alleviating crises rather than leveraging them. A crisis comes with a choice: we either move forward, stay where we are, or slide backward. Richard M. Nixon, a man who knew crisis, wisely said: "The easiest period in a crisis situation is actually the battle itself. The most difficult is the period of indecision—whether to fight or run away."

Families believe their very existence will crumble if they don't rescue the alcoholic at every turn. No crisis, big or small, is left unresolved. While in the throes of rescuing the addict, families can't see they are clearing the way for the next crisis. Problems come faster and bigger over time. Misery increases. Fear escalates. By keeping our eye on the problem, we perpetuate the problem. As long as we are managing the problem, we are part of the problem. When we shift our gaze to solutions, things begin to change.

Our brains develop patterns based on where we place our attention. When we focus on problems, we don't notice solutions. We may even lament that there are no solutions. When we focus on solutions, we don't see problems, we see opportunities. As Harry Truman said, "A pessimist is one who makes difficulties of his opportunities and an optimist is one who makes opportunities of his difficulties." Addiction will always present us with a crisis, so we have to become skilled at spotting the opportunity.

How do we turn an alcoholic crisis into a solution? Imagine that your brother gets arrested for driving under the influence. He calls and asks you to come and bail him out. Your normal reaction would be to run directly to the jail with the money. But if you step back for a moment and not allow yourself to be sucked into emergency thinking, you see the opportunity. Rather than bail him out, you call the rest of the family for a meeting. You and your other brothers and sister meet at your parents' house. You explain what happened and say, "But don't worry. I have a plan how this crisis will help get him into treatment." The family unites as a team with a single message: *We will bail you out of jail only if you agree to go directly to treatment.* Before the family goes to the jail, you call a treatment center and arrange for admission. You pack a suitcase for your brother and put it in the trunk of the car. Then the entire family goes to the jail, posts bail, and drives the alcoholic to treatment.

Here's another scenario. Imagine you have a divorced daughter who has shared custody of her three children. She is addicted to marijuana and alcohol. You stop over one evening, and she is stumbling and slurring her words. The children are all huddled together in the family room watching television. You immediately call the children's father and ask him to come and get them. The next day you meet with the father and discuss how to get your daughter into treatment. He's angry and says he's going to the court and ask that her custody be revoked. You point out that by reacting punitively, you lose a great opportunity to persuade her to go to treatment. She will always be the mother of his children, you explain, so her recovery must be a priority for him, too. The children win only if their mother gets sober. Whether they are wrenched from her arms in a court battle or left in her care while she's intoxicated, they bear the brunt of the pain. But if she gets well, everyone wins. The next day, you set up a meeting with your daughter at your home. You invite the entire family along with her ex-husband. You explain: "We are not taking your side or your ex-husband's side. We are taking the side of your children. You must go to treatment now. If you do not, you force us to stand with your children's father as he asks the court to remove them from your custody. Your drinking and pot smoking cannot come before their safety. Please, let's not break their little hearts. They love you. Choose to come with us and get well."

Here's yet another example. Imagine you are the father of a thirty-two-year-old crack-addicted son. You receive a call from him and, after fifteen minutes of small talk, your son finally gets around to asking you for money. His mortgage is overdue and he's broke. He's afraid he'll lose his house and have to live in his car. "I can't keep my job," he says, "if I don't have a place to live." This kind of reasoning always has you reaching for your checkbook, but this time you stop yourself from reacting. You need some time to think, so you ask your son if you could call him back in fifteen minutes. When you call your son back, you say, "I am willing to help you, but only in the right way. I will help arrange treatment for you. If you go to treatment and complete the twenty-eight-day program, I will make arrangements with your mortgage company. Then you and I can settle up when you're sober and back on your feet." You understand that if your son doesn't get help, his financial crisis will continue to grow.

If you offer treatment as a solution and your addict refuses, do not back down and fix the problem. You are being tested. When you fail the test, you empower the disease. You must follow through with your promises. Simply say, "This is your

choice. I can't tell you what to do. But I have made a choice, too.
I will only help you get better. Solving your latest crisis only
helps you stay sick. If you change your mind, you can always
come to me." Even if the addict continues to refuse the opportunity you are providing, you can feel good about doing the
right thing. You approached the addict lovingly, offered help,
and resisted being drawn into the dishonesty of the disease. You
left the door open for a change of heart. The crisis is left in the
addict's lap, giving him or her reason to think long and hard
about making a better choice and saying yes to treatment.

The Golden Rule asks us to take a particular action: do unto
others as we would have them do unto us if we were in the same
situation. I doubt one of us would want anyone to do anything
that would help us remain a debilitated alcoholic or addict.
George D. Herron, a journalist and former priest, was speaking
of the Golden Rule when he wrote the following:

> *We have talked much of the brotherhood to come; but brotherhood*
> *has always been the fact of our life, long before it became a modern*
> *and inspired sentiment. Only we have been brothers in slavery and*
> *torment, brothers in ignorance and its perdition, brothers in*
> *disease, and war, and want, brothers in prostitution and hypocrisy.*
> *What happens to one of us sooner or later happens to us all; we*
> *have always been inescapably involved in common destiny. The*
> *world constantly tends to the level of the downmost man in it; and*
> *the downmost man is the world's real ruler, hugging it close to his*
> *bosom, dragging it down to his death.*
>
> *You do not think so, but it is true, and it ought to be true. For if*
> *there were some way by which some of us could get free, apart*
> *from others, if there were some way by which some of us could*
> *have heaven while others had hell, if there were some way by*
> *which part of the world could escape some form of the blight and*
> *peril and misery . . . then indeed would our world be lost and*

*damned; but since men have never been able to separate
themselves from one another's woes and wrongs, since history is
fairly stricken with the lesson that we cannot escape brotherhood
of some kind, since the whole of life is teaching us that we are
hourly choosing between brotherhood in suffering and
brotherhood in good, it remains for us to choose the brotherhood
of a cooperative world, with all its fruits thereof—the fruits of* love
and liberty.

SUCCESS IN TREATMENT IS TIME IN TREATMENT

RECOVERING FROM ADDICTION is never easy. I was listening to an interview with Elton John, who was speaking of his own recovery. He said it was the hardest thing he'd done in his life, even harder than launching a successful music career. As one addiction expert has said: "Success in treatment is a function of time in treatment. . . . Time in treatment is often a function of coercion—being forced into treatment by a loved one." People often tell me that their loved one has been through treatment but never stayed sober. After asking a few questions, I find out that "treatment" was a three-day detox regimen. Detox is not treatment. Treatment takes time.

Once we've put our hearts and souls into getting loved ones into treatment, we want them to get the correct level of care. It is heartbreaking to learn that our alcoholic is being sent home because insurance won't pay for more than a few days. We need to find ways to keep our addicted loved ones in treatment longer. Treating addiction can't happen overnight. One study discovered that it takes twenty-one days of inpatient treatment, on average, for alcoholics and addicts to have a major breakthrough. A breakthrough isn't the same as being cured, of

course. It only means they now have a fighting chance to succeed. How likely is it that someone will remain sober after only
five or six days of treatment? Will she be capable of staying away
from the gin bottle or the crack pipe when she gets home? Her
brain is profoundly altered, she has had inadequate time in
treatment, and she is being sent back to her drinking or drugging environment. I'm surprised anyone ever succeeds under
such circumstances.

If a family has plenty of money, this isn't a problem. They can
choose from many excellent treatment centers throughout the
country and write a check. But when money is an issue, it takes
some investigation to match our treatment needs to our pocket-
book. There are programs that offer very good treatment at low
to moderate prices. There are also a few no-cost options for
families who lack the resources for treatment at any price.

If you have no money, or very little money, begin by calling
your county government offices and inquiring about funding for
treatment services. Be prepared to make several phone calls.
People staffing state agencies are often very busy, so know your
questions in advance. Be brief. If the person you are talking to
can't answer your questions, ask to be transferred to someone
who can. Find out what requirements your loved one must meet
to qualify for funding. Some agencies require addicts to call and
make an appointment for an evaluation. Sometimes the waiting
period for funding is one or two weeks. These delays make it
more likely that addicts will change their minds about treatment. When doing an intervention, we want the addict to go to
treatment immediately. If we can't get him in right away because
of funding, it is important to say: "You are eligible for funding
that will pay for your treatment. This will require jumping
through some hoops. We don't want you to give up or change
your mind, so we'd like you to choose one person from the family

to go through the funding process with you." Make the first call without delay, with the entire intervention team present.

If you have no resources for treatment and cannot access publicly funded treatment, search for privately funded treatment programs that help the disadvantaged. For instance, the Salvation Army has treatment centers throughout the United States. Alcoholics and addicts from many backgrounds access these programs. You'll find people from the streets as well as from the suburbs. Most people in them, however, have come to the end of the road and the Salvation Army is their last chance. When I spoke with a recovering twenty-eight-year-old cocaine addict from an upper-middle-class family, she said, "Things got really bad for me in my addiction, and my parents wouldn't pay for treatment. It was either the Salvation Army program or I was going to die. The program was pretty strict. There were a lot of people from the streets. But it worked for me. I'm sober two years now." The Salvation Army in Sacramento, California, describes their program: "Our addiction program offers a six-month curriculum of counseling, drug and alcohol education classes, twelve-step studies, twelve-step meetings, Bible studies, anger management and self-esteem classes, work therapy, and an in-depth Christian spiritual program. A three-month re-entry program is also available. This program focuses on job search, job interviewing skills, computers, finances, budgeting, as well as a continued focus on recovery issues." Call the Salvation Army in your home area and ask about the nearest rehabilitation program and what services it offers. Some offer beds on a first-come, first-served basis only, and beds aren't reserved or guaranteed.

If you have resources to pay for treatment but they are limited, there are low-cost centers that provide excellent care in a beautiful setting. You'll probably have to add the cost of an airline ticket to the price of treatment, but arranging for alcoholics to leave home for treatment is a smart idea. If they are having a bad day, for instance, they can't call a taxi to drive them home. The Resources section includes a list of low-cost treatment options.

Many people still get sober by going directly to Alcoholics Anonymous or Narcotics Anonymous, both of which are free of charge. Treatment is a preparation course for recovery, but recovery happens in the 12-step groups. Some people have great difficulty staying sober without the initial support of treatment, however. If you have no available way to send your alcoholic to treatment, ask him or her to start out by attending an Alcoholics Anonymous meeting every day for ninety days. People addicted to other drugs often prefer going to Narcotics Anonymous. Call and request a schedule of local meetings. If possible, invite a member of Alcoholics Anonymous to attend the intervention to answer questions and take the alcoholic to his first meeting. Present the schedule of meetings to the alcoholic at the end of the intervention and say, "We are asking you to begin attending meetings of Alcoholics Anonymous [or Narcotics Anonymous], get a sponsor, and begin working the twelve steps." Even when there is initial resistance, alcoholics who go to ninety meetings in ninety days usually do very well.

If Alcoholics Anonymous alone is not enough structure for our alcoholic to stay sober, we need to think more creatively. Find an inexpensive halfway house with a good reputation. Call local treatment centers for recommendations. If there are no halfway houses in your area, begin looking in nearby cities or out of state. Call any of the nationally known treatment centers for a recommendation. Many halfway houses take alcoholics and addicts who are fully detoxified and medically stable but have not completed a primary treatment program. They will be required to attend an intensive outpatient program, go to regular meetings of Alcoholics Anonymous, and find a full-time job. This can be an affordable option. Many insurance policies pay for outpatient treatment. If there is no insurance, no money, and no government funding, then ask the treatment center about patient aid, sliding scales, or scholarship funds. If you make enough phone calls and ask enough questions, you'll usually find a way to make it work. Insurance does not pay for halfway houses, but this isn't a problem. Many halfway houses are very affordable—a couple of hundred dollars a week—and alcoholics can finance it out of their wages. Halfway house stays typically range from three to six months. There are some transitional housing programs that offer yearlong programs. Quality can vary widely. I always recommend obtaining a referral from a reputable treatment center or talking with people in Alcoholics Anonymous before selecting a program.

Many alcoholics and addicts need to completely rebuild their lives in recovery. Some have never learned how to function in life in the first place. To succeed in recovery, they need long-term structure even after completing a twenty-eight-day inpatient program. They could be sent to an extended-care program (which is highly structured), halfway house, three-quarters house, or sober house (which has the least structure). These recommendations are part of aftercare planning. Everyone who completes a treatment program is given an aftercare plan before being discharged. This plan tells alcoholics and addicts what they need to do to stay sober. When people leave treatment and refuse to follow their aftercare plans, they almost always relapse. Families who attend the family program at the treatment center can ask about aftercare planning and discuss the plan for their loved one. The more information families have about aftercare requirements, the more accountability the addict feels. If addicts hide their aftercare recommendations from their families—or lie about them—they aren't taking recovery seriously. Here's

an example of an aftercare plan that includes a recommendation
to a halfway house:

> *When discharged from primary treatment, transfer directly to a*
> *halfway house for four months. Follow all halfway house*
> *requirements. Attend a minimum of four Alcoholics Anonymous*
> *meetings per week, or as determined appropriate by halfway house*
> *staff. Choose an Alcoholics Anonymous sponsor and work the*
> *twelve steps. Ask five members of Alcoholics Anonymous for their*
> *telephone numbers and talk to at least one every day. Visit a pain*
> *clinic to begin biofeedback to manage back pain. Follow all*
> *aftercare recommendations provided by halfway house staff upon*
> *completing the four-month program.*

Alcoholics sometimes say: "I didn't get anything out of attending AA." Alcoholics Anonymous isn't about *getting,* it's
about *giving.* The spiritual revelation about the twelve-step programs is that alcoholics stay sober by reaching out and helping
other alcoholics. Addiction was about "me," but recovery is about
"we." Alcoholics only get what they give. Bill Wilson, cofounder
of Alcoholics Anonymous, explains:

> *From the beginning, communication in AA has been no ordinary*
> *transmission of helpful ideas and attitudes. Because of our kinship*
> *in suffering, and because our common means of deliverance are*
> *effective for ourselves only when constantly carried to others, our*
> *channels of contact have always been charged with the language of*
> *the heart.*

FORMULATING A RELAPSE AGREEMENT

FAMILIES BEGIN TO WORRY about relapse before alcoholics are discharged from treatment. These fears are well-founded. The brain doesn't heal in thirty days of treatment or even after four months at a halfway house. The behavior control centers are still burnt out. The brain must work harder to control behavior. Environmental cues trigger drug cravings at an unconscious level. Profoundly powerful cravings occur in the area of the brain responsible for emotional memory. The addict is blindsided by these memories, which take over body, mind, and soul. The brain's decision-making regions are still defective. Judgment is poor. The ability to weigh risk against benefit is faulty. In many cases, choices are made without regard for harm or punishment and with no thought of the future. These brains still have trouble learning from past mistakes. When the addicts and alcoholics using these brains say, "I'm going to do it my way," it doesn't take too much imagination to know where "my way" is going to lead: back to alcohol and drugs.

Understanding the limitations of the addicted brain in early recovery makes it easier to understand the battle cry of recovery: "Just follow the directions!" In other words, you can't trust your own brain. So listen to what other people tell you to do if you hope to stay sober. The problem is, of course, that alcoholics and addicts are terrifically grandiose and feel extraordinarily unique. They don't think "follow the directions" applies to them. They are quite sure they possess special qualities and insights that make them different from everyone else. If they only knew how precisely they mimic every other addict, who is thinking exactly the same way.

Formulating a relapse agreement gives alcoholics a reason to follow the directions. People who follow directions rarely relapse. But if they do, it gives us something we can fall back on after the relapse. We want to create a sense of accountability in our alcoholics. Accountability is the capacity to account for one's actions and answer to the consequences of those actions. A strong sense of accountability is necessary when self-regulation cannot be trusted.

A relapse agreement gives families a plan to follow. I highly recommend that sometime during the last half of the treatment program, families meet with the alcoholic and her counselor and write a relapse agreement. Not all counselors are familiar with relapse agreements, so explain what you want to accomplish. If your alcoholic went directly into Alcoholics Anonymous, write this agreement with her and her sponsor. Ask the alcoholic directly: "It is my hope that you never have to face a relapse, but I'm told we need to talk about the possibility. What would you want us, as a family, to do if you begin drinking or taking drugs again?" The counselor will guide the alcoholic as she ponders this decision. Once the counselor is satisfied the alcoholic has designed a good relapse agreement, put it down on paper and sign it. Ask the alcoholic if everyone from the intervention team can have a copy, but let her make the final decision. This is a matter of dignity for the alcoholic. If she doesn't feel she has control over this agreement, it won't have value to her later. Don't engage in a power struggle or you'll create resentment, not agreement. It is the counselor's job to therapeutically encourage strong, healthy decisions. If the alcoholic does not make a good decision—for example, she says she wants you to leave her alone if she relapses—you should not sign the agreement. The counselor can explain to her that the agreement is not in anyone's best interest and then give her an assignment to ask her peers for feedback on this issue in group therapy. Later you can meet again and attempt to design a better agreement.

When we ask alcoholics about relapse, there are several important points to discuss. Not every relapse is the same. If the addict has a slip but is active in Alcoholics Anonymous and is honest about what happened, we will treat that differently than when someone has taken up drinking where he left off and has no program of recovery. These are some of the questions a relapse agreement should consider:

◆ *Is detox necessary?* This depends upon the drug, how much is being used, and for how long. If an alcoholic is drinking daily, detox may be necessary. If a prescription drug addict has been taking large doses of pills for a period of time, detox will be necessary. Heroin addicts will need detox, whereas pot smokers and cocaine addicts won't.

◆ *Is the addict currently involved in Alcoholics Anonymous or Narcotics Anonymous? If so, is she working with a sponsor?* If the answer to both of these questions is yes, the alcoholic may only need to go to more meetings and talk with her sponsor more often. If she is going to meetings but doesn't have a sponsor, the answer might be to get a sponsor, begin working the twelve steps, and attend more meetings. If she is not going to meetings and doesn't have a sponsor, the answer might be going back to treatment or into a halfway house.

◆ *How much support does the addict have in his home environment?* Do other people in the house drink or use drugs? Is he living alone? Does he have structure in his life? Perhaps the addict wasn't ready to return home, or the home environment isn't conducive to recovery. A halfway house or a sober house might be a good solution.

◆ *Is something blocking recovery?* Are transportation issues making it difficult to get to meetings? Is it difficult to find a babysitter? Are long hours at work getting in the way? I often ask alcoholics what they would do if one of these blocks had prevented them from getting a drink. They surely would have found a way around it. If a spouse is resentful of the time spent at meetings, invite him or her to attend Al-Anon and then go out for coffee with other recovering couples.

◆ *Are there signs that an undiagnosed mental health issue is blocking recovery?* Consult with a psychologist who is experienced in the field of addiction. Call a treatment center for a referral.

◆ *Is the alcoholic following all the directions, working a strong program of recovery, and still relapsing?* Something is missing in his program. He needs more support. Begin counseling sessions with an addiction specialist to determine what those needs are and what kind of support is required.

Relapse always tells us something is missing. Either the addict isn't working his program or he's doing it halfheartedly, or something is blocking his recovery. Relapse is not a sign that treatment or Alcoholics Anonymous doesn't work, and it doesn't mean an addict won't be successful eventually. It simply means that the addict needs to do something more. A relapse agreement helps us understand how to get alcoholics what they need to stay sober.

PART FIVE

Creating a Space for Grace

SPIRITUAL ACTION

When ADDICTION DAMAGES THE BRAIN and soul, healing doesn't occur by simply abstaining from alcohol or other drugs. That's why we differentiate between abstinence and recovery. Abstainers don't change much beyond not drinking. Sometimes their personalities go further downhill because they're so miserable without the drink. A recovering person heals his brain and soul, evolving into something quite different than his former addicted self, and his life begins working again. He does this by practicing the twelve steps of Alcoholics Anonymous.

Recovery works the brain like an atrophied muscle. It forces the brain to reach to a deeper level and do things it hasn't done before. It coaches the brain, stretches it, and reshapes it. Working a program of recovery provides the brain with challenges that help heal it. Most alcoholics and addicts insist they are far better people after working a program of recovery than at any other time in their lives. They've learned a way of living far superior to anything they'd known before.

The twelve steps of Alcoholics Anonymous clear up the distorted thinking caused by addiction's assault on the brain and spirit. Even after addiction has taken everything from an addict, alcohol and drugs have an almost romantic pull on the person. There's an old joke about a man who lost everything to his alcoholism. His wife was gone, he was fired from his job, and he was broke. Moving into a flophouse, he owned the clothes on his back and a half-empty bottle of whiskey. Alone in his room, he sat on the sagging bed and held the bottle in front of his face. He said: "I thought you were my friend. I trusted you. Look at me now. I have nothing. I am a broken man." Then he got up and opened the window. "I'm through with you," he said. "I'm throwing you out the window and ending this for good." As he cocked his arm behind his head, getting ready to pitch the bottle out, he heard it go *swoosh*. He looked at the bottle quizzically and said, "Was that an apology?" With everything lost, alcoholics still look at the bottle and see a friend. "It's you and me against the world," they'll say. Alcohol never remains the enemy for long. To the addicted brain, it's the ultimate solution.

Long before researchers uncovered the scientific evidence, Alcoholics Anonymous had an uncanny understanding of how addiction fundamentally changes the functioning of the brain. The twelve steps of Alcoholics Anonymous, practiced as a way of life, enable alcoholics to become "happily and usefully whole." These steps have healed alcoholic brains, repaired souls, and rebuilt lives. Some who have been saved by these steps say the twelve steps must have been divinely inspired. Whatever the impetus behind the writing of the twelve steps, nothing else, before or since, has ever emancipated such large numbers of alcoholics.

Each of the twelve steps works the brain in a deep and meaningful way, hastening the healing process. For example, the brain must be trained to focus. Step one focuses the brain on truthfulness, integrity, and honor: *We admitted we were powerless over alcohol—that our lives had become unmanageable.* To the casual observer this may seem an obvious realization, but to the addicted brain it is monumental, nothing less than a spiritual breakthrough. Rationalizations are unmasked and the truth is revealed: "I'm not different. I am an alcoholic. My life is unmanageable." By admitting their powerlessness over alcohol and other drugs, alcoholics achieve what is explained by Bill Wilson as the paradox of Alcoholics Anonymous: "strength arising out of complete defeat and weakness, the loss of one's old life as a condition for finding a new one." Step one is the foundation for building a new life.

Before the brain can heal, it must recognize it cannot help itself. This realization arises from a conversation between the brain and the soul. The addicted brain insists the addict can do it on his or her own. From the depths of despair and desperation, the soul replies that the addict cannot—he or she must reach out for help. *Came to believe that a Power greater than ourselves could restore us to sanity.* Step two is not a quasi call to religious faith; it is a refutation of addiction and an affirmation that answers come from a place other than the addict's mind. This is a critical step each addict must take, disassembling the rationalization machine that is the addicted brain. Alcoholics and addicts bristle at the idea of having to be "restored to sanity," but their genius for self-destruction is unparalleled. This step brings a message of hope and possibility: they may be powerless, but something other than the will can restore them to soundness of mind and spirit. It is the story of recovery—what alcoholics must do to regain their lives.

The brain must begin following directions before it will heal. Sobriety isn't achieved when alcoholics put their intellectual resources to work; it happens when alcoholics follow directions and do what they are supposed to do. *Made a decision to turn our will and our lives over to the care of God as we understood*

Him. Step three is the first action step: an outward display of *willingness.* Alcoholics willingly step out of the driver's seat and put their recovery in the care of a Power greater than themselves. Many alcoholics come into the program angry with God or denying His existence. They may have been raised in fear of a revengeful, punishing God. Alcoholics Anonymous espouses a loving, forgiving God, but still, some prefer to define God as "good orderly direction" or as "a group of drunks." However God is understood, when alcoholics put their lives into the care of a Higher Power, they shield themselves from self-will run riot. Step three offers safe harbor. It is the foundation for the spiritual awakening that comes from working the rest of the twelve steps.

These first three steps of the 12-step program take the pressure off alcoholics. The importance of this can't be overestimated. The alcoholic doesn't know how to navigate his way through sobriety. These steps allow him to follow the experience of others. Working steps one, two, and three brings a sense of belonging into the alcoholic's life. A recovering friend of mine recounts his early days recovering from alcoholism and drug addiction.

Every day I went to work and everything was incredibly frustrating as my brain tried to readjust to being sober. It was the relentless consciousness that I found intolerable. My very soul was weary. But every night I went to a meeting of Alcoholics Anonymous. I felt tremendous relief being in the company of people who understood me completely. They shook their heads knowingly when I talked about the littlest things setting me off, and we laughed about it. We wouldn't analyze all the little irritations, and we wouldn't medicate them. We just laughed. And that's how God worked through people and helped me make a new group of friends who I could build a sober life around.

The brain must clean house. Alcoholics cannot stay sober without purging resentment, guilt, remorse, anger, and loss. Steps four and five provide the opportunity for complete honesty. Step four is the first step in which a palpable, concrete outcome of spiritual action is produced: a written history of strengths and defects. *Made a searching and fearless moral inventory of ourselves.* This is where the last vestiges of denial are swept away, and the light of truth shines in the darkest corners. But this alone is not enough to keep addicts sober. False pride and overconfidence have fueled many relapses. A healthy dose of humility and soul-searching honesty completes the process. *Admitted to God, to ourselves, and to another human being the exact nature of our wrongs.* Step five requires that addicts share their personal inventory with another person, usually an AA sponsor or clergy member. With this step comes the redemptive power of confession: the unburdening of the soul by speaking these things out loud. The alcoholic finally gives and receives forgiveness. After completing steps four and five with uncompromised thoroughness, the probability of relapse is diminished and a sense of self-confidence is restored. After quitting drinking, this is one of the most important milestones in recovery.

The brain must become willing to do difficult things. This is where the twelve-step program broadens to include all aspects of a moral life. *Were entirely ready to have God remove all these defects of character.* Step six shows alcoholics that their wrongs are rooted in character defects. Alcoholics recognize that they can't remove their defects on their own any more than they could stop drinking on their own. *Humbly asked Him to remove our shortcomings.* Step seven requires asking for help. Grandiosity is a common character defect among alcoholics; humility opens up a healing strength. With these steps, alcoholics are filled with a sense of self-betterment.

The brain must bond with other people in a healthy way.

Steps eight and nine consider how addicts can develop the best relationship with every person in their lives. To do this, they must first consider whom they have harmed. *Made a list of all persons we had harmed, and became willing to make amends to them all.* This is the step that surveys the human wreckage caused by addiction. It leads to character and integrity and is the beginning of the end of isolation. However, it is not enough for addicts to know whom they must apologize to; they must make the apology. *Made direct amends to such people whenever possible, except when to do so would injure them or others.* Step nine should be completed under the guidance of a sponsor and with good judgment and courage. It requires accepting consequences for past acts, but doing so without hurting others. This step is more difficult than some people can imagine. Often, addicts are responsible for embarrassing and unseemly deeds for which they must apologize. In the words of Bill Wilson: "The alcoholic is like a tornado roaring his way through the lives of others. Hearts are broken. Sweet relationships are dead. Affections have been uprooted. Selfish and inconsiderate habits have kept the home in turmoil."

The brain must maintain spiritual fitness through the habit of daily housekeeping. Alcoholics are not cured of their obsession to drink. They are given a daily reprieve that is dependent upon maintaining a positive spiritual condition. *Continued to take personal inventory and when we were wrong promptly admitted it.* Step ten requires a daily spiritual action: when wrong, admit it without delay. This is important because alcoholics cannot afford the luxury of negative emotions. By promptly admitting wrongs, they remain free of guilt and worry and avoid emotional hangovers. This step leads to character building and good living.

The brain and soul must come together in harmony. To flourish in recovery, alcoholics need to find purpose in life. *Sought*

*through prayer and meditation to improve our conscious con-
tact with God as we understood Him, praying only for knowledge
of His will for us and the power to carry that out.* Step eleven
is a recipe for a spiritual life in one sentence. It directs alcoholics toward a meaningful and purpose-driven life. Working this
step, alcoholics acknowledge that real power doesn't come
from "big alcoholic ideas" but from a source outside themselves. With this step, addicts attain wisdom, strength, and
peace of mind. "More than most people," says Bill Wilson, "I
think alcoholics want to know who they are, what this life is
about, whether they have a divine origin and an appointed des-
tiny, and whether there is a system of cosmic justice and love."

The brain and soul must seek spiritual growth above all
other desires. The key to growing spiritually is giving to others
without expectation of reward. *Having had a spiritual awakening as the result of these steps, we tried to carry this message to alcoholics, and to practice these principles in all our affairs.* Step
twelve turns principle into action. The ultimate display of gratitude is giving back to others. Alcoholics stay sober by helping
other alcoholics; it is a continuous circle of giving and receiving.
With this step of giving, alcoholics find friendship, accomplishment, and self-worth.

These twelve steps bring with them a gift: *renewed life.*
Emotional sobriety is the final achievement. Alcoholics are right
with themselves and with the world. But the gift doesn't end
there. Every family of a recovering alcoholic is given the gift.
Sister Molly Monahan, in *Seeds of Grace,* explains:

> *Driving home after the meeting, I found myself grateful for AA
> in a new way. Imagine the life of those babies if their alcoholic
> parent or parents were still drinking. The erratic behavior, the
> emotional turmoil, the fights, the terror, the shame they would
> experience . . . These children will be raised by parents with all of*

the resources of Alcoholics Anonymous at their disposal, parents with a degree of emotional stability, responsible, who are committed to living a spiritual life, and who have the tools of the program and the support of the fellowship to help them deal with the inevitable disappointments of life. "It's a God-given program," we say. I believe it.

IN THE BEGINNING:
ACTION

BILL WILSON, the cofounder of Alcoholics Anonymous, had a miraculous thought: *an alcoholic can stay sober by helping another alcoholic.* To save *your* life you must help others save *their* lives. As long as he was helping someone else, Bill didn't drink. For years, he had been drying out in sanatoriums and consulting with doctors and psychiatrists, but nothing gave him relief from his chronic alcoholism until he came upon this simple solution. Bill had been an atheist, but after a spiritual awakening he found saving grace through the greatest tenet of all the world's religions: *give and you shall receive.* In five thousand years, mankind had made no headway in helping alcoholics recover. But to this day millions of alcoholics stay sober primarily by implementing Bill Wilson's idea of helping another alcoholic. Those who say, "I'm not getting anything from AA," haven't grasped the basic premise of recovery: *you only get what you give.*

Alcoholics don't have to want help to be helped. This is clearly illustrated in the story of how Alcoholics Anonymous began: two drunks got together and talked, one eagerly and the other reluctantly. If the belief that no one can help an alcoholic until he wants help prevailed in those early days, it is questionable whether or not this program of recovery would exist today. The only reason this first meeting took place was because two women insisted upon it.

This is how it all began. Bill Wilson was standing in the lobby of the Mayflower Hotel in Akron, Ohio, after a business deal fell through. He was devastated, and he wanted to get drunk. For the first time in his life, he panicked at the idea of drinking. The hotel bar was filled with people laughing and drinking. At the other end of the lobby was a church directory. He had a decision to make: was he going into the bar or over to the directory? At that moment, he did something miraculous for an alcoholic— he turned away from the bar and walked over to the list of churches and clergy. He needed to find an alcoholic to help and was inexplicably drawn to the name of Reverend Walter F. Tunks. He put money into the pay phone and called the preacher. He told him he was looking for an alcoholic he could help. He had found a way to help them stay sober, he explained. The fact that he had not yet succeeded at keeping a single alcoholic sober after six months of trying didn't deter Bill. He had stayed sober because he was trying to help others, and that was miracle enough. He told himself, *I need another alcoholic to talk to, just as much as he needs me.* Without hesitation, Reverend Tunks gave Bill the names of ten people he thought might be of service. Bill called name after name. It wasn't until the tenth name that he found someone willing to help.

"I'm leaving for New York right now," the fellow at the other end of the line told Bill, "but I'm going to give you the telephone number for Henrietta Seiberling. She can probably help you." In his better days, Bill had met Jack Seiberling, the founder of Goodyear Tire Company. Henrietta must be his wife, Bill thought. He was mortified by the idea of calling this prominent family with such a request. He paced back and forth, but the thought persisted: *You better call this lady.* When Henrietta answered, Bill introduced himself as a "rum hound from New York." He told her he had figured out a way to keep alcoholics sober. "You come right out here," she said. Later she told people she silently thought: *This is manna from heaven.*

As it turned out, Henrietta wasn't Jack Seiberling's wife but his daughter-in-law. She was not an alcoholic herself but knew a surgeon, Dr. Robert Smith, who was in desperate need of help. His fellow doctors and patients no longer trusted him. His practice was dwindling, and he was just one step ahead of bankruptcy. He was a devotedly religious man who had tried again and again to stay sober using various religious approaches but always failed. She called Dr. Bob's wife, Anne Smith, and told her to send him over right away. "I've found a man who can help Bob," she said. Anne hedged, saying it wasn't a good time. Henrietta was insistent. Finally Anne admitted that Bob was passed out drunk and in no condition to talk to anyone. It was the day before Mother's Day, and Bob had come home with a potted plant for Anne. He'd walked into the kitchen, put the plant on the table, and promptly passed out on the kitchen floor. Henrietta said, "All right, come over tomorrow at five o'clock for dinner."

The next day, Anne informed Bob of Henrietta's invitation. She explained there was a fellow who had a way to keep alcoholics sober. Bob had a terrible hangover and no interest in meeting this man. But saying no to Henrietta was difficult. Bob had a great deal of respect for her. She had known suffering in her own life and wasn't one to give up easily. Bob decided he might as well get it over with and agreed to see Bill Wilson, but he made Anne promise they'd stay only fifteen minutes. Dr. Bob later described his thinking at the time: "I didn't want to talk to this mug, or anybody else, and we'd really make it snappy."

Arriving at Henrietta's house, Bob was shaky. He hadn't had a drink all day. Henrietta introduced him to Bill Wilson, who promptly said, "You look like someone who needs a drink." Bob was embarrassed but relieved. He did need a drink. Henrietta served dinner, but Bob couldn't eat. Afterward, Henrietta ushered Bill and Bob into another room to give them some privacy. Bill shared his story with Bob, one drunk to another. The fifteen-minute visit turned into six hours. This was the beginning of Alcoholics Anonymous. Bill Wilson later described his conversation with Dr. Bob in *Alcoholics Anonymous Comes of Age:* "You see, our talk was a completely *mutual* thing. . . . I knew I needed this alcoholic as much as he needed me. *This was it.* This was how to carry the message. And this mutual give-and-take is at the very heart of all of AA's Twelfth Step work today."

Taking action was as crucial in the beginning as it is today. Bill Wilson knew he needed to talk with another alcoholic to stay sober. Not drinking wasn't enough; he had to take action. He wasn't out preaching or evangelizing, but he knew it was spiritually incumbent upon him to connect with another alcoholic. He couldn't remain isolated and passive if he was to stay sober. He had to step outside himself, swallow his pride, and venture out on faith. From the very start, it was the mutual action between two drunks that led to sobriety, not wishful thinking or waiting for things to change on their own.

Yet Bill Wilson's efforts were not enough to initiate the beginning of Alcoholics Anonymous. His meeting with Bob never would have occurred had it not been for the cooperative efforts of Anne Smith and Henrietta Seiberling. Even though Bob had repeatedly tried and failed to get sober on his own, he wasn't interested in accepting outside help. In all of Bob's desperation—

a failing career, financial ruin, and a wife on the verge of a nervous breakdown—he couldn't manage to extend himself *of his own accord* to this man with a solution. It was the influence of Henrietta and Anne that gave Bob the impetus to agree. The beginning of Alcoholics Anonymous, and the salvation of millions of alcoholics, might never have happened if it weren't for two women pressuring a recalcitrant alcoholic into meeting with another alcoholic on Mother's Day in 1935.

Today, there are meetings of Alcoholics Anonymous in neighborhoods throughout the United States and in 177 other countries. Over two million alcoholics are sober. But many more continue to resist recovery. They perceive Alcoholics Anonymous as the worst thing that could happen to them, even while their families suffer noticeably. As they lose everything, they continue to hang on to the idea that they can handle drinking. Many die before ever reaching out for help. We must begin to live up to the legacy of Henrietta and Anne. We don't need to wait. We can influence alcoholics to do what they don't want to do. Addicted people don't change by themselves. Those of us who love them must steer them in the right direction. We are no longer obliged to silently tolerate untreated addiction.

Two years after that fateful first meeting, Bill sat in Bob's living room and the two men discussed how they were doing at helping other alcoholics. This is how Bill Wilson describes that conversation in *Alcoholics Anonymous Comes of Age:*

> *There had been failures galore, but now we could see some startling successes too. A hard core of very grim, last-gasp cases had by then been sober a couple of years, an unheard-of development. There were twenty or more such people. All told we figured that upwards of forty alcoholics were staying bone dry. As we carefully rechecked this score, it suddenly burst upon us that a new light was*

shining into the dark world of the alcoholic . . . a benign chain reaction from one alcoholic carrying the good news to the next, had started outward from Dr. Bob and me. Conceivably it could one day circle the whole world. What a tremendous thing that realization was! At last we were sure. There would be no more flying totally blind. We actually wept for joy. And Bob and Anne and I bowed our heads in silent thanks.

JUSTICE:
LOVE AND TRUST IN ACTION

JUSTICE IS THE QUALITY OF BEING FAIR. It is trust in action. Most religions use the word to mean *right relationships:* honorable dealings with others, integrity of action, and goodness. We are called upon to mold ourselves to what is morally right and embrace truth, correctness, and propriety. But when addiction infiltrates our families, evenhandedness and fairness fall away. The inherent dishonesty of addiction diminishes trust. Addiction claims all rights and privileges for itself and shuns responsibility for any of its actions. It shifts blame onto the family and expects others to make sacrifices for its sake. Our right to a rewarding and loving family life is ultimately sacrificed. Addiction demands high standards from everyone else but places itself beyond reproach. But justice is aimed at the good of the entire family, not just one individual. And addiction doesn't have the God-given right to take that away from us.

Many families give alcoholics and addicts whatever they demand in hopes of receiving fair treatment in return. But addiction does not concern itself with fairness. Waiting for justice from alcoholics and addicts is fruitless, for their very brains are affected in ways that make it difficult for them to feel compassion

or consistently act in thoughtful ways. They lack strong character because the part of the brain that controls character is compromised. Instead, justice must come from the family. It is we
who must stand up, reclaim our power, and do the right thing.
As Martin Luther King Jr. said, "Power at its best is love implementing the demands of justice. Justice at its best is love correct-
ing everything that stands against love."

Mother Teresa upheld the belief that "love requires action."
I think she was speaking not of a sweet, sentimental love but
rather of a tangible, hands-on love that does the tough work of
righting what is wrong. We may lament the adversity that addiction brings to our family, but it also presents us with a higher
purpose. When Jesus was asked why a man was born without
sight, He responded by saying: "He was born blind so the power
of God could be seen in him." Alcoholics, addicts, and their
families are freely given a gift, which they often resist accepting.
Once they take the gift, however, the power of God is seen in
them. The gift, of course, is recovery.

Rainer Maria Rilke wrote: "Perhaps everything terrible is in
its deepest being something helpless that wants help from us."
Certainly when we hear the stories of recovering alcoholics and
addicts, we learn this is true. I'd like to revisit Jeff's story, which
I told earlier in the book. This is a story very dear and near to my
life. Jeff broke everyone's hearts as alcoholism consumed his
life. His mom and dad tried everything to help: giving him
money, putting him back in school, finding him jobs. But alcoholism persisted, and their child of great promise failed at every
turn. In time, he left home and hitchhiked around the country.
He was lost to his family. They prepared themselves for the possibility that someday they would hear he had died. After losing
touch for over a year, they did receive a phone call about their
son. The news wasn't good, but they saw the opportunity presented by the crisis. They had learned about crisis intervention

and used the technique to convince their son to accept help. Here's Jeff's story again, but this time in his own words, through his eyes as an alcoholic:

After years of chronic alcoholism and drug addiction, I was unable to help myself in any way. Although I had been a National Merit Scholar, president of my high school student association, and head of the altar boys, I was now homeless and penniless. I had a bleeding ulcer, a bleeding colon, and neuropathy of the legs. I was unable to eat solid food, and I was sleeping under bushes in city parks. But I still didn't think I had an alcohol or drug problem. I thought I had a little cash flow problem. Sitting on a park bench on a cold and rainy day, I told myself: "If I can just get another twenty bucks together, everything will be all right." But in short order, suicide became my solution. I didn't know I was suffering from a disease, much less that effective treatment was available. All I knew was I couldn't go on and didn't think I could turn to my family for help. I was alone in the world, bleeding internally, and racked with pain. I was twenty-six years old.

I'd made all the necessary preparations to kill myself, including renting a four-dollar-a-night room in a flophouse. I planned my suicide for the next day so I could give myself a one-man going-away party. I frequently drank myself into blackouts, and this night was no exception. Apparently, I made a phone call across the country to an ex-girlfriend and told her of my brilliant plan. Realizing I was serious, she called my parents.

My mother and father phoned me at the flophouse early the next morning. I was passed out and fully clothed, lying crosswise on the bed, when someone pounded on my door and bellowed something about a telephone call. I stumbled down the corridor and three flights of stairs to the basement. There was a pay phone on the wall with the receiver dangling by its cord. I picked up the phone and heard my father's voice. I hadn't spoken to my parents in over a year. I quickly said, "I can't talk to you now. I'll call you back." I hung up the phone.

I cannot begin to describe the depth of my humiliation and depression. I couldn't even commit suicide right. I headed out to the liquor store across the street and then to the city park to drink my freshly purchased bottle of port wine. Folding back the brown paper bag, I slumped down onto the grass to drink. The tiny park, in the middle of a big city, was alive with people going to work and taking their morning exercise. My first chug brought up bloody sputum, as usual, but I continued to pull on the bottle, drinking the only medicine I knew.

Fortified and determined to carry out my suicide plan, I finished off the small bottle. I would not be distracted this time. First I resolved to call my parents. I had promised my father, and I didn't want to jinx myself by breaking my word. Naturally, I would reassure them everything was fine. Then I'd get down to the simple business of ending my life.

There was a small bank of pay phones at the corner of the park. I placed a collect call to Michigan. I learned later that my parents had been talking with someone about intervention and had learned a new way of approaching me. There was no anger or recrimination in their voices. They were very calm and loving. Their tone was disconcerting to me, because we hadn't had a calm conversation in years.

My father asked me a very simple question, which momentarily stunned me. There was nothing magical about this question, but it stopped me in my tracks. He asked, "Jeff, how are you doing?" I simply couldn't reply. I thought to myself, Well, how am I doing? I'm bleeding internally, I can barely walk, and I can't eat solid food. It's a beautiful day, the sun is shining, the birds are singing, and I'm getting ready to commit suicide. How indeed am I doing? *For some reason, I finally replied with the single most intelligent thing I've ever said. I'm not even sure where my response came from. I answered my father by saying: "I think I need to go into a hospital."*

My parents purchased a plane ticket for me immediately. Upon arriving home, they admitted me into a hospital for ten days. Then I was transferred to a thirty-day residential treatment program for alcoholics. I remember thinking, Has my life come to this? *Every day I wanted to leave treatment, but I stayed. When I was finally discharged, I went to an AA meeting and asked a fellow sitting next to me how often I should attend. He replied, "How often did you drink?" So I went to an AA meeting every day for a very long time. I knew I would die if I drank again, and the only thing between me and a drink was a meeting. Twenty-four years later I'm still sober, thanks to my mother, my father, and Alcoholics Anonymous."*

I met Jeff ten years after his mother and father saved his life, and he changed my life. I personally owe his parents a debt of gratitude. If they had not saved their son, I never would have known him and my life would not be what it is today. Whenever we intervene on the disease of addiction, it isn't only an alcoholic we are saving. We save family, friends, and countless others known only to the future.

RESOURCES FOR TREATMENT AND RECOVERY

WEB SITES

General Information

Alcoholism at About.com. *www.alcoholism.about.com.* A compendium of the latest research, articles, and resources on alcoholism. Information for special populations, how to find meetings, support for families, and more.

Brainplace. *www.brainplace.com/bp/atlas.* This online atlas shows excerpts from Dr. Daniel Amen's book *Images into Human Behavior: A Brain SPECT Atlas.* Use the drop-down menu to access brain scans of brains affected by alcohol and other drugs. Compare them to normal brain scans and brains one year after recovery.

Cyber Sober. *www.cybersober.com.* A search tool for locating 12-step meetings throughout the United States, Canada, and seventy-five other countries. Also, search for treatment centers and Veterans Administration facilities. Information for parents and teens. Online 12-step meetings and chats. Membership fee.

Love first. *www.lovefirst.net.* Extensive information on intervention and treatment resources.

National Clearinghouse for Alcohol and Drug Information. *www.health.org.* A source for publications, statistics, videotapes, and other resources. Information organized by drug type. Resources are available for families, youth, schools, workplace, and community. Most publications are free.

National Council on Alcoholism and Drug Dependence. *www.ncadd.org.* Founded in 1944, an advocacy group fighting the stigma attached to addiction. Interviews with medical and scientific experts and recommendations from leading health authorities. Information is available for parents and youth. Publications and videos available.

National Inhalant Prevention Coalition. *www.inhalants.org.* Teaches parents about inhalant abuse, what to watch for, and how to approach a child high on inhalants. Education and prevention programs are available for youth, parents, and educators. English and Spanish.

National Institute on Alcohol Abuse and Alcoholism. *www.niaaa.nih.gov.* Conducts and supports research in a wide range of scientific areas: genetics, neuroscience, epidemiology, health risks, prevention, and treatment. Publications can be read online.

National Institute on Drug Abuse. *www.nida.nih.gov.* Studies how drugs of abuse affect the brain and behavior. Offers information on all drugs of abuse. Resources for parents and teachers, students and young adults. English and Spanish.

Recovery Is Everywhere. *www.recoveryiseverywhere.com.* A public education campaign designed by a small group of recovering addicts who want to change the way people see and think about people who are addicted. Their purpose is to reduce stigma, offer hope, and challenge stereotypes. They provide a series of print ads that can be reprinted without charge in local newspapers or other publications. Posters, postcards, and wristbands available.

Serenity Quest. *www.serenityquest.org.* Dedicated to the physical, emotional, and spiritual growth and healing of recovering people and their families. Features articles, topic of the day, jokes, slogans and sayings, book reviews, health, fitness, and more.

Steps for Recovery. *www.steps4recovery.org.* An online magazine and guide for sober living. The mission is to provide insight into the twelve-step process. Articles explore topics such as finding natural highs, teens in recovery, eating disorders, debt problems, self-pity, and more.

Stop Drugs. *www.stopdrugs.org.* Offers an interactive tool for identifying drugs, up-to-date information on the crystal methamphetamine epidemic, information pertaining to the safety of children of drug-addicted parents, and more.

Recovery Information for Alcoholics and Addicts

Alcoholics Anonymous. *www.aa.org.* Welcomes anyone who wishes to stop drinking. Offers online pamphlets such as "Is AA for You?" and "Do You Think You're Different?" Locate local AA groups. English, Spanish, and French.

Alcoholics Anonymous Big Book Online. *www.recovery.org/aa/ bigbook/ww.* Read the *Big Book* online. A special section highlights important information such as "The Promises" and "How It Works."

Alcoholics Anonymous Speaker Tapes. *www.aaprimarypurpose. org/speakers.htm.* Listen to Alcoholics Anonymous members tell their stories. New tapes are added on a regular basis. Tapes of Bill Wilson and Dr. Bob Smith are available. Taped workshops on various topics and *Big Book* study tapes. Requires Real Audio player. Listening to tapes is free, but donations are welcome.

Astrofysh. *astrofysh.tripod.com.* Recovery wit, wisdom, humor, and prayers. Offers creative ideas to help those working a program of recovery.

Cocaine Anonymous. *www.ca.org.* Welcomes all people interested in recovery from cocaine addiction. Find meetings, take a self-test, and order literature. Download "Infoline Numbers" brochure.

Dick B's Web Site. *www.dickb.com.* Articles on the history of AA, early AA resources, AA tributes, and more.

Debtors Anonymous. *www.debtorsanonymous.org.* For people whose lives have become unmanageable because of credit card debt and overspending. Lists signs of compulsive overspending. Online and telephone meetings. Meeting locator.

The eAA Group of Alcoholics Anonymous. *www.e-aa.org.* Offers forums, chats, and sober mail. Specialty meetings for women, new members, and the blind.

Gamblers Anonymous. *www.gamblersanonymous.org.* For people who desire to stop gambling. Meeting directory. Gam-Anon offers help for families and friends.

Gopher State Tape Library. *www.gstl.org.* Maintains an extensive CD and audio tape library of speakers from Alcoholics Anonymous, Al-Anon, Overeaters Anonymous, Emotions Anonymous, and Narcotics Anonymous. Tape-of-the-month club and listening room available.

Narcotics Anonymous. *www.na.org.* Membership is open to all drug addicts wishing to get sober, regardless of the combination of drugs used. Links to meetings throughout the United States and the world.

Online Intergroup for Alcoholics Anonymous. *www.aa-inter group.org.* Serves all online AA groups around the world. Real-time meetings, audio meetings, and e-mail meetings.

Renewal Center of the South. *www.rcsouth.org.* A nonprofit retreat center for recovering people. Members of the 12-step fellowships come for sharing, learning, and recreation. Not a treatment center, but a place for intense renewal and study of the principles of recovery. Located in North Carolina.

Sex Addiction Anonymous. *www.sexaa.org.* Membership open to anyone wishing to overcome sexual addiction. Find local or online meetings. Books, literature, and tapes available. English and Spanish.

Twelve Steps for Recovery. *www.12step.org.* A helpful tool for working the twelve steps. Downloadable worksheets and workbooks.

Recovery Information for Special Populations

Birds of a Feather. *www.boaf.org.* Assisting troubled airmen in their sobriety, saving lives and careers. List of meetings and contacts in the United States, Canada, and United Kingdom.

Christians in Recovery. *www.christians-in-recovery.com.* Recovering Christians who discuss the twelve steps, the Bible, and personal experiences. The Web site has a members-only section offering private chat rooms, support groups, daily recovery meetings, 12-step Bible studies, and more.

Council of Special Mutual Help Groups. *www.crml.uab.edu/%7ejah.* Provides networking for special-interest recovery groups: nurses, anesthetists, pharmacists, ministers and pastors, nuns, academics, psychologists, social workers, and veterinarians.

Deaf and Hard of Hearing. *www.dhh12s.com.* AA meetings and special events for the deaf.

International Doctors in Alcoholics Anonymous. *www.idaa.org.* Provides support, fellowship, and resources for recovering health care workers and their families worldwide. Contact numbers for meetings in the United States and internationally. Help line for professionals and their families seeking another doctor to talk to about recovery.

International Lawyers in AA. *www.ilaa.org.* A group of recovering lawyers and judges working to help other alcoholic lawyers and judges who are reluctant to join Alcoholics Anonymous. Directory of local meetings.

Jews in Recovery. *www.jacsweb.org.* Supporting Jews in recovery and their families. Conducts retreats and other events. List of anonymous Jewish recovery meetings. Stories, prayers, and writings about Judaism as it relates to recovery.

Out of Sight. *www.aa-intergroup.org/directories/email_blind.html.* An e-mail AA group created primarily for alcoholics who are blind and use screen readers.

Recovery Information for Families and Friends

Adult Children of Alcoholics. *www.adultchildren.org.* For men and women who grew up in alcoholic homes. Offers literature and meeting locator.

Al-Anon and Alateen. *www.al-anon.alateen.org.* Offers hope and help to families and friends of alcoholics. Alateen is for younger people. Meeting locator for United States, Canada, and other countries. English, Spanish, and French.

Families Anonymous. *www.familiesanonymous.org.* Dedicated to doing something constructive about the approach to someone else's addiction problem. Meeting directory.

Nar-Anon Resources. *www.alcoholism.about.com/od/naranon resources.* Articles and resources on Nar-Anon, the 12-step group for families and friends of people addicted to drugs.

Nationally Recognized Treatment Centers

The following full-service centers are known for their excellence in treatment. They offer medical detoxification and specialized services tailored for individualized treatment. Support services for the family are available. The facilities and campuses are well designed, inviting, and comfortable.

Advanced Recovery Center. *www.arc-hope.com.* 877-272-4673. Extended care for chemical dependency, post-traumatic stress disorder, and other issues. Upscale, independent living quarters. Tennis court, swimming pool, and fitness center. Pet friendly. Delray Beach, Florida.

Betty Ford Center. *www.bettyfordcenter.org.* 800-854-9211. Nonprofit chemical dependency treatment center with a special emphasis on child and family issues. Also offers a program for impaired professionals. Walking trail and swimming pool. Rancho Mirage, California.

Caron Foundation. *www.caron.org.* 800-678-2332. Offers treatment services for adults and adolescents. Also offers an extended family program for addressing codependency issues and a one-week compulsive eating disorder workshop. Online virtual tour. Wernersville, Pennsylvania.

Cottonwood de Tucson. *www.cottonwooddetucson.com.* 800-877-4520. Dual-diagnosis facility in the foothills of the Sonoran Desert. Provides services for adults, young adults, and adolescent girls. Offers an addiction and behavioral health program for lawyers. Treats addiction, gambling, depression, anxiety disorder, codependency, food issues, sex issues, and more. Family program. Tucson, Arizona.

Crossroads Centre. *www.crossroadsantigua.org.* 888-452-0091. Eric Clapton's beautiful inpatient treatment center overlooking the ocean in Antigua, the West Indies. Treats alcohol and drug addiction. Yoga, massage therapy, and fitness program. Family program. Reasonably priced.

Cumberland Heights. *www.cumberlandheights.org.* 800-646-9998. Inpatient treatment program in the rolling hills outside Nashville, Tennessee. Special programs for women, adolescents, and young adult males. Family and children's program. Relapse prevention program. Equine therapy and ropes course. Reasonably priced.

Father Martin's Ashley. *www.fathermartinsashley.com.* 800-799-4673. A beautiful treatment facility on the banks of the Chesapeake Bay, founded by Father Martin. Relapse program and family wellness program. Worship services and a Catholic mass are offered on a regular basis. Havre de Grace, Maryland.

Hanley Center. *www.hanleycenter.org.* 800-444-7008. Inpatient services for men and women age eighteen and older. Offers a specialized program for adults fifty-five years and older. Three-day family program. Meditation center. Beautifully landscaped campus with pool, exercise course, and small lake. West Palm Beach, Florida.

Hazelden Foundation. *www.hazelden.org.* 800-257-7810. World-renowned and the pioneer of modern addiction treatment. Located in a beautiful, rural lakeside setting. Offers programs for adults, young adults, adolescents, and families. Mental health services, tobacco recovery, and extended care are available. Renewal center offers workshops for recovering people. Five-to-seven-day family program. Online bookstore. Center City, Minnesota. Other locations listed on Web site. Founded the well-known Fellowship Club halfway house (intermediate care) in St. Paul, Minnesota.

Keystone. *www.keystonetreatment.com.* 800-992-1921. Offers thirty-day treatment program with a Christian emphasis. Specialty programs include gambling, dual diagnosis, adolescents, Native Americans, and more. Reasonably priced and will adjust costs for families who don't have insurance benefits. Two-day family program. Canton, South Dakota.

The Meadows. *www.themeadows.org.* 800-632-3697. Trauma and addiction treatment program created by Pia Mellody. Eating disorder and sex addiction treatment. Family program. Five-day workshops on various topics. Free nationwide lecture series. Call for free video. Wickenburg, Arizona.

Pride Institute. *www.pride-institute.com.* 800-547-7433. Addiction treatment for gay, lesbian, and bisexual alcoholics and addicts. New York, New York, and multiple locations nationwide.

Ridgeview Institute. *www.ridgeviewinstitute.com.* 800-329-9775. Highly individualized, dual-diagnosis treatment center with a wide range of services, including older adult program, adolescents, impaired professionals, women's center, family program, young adults, relapse prevention, adult addiction, and psychiatric. Smyrna, Georgia.

Sierra Tucson. *www.sierratucson.com.* 800-842-4487. Provider of chemical dependency and dual diagnosis services, including trauma, eating disorders, gambling, depression, anxiety, and sex addiction. Integrative therapies include psychodrama, EMDR, acupuncture, chiropractic services, and yoga. Equine therapy. Tucson, Arizona.

Talbott Recovery Campus. *www.talbottcampus.com.* 800-445-4232. Offers a ninety-day treatment program. Reasonably priced. Originally developed for addicted physicians but now open to all people. Offers a professional effectiveness program for individuals having emotional or behavioral problems in the workplace. Atlanta, Georgia.

Wilderness Treatment Center. *www.wildernessaltschool.com.* 406-854-2832. Offers a sixty-day treatment program for young males ages fourteen to twenty-four. The program has a 12-step foundation with challenging activities such as backpacking, cross-country skiing, rappelling, ranch work, and a wilderness expedition. Reasonably priced. Marion, Montana.

Willingway Hospital. *www.willingway.com.* 800-242-9455. Family-operated treatment center founded by Dr. and Mrs. John Mooney. Offers four to six weeks of inpatient treatment services and a five-day family program. Accepts ages fourteen and older. Reasonably priced. Statesboro, Georgia.

Moderately Priced Treatment Centers

The following centers are known for quality care at a moderate price. Medical detox and physical examination are included.

Edgewood. *www.edgewood.ca.* 800-683-0111. Offers an intense inpatient program in a beautiful, rustic-style facility. Length of stay is determined by individual needs. Average stay is two months. Dual-diagnosis capability. Extended-care program available. Additional intensive, six-day therapeutic program is available for family at an additional cost. Nanaimo, British Columbia.

Sober Living by the Sea. *www.soberliving.com.* 800-642-0042. A unique residential treatment program situated near the ocean is especially conducive to helping young adults rebuild their lives in sobriety. Requires a 90-day stay. Extended care available. Option of attending college while in treatment. A separate program for eating disorders is offered. Newport Beach, California.

Valley Hope. *www.valleyhope.com.* 800-544-5101. Offers inpatient, outpatient, and day treatment. Accepts ages sixteen and over. Located in Kansas, Missouri, Arizona, Oklahoma, Texas, Nebraska, and Colorado.

Low-Priced Treatment Centers

These treatment centers are known for offering quality care at a low price. Not all programs offer medical detox services, but rather require patients to be medically stable upon admission.

St. Christopher's. *www.stchris-br.com.* 877-782-4747. Residential treatment program for males ages eighteen and over. Seventeen-year-old males are considered on an individual basis. Inpatient treatment program is thirty to ninety days. Extended care program is a minimum of six months. Males who've completed inpatient elsewhere can go directly into extended care. Family program available. Baton Rouge, Louisiana.

Dawn Farm. *www.dawnfarm.org.* 734-485-8725. Three-month residential treatment program located in a rural setting outside of Ann Arbor, Michigan. Transitional housing is available for six months to two years. Pregnant women and women with children are accepted.

High Watch Farms. *www.highwatchfarm.com.* 888-493-5368. Located on a 200-acre farm and admits people eighteen years and older who have been drug- and alcohol-free for seventy-two hours. They do not offer medical detox. Minimum stay is twenty-one days. North Kent, Connecticut.

The Retreat. *www.theretreat.org.* 877-446-9283. Program provides supportive, educational services based on the spiritual principles of Alcoholics Anonymous and a back-to-basics philosophy. A 42,000-square-foot retreat in a beautiful wooded setting. Admits adults who are medically stable. They do not provide medical detox. A residential continuum care program is available for a six- to twelve-month stay. Wayzata, Minnesota.

Sundown M Ranch. *www.sundown.org.* 800-326-7444. Situated on thirty acres at the entrance to the Yakima River Canyon. Offers treatment for adults and adolescents. It also offers gender-specific groups, elders groups, pregnant and postpartum women's group, relapse prevention, and family counseling. Adult treatment at the time of this writing costs $4,000 for twenty-one days. Adolescent treatment is just over $6,000 for twenty-eight days. Call for updates on costs. Selah, Washington.

INTERVENTION BOOKS

Intervention: How to Help Someone Who Doesn't Want Help, Hazelden, 1986. Author: Vernon E. Johnson. This classic text explains the disease of addiction, including the emotional and delusional syndromes of addiction. Provides the reader with a good introduction to family intervention and information on families getting help for themselves.

Love First: A New Approach to Intervention for Alcoholism and Drug Addiction, Hazelden, 2000. Authors: Jeff Jay and Debra Jay. *www.lovefirst.net.* The book offers a complete road map for structured family intervention. Emphasizes a dignified and loving approach. Answers the many questions families have while planning an intervention. Easy to read and thorough. Can also be used for eating disorders, gambling, and other issues. The Web site offers extensive information including articles and resources.

OTHER HELPFUL BOOKS

Aging and Addiction: Helping Older Adults Overcome Alcohol or Medication Dependence, Hazelden, 2002. Authors: Debra Jay and Carol Colleran. This book is a definitive guide for recognizing and addressing substance abuse among older adults. Key topics include understanding the relationship between aging and addiction, finding help for a loved one, and recognizing the treatment needs of older adults.

Another Chance: Hope and Health for the Alcoholic Family, Science and Behavior Books, Inc., 1981, 1989. Author: Sharon Wegscheider-Cruse. Describes the impact addiction has upon family members and the roles individuals play within alcoholic families.

Beyond the Influence: Understanding and Defeating Alcoholism, Bantam Books, 2000. Authors: Katherine Ketcham, William F. Asbury, Mel Schulstad, and Arthur P. Ciaramicoli. Explains the effects of alcohol on the human body and brain in both alcoholics and nonalcoholics. Offers information on topics such as the importance of nutrition and identifying early-to-middle-stage symptoms of the disease. Encourages intervention rather than waiting for alcoholics to "hit bottom" and seek help on their own.

It Will Never Happen to Me and **Changing Course**, Mac Publishing, 1982, and Hazelden, 2002. Author: Claudia Black. *It Will Never Happen to Me* extends a helping hand to people raised with addiction. It provides a framework for understanding what it means to grow up in fear and shame and gives a voice to those who have suffered in silence. *Changing Course* is the sequel to *It Will Never Happen to Me,* and offers guidance for letting go of a painful childhood and living a life that is free and without fear.

Seeds of Grace: Reflections on the Spirituality of Alcoholics Anonymous, Riverhead Books, 2001. Author: Sister Molly Monahan. An enlightening assessment of Alcoholics Anonymous by a Catholic nun. She describes what she found in AA and how it surprised her. She tells of a deeper spirituality than she had ever experienced in her religious community, even though AA is a nonreligious organization.

The Selfish Brain: Learning from Addiction, Hazelden, 2000. Author: Robert L. DuPont, M.D. Appropriate for addicts, their families, and professionals. Discusses the biological roots of the disease, confronting the disease, and preventing behavioral reinforcement from well-meaning family members and friends.

Teens Under the Influence: The Truth About Kids, Alcohol, and Other Drugs, Ballantine Books, 2003. Authors: Katherine Ketcham and Nicholas A. Pace, M.D. A parenting resource offering a factual look at the problem of teenage substance abuse. Valuable both to parents of children who are abusing drugs and alcohol and to those who want to prevent their kids from using. The book provides a detailed chapter on each drug and how it works.

The Wellness-Recovery Connection: Charting Your Pathway to Optimal Health While Recovering from Alcoholism and Drug Addiction, Health Communications, Inc., 2004. Author: John Newport, Ph.D. *www.wellnessandrecovery.com.* Addiction produces poorly nourished bodies, and some former alcohol and drug addicts develop compulsions for caffeine, nicotine, or junk foods. Discusses ways to prevent this from happening. Outlines meaningful applications of physical wellness to accompany the spiritual dimension of recovery. Challenges readers to set long-term goals to enable them to enjoy the full benefits of recovery.

INDEX

ABOUT THE AUTHOR

Debra Jay is the co-author of the Hazelden Guidebooks *Love First: A New Approach to Intervention,* and *Aging and Addiction.* A graduate of the Hazelden Addiction Professional Training Program, she currently provides private intervention consultation to families throughout the United States and Canada. Debra appears regularly on *The Oprah Winfrey Show,* has been featured in *Prevention Magazine,* and is a national speaker and workshop leader. She resides in Grosse Pointe, Michigan, with her husband, Jeff Jay. Her website is www.lovefirst.net.